M000191239

"M.H."
MEETS
PRESIDENT HARDING

Also by Michael Zagst
The Greening of Thurmond Leaner

"M.H."

MEETS

PRESIDENT HARDING

A NOVEL BY

MICHAEL ZAGST

DONALD I. FINE, INC.

New York

Library of Congress Catalogue Card Number: 86–8210

ISBN: 1–55611–010–3
Manufactured in the United States of America

10 9 8 7 6 5 4 3 2 1

This book is printed on acid free paper. The paper in this book
meets the guidelines for permanence and durability of the Committee on
Production Guidelines for Book Longevity of the Council on Library Resources.

"Yes, We Have No Bananas" © 1923 by Skidmore Music Co., Inc.
Renewed. Used by permission.

Although some of the characters in this book were real people, and at
times their dialogue consists of their actual words as recorded in speeches,
interviews, and biographies, the story is fictional. My account of the
incidents in their lives is not intended to be a reflection of their character,
and is to be considered only a work of the imagination.

For my mother, and also for
JEAN, JOHN, and CATHERINE

1

DEBBIE TELEPHONED THIS MORNING, AS SHE DOES
every morning. Debbie is a volunteer, a member of a group
of charitable people that has taken it upon itself to phone
old men and women who live alone to make sure they are
still alive. I do not mind the calls. In fact, I look forward to
the ring of the telephone. The pleasures and activities of a
man as he approaches a century of life can be somewhat
restricted.

When she calls, I have already been up for hours. Early in
the day, I tend my vegetable garden, and my conversations
with Debbie have a definite agricultural slant to them. You
might say that the garden is the center of my life. It is not
only a conversation piece; it also satisfies my need for exercise and my taste for fresh vegetables. For a person like
myself living on a fixed income, a garden can be a near-
necessity.

I was born in 1892. My doctor tells me that I am in
excellent physical condition for a man of my age. He says I
have the body of a seventy-year-old. My doctor is the fun-
niest man alive. I am not without a sense of humor myself.
My faithful companion is my Irish setter, a dog as red as a
fire engine whose name is Blue. Blue runs in circles around
me when I work in the yard, picking black-eyed peas or corn
or squash. At this time of year, which is autumn, Blue runs
in circles around me when I pick pecans off the ground. Oh
yes, the doctor has said my mind is still fine. He says I am as
sharp as a tack, but I wouldn't know about that.

Memory is a funny thing. It is my understanding that
when a body cell dies, a new cell forms and replaces it. This
is a constant thing, this cellular relay race we call growth
and aging. After six or seven years, each and every cell in
your body has been replaced. But memory hangs as tough as

a barnacle, passing along through the various stages of life, somehow not losing its way in the shuffle, as do hair cells and good eyesight.

I have outgrown a dozen bodies since 1892, and as near as I can tell, my memory is fairly intact. I find this fact utterly remarkable, almost miraculous. Exactly what is a recollection from long ago? It is like newsreels of marching dough-boys on Fifth Avenue at the end of the Great War. Movement is stiff and jerky. A wave from someone in the ranks becomes a flyswat. Confetti clouds the air. Smells and sounds are muted in black and white. Memory is an old man standing in a creek, water to his knees. See that shadow on the bottom, filtered through murky, flowing water and cast on uneven rocks? That is memory. It is up to my interpretation to say what these shadows are. The face reflected is hardly my own.

To answer the question of why this particular memory I will shortly describe remains intact, well, it was simply the highlight of my life. It was an adventure. I was in love. I was not an old-timer unearthing new potatoes. Let me remove my present self, then. Let me step back, at least for now, until my focus is sharp. I will crack pecans and comb Blue's ears.

It is 1923.

2

SIDNEY MARTIN HALVERTON WAS A SUPERVISOR WITH the Trenton Canvas Company. He oversaw workers whose job it was to manufacture boat sails, store awnings, tents of every size, camp stools and deck chairs, trampolines, tarpaulins, even lamp shades and boxing ring mats. In the event of rain in the 1923 World Series, wherever it would be played, chances were that the field would be protected by canvas assembled in the Trenton factory.

In the beginning of April, a sketch for twenty tents reached Halverton's desk. The plans called for six designs of various sizes, including an enormous dining tent. Halverton unrolled the plans, anchoring the paper with ink bottles, erasers and pads. He bit off a chew of tobacco and made notes on the most efficient and least complicated method of producing the job. He saw that the order was being billed to Mr. Thomas Edison in nearby West Orange, and it gave Halverton great satisfaction to know that his work would end up in the hands of such a man. He had read that Edison, now 76 years old, had been in Florida since the first of the year in poor health.

He gave the tent order priority, and it was filled within two weeks under Halverton's supervision. Another week passed. The tents had been trucked to West Orange, and Halverton was at work on a huge order from the Ringling circus. He happened to glance from his desk in his glass-enclosed office. There was an entourage worming its way through the work area, and Halverton was astonished to see Thomas Edison among its members. Halverton opened the office door and watched him. Edison's features were without a trace of illness, his eyes vibrant. As various machines and procedures were pointed out to him, Edison would cup a hand behind one ear. But the noise of the machinery was overpowering, and Edison was all but deaf. Halverton joined the group now and was introduced to the famed inventor. After shaking hands, he tapped on Edison's wrist in Morse code, "Good morning, sir."

Edison beamed. "Ah, a man who speaks my language!" The old telegrapher latched on to Halverton's arm for the remainder of the tour. Halverton had been part of the radio crew aboard the USS *Delaware* during the World War, and though he had not used his knowledge of Morse code since his discharge from the Navy, he was able to tap out the highlights of the factory for their guest. Edison wanted to know all sorts of things, from the life expectancy of the average needle to the components of a waterproofing compound used on some of the tarps. When he asked who their most difficult customer was, Halverton named the present one, Ringling.

"The circus," Edison said. "Myself, I prefer large-scale problems. The larger the better."

The group posed for photographers in front of the building, some of them holding their hats. Their expressions were more serious than the situation demanded. Someone helped Edison into his car, and he motioned for Halverton from the front seat.

"I want to thank you personally for the work on the tents," he said, almost shouting. "I'd like you to join us on the campout if you can."

"I'd be honored," Halverton said. At that moment he would have walked away from his job had Edison asked.

"It'll be the first part of June," Edison added. "There's a part of West Virginia the crowds haven't discovered yet. The caravan disembarks from West Orange. We can send a vehicle for you, or you can drive your own car. If it's a Ford."

Halverton smiled. "It's a Ford," he said.

"Good," Edison laughed. "Henry won't allow us to bring nothing but Fords. You just write down where a letter can reach you, and I'll see you get instructions for the trip."

A picture of Edison and Halverton appeared in the paper the following morning. It was reported that an invitation had been extended to Halverton for the campout in June. Henry Ford, Harvey Firestone and possibly President Harding were expected to be among the campers.

Sid Halverton felt like fainting when he read his name in association with those luminaries. He bought several copies of the paper and mailed clippings to his relatives. At work, he was kidded about hobnobbing with the upper crust.

The following Sunday, Halverton played the piano for an hour at the YMCA. He then took in a double bill, a forgettable feature shored up with a fine unbilled Stan Laurel Comedy. Halverton laughed out loud more than once in the darkened theater, and as he rode the streetcar to the park, he found himself in a pleasant and receptive mood.

He unbuttoned his collar and lay in the grass, watching a group of children kicking a ball. He leaned on his side, lost in thought. So deep was he into his reverie that he failed to notice where the woman had come from. In fact, he wasn't conscious of her at all until he realized he was staring at her. Her dress was softly fluttering in the afternoon breeze like a flag. She was majestically tall, and he could see in the few steps that she took, graceful. She was slim, with radiant amber skin. Her black, black hair was tied above her, accented here and there with single strands of grey. She was, perhaps, forty years old. Halverton couldn't take his eyes from her.

Plainly, he was attracted to her at first sight. But protocol of the day prevented him from speaking out and introducing himself. It just wasn't done. In the war, it was easy. On leave in London and Aberdeen, Halverton could sit at a piano, give a wink, tap the bench lightly with his hand, and he'd have a girl on each side for the rest of the night. When he thought about it, that's what war was to him — total abandonment of all manners. If society permitted a young man to kill, it certainly wasn't about to frown on his attempts to find companionship and love. The leeway there came with the territory. He would be crazy to say that he missed the war, but if Halverton was honest with himself, and he usually was, he had to admit that some of it wasn't so bad.

But lying there in the park, who was there to censure him,

other than himself? If he didn't speak, the moment would be gone.

"You're very pretty," he said.

She caught his eyes with her own and seemed to smile.

"That's an awful thing to blurt out to a total stranger, I know. If it embarrasses you, I apologize right here and now. But any man within a mile of here would say the same thing if he spoke his mind. You are very pretty."

"Do you always speak your mind?" she asked him.

"Of course not," he said.

"Not when you wish to spare the feelings of those you care about," she said.

Halverton brought himself to his feet and found himself straightening his clothes. "That's right," he said. Suddenly, he was the self-conscious one. She recognized his discomfort.

"That's nothing to be ashamed of," she said. "I wish more people cared enough to be a little less than honest. I've always believed that absolute honesty will bring pain, sooner or later. I say, if you care about someone, make them feel good. Learn to lie to them now and then."

Halverton smiled at the remark. There was something in the cockeyed logic he liked. He didn't know whether she was serious or just trying to be entertaining. But he knew he liked her. He liked talking with her. And she really was very pretty. No, she was beautiful.

3

IF QUESTIONED ON THE CHARACTER OF HER boarders, Mrs. Meek was quick to point out that, when Prohibition was about to be enacted, only one, Sidney

Halverton, had not run wildly into the streets for one last legal bottle. If pressed, she would further state that she not only believed Halverton to be a teetotaler, but that he had never taken a woman to his room. Prone to exaggerate, Mrs. Meek could truthfully say with the flair of a Holy Roller testimonial that not a single creditor had knocked on her door looking for Halverton since he had moved there in 1919.

And if asked of her own marital status, or of the where-abouts of Mr. Meek, she would not utter a sound until the subject was changed.

Halverton stopped for a shoeshine on the way to Marga-rete's hotel and entered the expense in a meticulously kept ledger he carried in his vest. "Shine .15," he wrote. Accumu-lated during the week were such investments as: Tobacco .10, Stamps .20, Lunch .45, Moving Picture .50, Haircut .30. Halverton's handwriting was a piece of art, flowing and rolling with such beauty that an illiterate could appreciate it at a glance.

Stopping to adjust his tie in the window of a shop, he absentmindedly whistled a song that was sweeping the coun-try, its lyrics as simple as the tune. The words went:

> *Yes, we have no bananas,*
> *We have no bananas today*
> *We have stringbeans and onions,*
> *Cabbages and scallions,*
> *All kinds of fruit, and say . . .*
> *Yes, we have no bananas,*
> *We have no bananas today.*

Margarete was a striking woman. Halverton had called for her from the lobby, and as she descended the stairs to greet him, his were only one pair of eyes among a dozen men's that watched her. She moved like a feather floating to earth.

When he had first walked her to the hotel, Margarete had

told him that she was Dutch. This frankly astonished Halverton, since she didn't have a trace of an accent. She went on to say that she was in Trenton visiting a distant relative of hers.

"My cousin was to join us, but he was suddenly taken ill," she told him. "I'm afraid he's indisposed for the evening."

"I hope it's not serious," Halverton said.

"No," Margarete said. "Vincent has a flair for the dramatic and a low resistance to pain. I've seen a headache put him to bed for two days. I have decided that he is a very odd fellow, and if one had a say in such matters, I would never choose him as a relative. Shall we go?"

In the restaurant, Halverton was at a loss for words. He was so taken with Margarete's appearance, her hair, the flush in her face, her amber skin, her presence, that he didn't know whether to make conversation by saying that his sister had bobbed her hair or that he had met Edison.

"I met Thomas Edison last week."

"Really?" Margarete said. "What was he like?"

"Very nice," Halverton answered. "I'm sure he's been taken advantage of through the years. Because of his fame and all. But he seemed to me to be unspoiled by all the attention. I liked him."

"How did you meet him?"

"It was through a project that the company I work for did for him. We made him some tents, and he invited me on his campout in June. It's an annual event for him. Henry Ford's supposed to be there as well."

Margarete fanned herself with a menu. "You have some high-class friends," she said.

"I just met Mr. Edison," Halverton said. "I'm no big shot. But I'll tell you something. I don't mind being a wage-earner. I know that you're supposed to have the ambition to own the company one day, but I like my job. I've had it since I was discharged from the Navy in Boston. That may show a lack of aggressiveness, but so be it. Being in charge of the whole works sounds like nothing but headaches to me."

"Where are you from, Sid?"

"Texas," Halverton said. "Houston. My father's in politics down there. Right now, he's a city commissioner. He used to represent our ward as an alderman when the city was set up that way. He gets his name on plaques set into buildings and bridges, and he does a lot of good. I'm proud of him. He's a Democrat. If he loses an election, someone just appoints him to a post. In Houston, I'm known as H.A. Halverton's son. And that's fine with me. I have a brother and three sisters back home too."

"And why did you not marry some nice Houston girl?" Margarete asked.

"I was going to," he said. "I was on leave in Aberdeen, Scotland, when her letter arrived. She married a friend of mine. They have two children now."

"I used to be married," Margarete said. "I found out how little I knew him in a year. He was French. He became an officer and died in the trenches."

"The war was the worst thing that has ever happened," Halverton said. "That must have been terrible for you."

"He used to beat me," she said blankly, then a waiter arrived, and they ordered their food.

In the following weeks, Margarete did not mention her relative again, and Halverton did not inquire about the cousin. Perhaps she had invented him. She lived in the hotel, and whether or not her cousin actually existed was of no great concern to him. They took walks in the evenings of his workdays or sat in the porch furniture of Mrs. Meek's rooming house. Since they were respectable people, discretion was used. When they met at her hotel, it was usually for the night.

For the first time, Halverton was allowing his work at the

canvas company to pile up. On weekends, he and Margarete
would be found in the audience of a New York vaudeville
show, bellylaughing along with the crowds. They saw Will
Rogers in a matinee, bought tickets to the evening perfor-
mance and were delighted to discover that he did not repeat
a single joke. They wept with laughter when they saw the
Marx Brothers on stage. Other days were spent at the ocean
where they rented weekend cottages. He was spending
money he didn't have, and he had lost his expense ledger.

Halverton's stomach ached. He did not sleep well, and he
ate irregularly. His attention drifted. He was in love, and it
was making him miserable.

4

WHEN HALVERTON RECEIVED EDISON'S CAMPING
instructions in the mail, he mentioned to Margarete that he
simply would not go without her.

"There's not a reason in the world for us to be apart,"
he said.

"Sid, it's the middle of June and could hardly be hotter,"
she said. "I don't like tents. I'm allergic to a variety of insect
bites. It might be for men only, then where would I go?"

"It doesn't mean that much to me," Halverton said. "If
you won't come with me, then I'll stay here."

"That's foolish," she told him. "Can't you see that the
men on this trip have shaped our society and are still writing
our history? You have a rare chance to see them as few
others are in a position to. Whenever you come across the
name of Edison or Ford, you'll have the satisfaction of
remembering them as you knew them. They will still impress
you long after you've forgotten me."

"Why do you say things like that?" he said. "I love you. There's no end to that."

"You're *in love* with me," she said. "And I don't expect you to be reasonable under the circumstances. You told me once you were no big shot. What do you think I am? I am the Dutch widow of a French soldier." She removed a silver bracelet from her left wrist and showed her arm to Halverton. "It's a tattoo," she said. "A snake swallowing its own tail. I used to dance the tango until dawn with young men who would be sent away to die, while my own husband was out there himself dying somewhere. Like all of Paris, I was starving. But I made the soldiers forget that they were dying, and they saw to it that I was well nourished. Over the years there have been many other men as well."

One day Halverton hoped to marry. He just assumed it would happen. And he would have sons and daughters to bounce on his knee in his own home. In his gut he knew that Margarete was not the woman to fulfill that dream with him. You didn't marry a woman like her. But, somehow — at that moment — it didn't seem to matter. He couldn't imagine his life without her.

"I don't know why you're telling me all of this," he said.

"Love is many things, Sidney," she said. "That's all. When are you leaving?"

"The day after tomorrow."

Margarete consented to accompany him, but made him promise that she could stay in a hotel if she became uncomfortable. This was fine with Halverton, since he was skeptical that they would be anywhere close to a hotel.

The morning of June nineteenth was cool — cool enough to drench the ground in dew and suspend a fog as thick as clouds in the low spots. Margarete wore a scarf to tie down her hat, and she had begun to look forward to the drive. Not owning a car of her own, it was a luxury for her to travel by private means. They were on the road to West Orange, where they would meet up with the start of Edison's caravan.

Halverton could never have found the actual campsite on his own, because Edison in his note had pinpointed it no more specifically than the Monongahela Forest, nearly a million acres of West Virginia's wilderness.

They drove onto the grounds of the huge Edison complex. It looked as if everyone had been given the morning off. Thousands of workers, in overalls, in lab coats and street clothes, were walking in one general direction, coming down every street and flowing together to form an enormous crowd.

"What do you think it is?" Halverton asked.

"I don't know," Margarete answered, sitting high in her seat for a better view. "Ask somebody."

Halverton pulled over to the curb. He stepped onto the running board and looked ahead as far as he could see. "What's all the excitement?" he asked of a passerby.

"The old man's getting a sendoff. On up ahead."

Halverton sat in the car again.

"They're getting ready to leave. I don't know if we can drive through all these people."

"You'll have to," Margarete said. There was a panic in her voice. "Let's go, Sid. They'll get out of our way."

Halverton stepped to the front of the car and cranked the engine, then idled his vehicle through the crowd. The workers were a genial bunch and willingly parted to allow them through. There was a line of three huge trucks overloaded like gypsy wagons and a string of cars in the rear of them that Halverton parked behind.

Then they saw Edison as he stood in the seat of the lead car. He made a short statement that Halverton was unable to make out, then waved his derby. Edison's employees, all 8000 of them, cheered enthusiastically. Halverton could hear a single voice sing out, "Hip hip," followed by an artillery of hoorays. After three cheers Edison waved again. Then he sat down and the vehicles began to move. Hats sailed in the air.

"This is wonderful," Margarete shouted, leaning over to kiss Halverton's cheek. "Thank you for talking me into it."

They heard the enthusiasm of the employees dim with distance, and before long they found themselves back in Trenton, where they turned south to pass within two blocks of Mrs. Meek's house on Perry Street. Philadelphia, Baltimore and Washington were obstacles in their path, and the circuitous route Edison had mapped led them around the larger cities. There were fifteen cars in all. Occasionally Margarete and Halverton caught a glimpse of Edison when there was a turn in the road and they were able to see a distance ahead.

"Look," Margarete would say. "There he is again."

"I see him," Halverton would answer.

At the same time, another fleet of vehicles was traveling southeastward out of Columbiana, Ohio. Its cargo included one hundred cleaned and dressed chickens and dozens of cakes, pies and cookies prepared by Harvey Firestone's Aunt Nannie and the Columbiana Ladies Aid Society. Among the passengers were six cooks, three assistant cooks, a cameraman, two journalists, a Methodist bishop and various wives, sons and in-laws.

In the lead truck, which was equipped with an oversized refrigerator on one running board and an oven on the other, Firestone was making a point to his friend Henry Ford.

"Henry, I'm telling you it's balloon tires from here out," he said. "They're safer, they give you a smoother ride, which won't make the car shake itself apart, and they cost a fraction of the amount to produce."

"All right," Ford said. "Now let me ask you this. What if one blows up when a man is changing it? What if an infant happened to crawl by when one gave out? It would be good-bye baby."

"You don't understand. Look, you're filling the tire with about thirty pounds of air, not dynamite."

"I'm not sold yet, Harvey."

"Well, what is it you don't understand? Will you listen to what Edison has to say about them? You trust Al's opinion, I *know*."

"We'll see, Harv," Ford said. "Oh, by the way, a Ford does *not* shake itself apart under any circumstances — with or without the miracle Firestone balloon tire."

In Washington, President Harding's train car, the *Superb*, was delayed from leaving for one day by a convention of the Nobles of the Mystic Shrine. The press had reported the President's itinerary for what he was calling his cross-country "Voyage of Understanding." But the scheduled dates of speeches were not firm, and the Shriners were fitted in before his departure. For the occasion, Harding had dressed the capitol in the Shriners' colors. Red, green and yellow bunting drooped in the heat of his viewing platform. Platoons of Shriner brass bands passed before him, and Harding welcomed the 20,000 members and their families that day to the White House. He was pleased to shake every man's hand, but by the end of the day his own hands were swollen as if they'd been crushed.

He was soaking them in warm water, standing at the sink in his bedclothes.

"Wurr'n, that was a foolish thing to do," the First Lady chastised him. "Your poor hands. Look at them, Wurr'n."

Harding raised his hands from the bowl. "I *love* to meet people," he said. "It's the most pleasant thing I do. It's really the only fun I have. It doesn't tax me, and it seems to give them great pleasure."

"They don't care about you," Mrs. Harding said. "They wouldn't even let you join them until you were President. Your influence is all they care about."

"They don't care?" Harding said. "I'll have you know, my dear Duchess, that they inducted me into the Tall Cedars of

Lebanon today. It's a new order, and a very prestigious one."

"Some honor. You get to wear a hat that's sillier than most of the others. Shaped like a pyramid. It's an insult."

He reached for a towel and made his hands into fists within it. "God damn it, Florence," he said. "Would you please just shut up?"

Harding walked into the hall, where he was greeted eagerly by his Airedale, Laddie Boy. They went wearily to his bedroom, and Mrs. Harding retired to hers.

5

THE FIRST GROUP OF CAMPERS — THE ONE LED BY Edison — had reached Elkins, West Virginia. Elkins was a small town, and a string of automobiles the length of the campers' never passed through it unless someone important there was being buried. Because of this, townspeople removed their hats as the cars drove past them, and they wondered who it might be who had died.

Outside the town, Edison directed the lead car to pull off the road, instructing someone to go back into Elkins to rendezvous with Ford's and Firestone's gang. "Word of our arrival," he said, "will not be far behind. We could have a thousand people on our hands if Henry and H.S. are lagging along the roadside somewhere. Go wait for them at the post office."

Halverton felt conspicuous at best. He had been thinking that he was the only person in the entire expedition who wasn't some sort of scientist, entrepeneur, or Edison confidante. He had waved when anyone in a car ahead of him had turned in his direction, and now that they had halted, he felt completely out of his element. Some of the passengers were getting out of their cars now, and he and Margarete did the same.

"I never know what to do around new people," he said to her. "I don't know what to say."

She took him by the arm. "We'll simply walk up there," she said. "We'll introduce ourselves, keeping in mind that we are all equals."

"And forget that some of us are millionaires," Halverton added.

Halverton had a tendency to take his own skills and virtues for granted. He didn't find the ability to decipher and execute a set of plans at his job the least bit unusual. But he was in awe of Edison, someone who could dream up projects with no apparent effort. And he assumed that Edison's friends and employees were just as distinctive and creative. So he held back, rather than place what he felt was his obvious ignorance on display.

They joined a group in some shade at the side of the road. Halverton had been wearing a straw hat, and he held it now by the brim with both hands as he talked with the others. Most of them were older than he, but many were near his own age. He didn't recognize any of their names.

"And how are you connected with Mr. Edison, Mr. Halverton?" someone asked him.

"Just barely," was the answer. "I have the idea that I was invited on a whim." He related the incident at the canvas factory.

"No, if he took a shining to you — and he certainly doesn't to everyone — it was no whim," Halverton was assured. "Have you spoken with him yet today?"

"No, I haven't had the chance."

"He'll remember you. He's not one to forget someone."

Halverton could see Edison in the background. Mrs. Edison had brought him a pillow a minute earlier, and he was now sound asleep in the gravel, as comfortable as if he were at home in his own bed.

Sandwiches were passed around, and Halverton sat on a blanket with Margarete. "Does it bother you that I'm so much younger than you?" he asked her.

"And how old do you think I am?"

"I don't know. Forty maybe."

"That's exactly it," she said. "In Europe, it's very common for a woman to have a younger husband, a younger lover." She watched his reaction, or lack of one. "Does it matter to you?"

He shook his head and squeezed her hand. Horns began to sound from the direction of the town, strained, joyous toots that were an integral part of the wooden-spoked, simple machines. The campers began to stand, some of them holding their plates, smiling to themselves as the first truck rounded a curve into view. It was a boxlike thing with the words *Buy Firestone Tires* emblazoned across its hump. Someone stirred Edison from his sleep, and the old man jumped to his feet, the first to meet the reinforcements.

"Another quarter hour, and we'd have left you behind," he shouted.

Henry Ford opened the door and stepped onto the ground. "We found a family whose car had broken down on the road," he said. "It was a Chrysler. Couldn't leave them in that condition. Fixed their car and sent them on their way. If not for that, we'd have beat you here."

"And what's your excuse, Mister Firestone?" Edison asked. "Are you sticking to that lame story?"

"We stopped once or twice," Firestone said. "I knew you'd lay down the rules once we got together, so I took the chance to shave when I had it."

"You're a tenderfoot, Harvey," Edison said. "Before you know it, you'll be dressed as a dude. No baths except in rivers, and no shaves. Period. We've left that back in civilization."

Firestone slowly broke into a grin, his face suddenly show-ing the cause of its wrinkles. The youngest of the trio at fifty-three, he didn't mind being the butt of their ribbing. He stepped forward and hugged Edison warmly.

"Harvey's got an announcement to make," Ford said. "Let's get everyone together for it, and we can get on our way."

Firestone gestured and shouted the group closer to him. There were nearly sixty people around him now.

"Gentlemen and ladies," he spoke from the running board. "This little excursion has become an annual event. It's our seventh year in a row now, our third since we lost our partner, our good and gentle friend John Burroughs. We're just a bunch of Ohio boys ourselves. For those of you joining us for the first time, take it from me that we'll do our share of the chores. Mr. Edison here claims to have a camp-site staked out. Experience has shown that to mean that we'll follow his nose."

Firestone calmed the laughter with a hushing motion of his hands before continuing.

"There's another Ohio boy starting a trip to Alaska in the morning. I invited him to meet up with us weeks ago, and I talked with him by telephone last night. He said if we can leave a trail he can follow, he'll be happy to be our guest for a few days. President Harding has a speech northeast of here in Martinsburg tomorrow and will motor into our camp sometime in the late afternoon or evening."

Halverton squeezed Margarete's arm at the announce-ment. "Then it's true," he said. "It was rumored he was coming, but I could hardly believe it. I still can't."

Margarete strained to hear whatever else Firestone was saying, but he had finished. "Now aren't you glad you're here?" she asked.

Edison did not appear impressed by the news. He either hadn't heard it clearly, or it just was not a matter of great importance to him. He turned his back on Firestone when he had finished speaking and began to walk through the congregation toward his automobile. Seeing Halverton for the first time that day, he stopped abruptly and sought him out.

"Mr. Halverton," he said. "I'm so happy you could come. Didn't have any trouble getting off work, did you?"

"Not when I told them why," Halverton answered.

"You've surely put a roof over our heads with those tents of yours. Seems I neglected to design a presidential model, though."

Halverton was embarrassed, overwhelmed actually, at being face to face with Edison. "I don't know what to say," he said.

"Then introduce me to the pretty lady you're with," Edison said, cupping his hand behind his ear.

"Yes, of course," he said. "This is Margarete Fabry."

Margarete was six feet tall and towered impressively over Edison, who reached out and shook her hand. "A lovely lady," he said. Then he turned and walked to his car where he gathered his hat from his wife. He made his way back to Firestone's truck in order for the expedition's leaders to ride three abreast.

"You were right about him, Sid," Margarete said. "He could charm the salt out of the sea. A nice old man."

Engines began to start. Halverton had one of the few cars without an electric starter, and while he was cranking the thing up, vehicles began to pass him on their way into the woods. Edison was again in the lead, and true to Firestone's prediction, he began to take the campers as far from the beaten trail as the cars and trucks would carry them. They bounced in and out of ruts, on occasion jarring a passenger out of his seat, vaulting him a foot into the air amid shrieks of delight. They discovered Sully, a town of a few dozen mountain people. There the power lines came to an end, but deeper into the Monongahela Forest they drove. If a crossroads looked more promising, that is, more difficult to traverse, Edison would halt the progress of the fleet and direct the lead car that way. Once, the entire string of vehicles had to back up nearly half a mile after Edison's choice of a dead-end logging trail. They wound through the mountains for an hour. Birds crisscrossed above them, and views of valleys and mountaintops when they could be seen through the trees were breathtaking. They passed the last sign of civilization, a cabin on a ridge, the smoke of its chimney its only hint of habitation. Ahead was a small clearing. It lay spread out on the banks of a creek. The cars and trucks drove over a wooden bridge and at last shut off their motors.

The workers in the party swarmed like drones around a hive to put the camp in order. Several projects were simultaneously shaping up, Ford supervising the management of a pile of wood, taking his own turn with the ax when someone needed a breather. Firestone was discussing with the cooks the evening meal and the most efficient arrangement of the galley with the dining area. Edison offered only a suggestion or two to some young men climbing trees, stringing from one to the next a wire that unreeled from the rear of one of the trucks. He walked beneath them and pointed with a stick to strategic places that would best support the cable. It was Edison's intention that the camp would not only be supplied with lights, including electricity in the individual tents, but the galley would have the latest electric conveniences, from fist-sized marshmallow toasters to a walk-in refrigerator. For their entertainment, an electric player piano could provide background accompaniment to the dozen films that were stowed away with the movie projector.

The source of the electricity was a single storage battery perfected by Edison and his "insomnia squad," as he called them. Once developed, the Edison storage battery vaulted into immediate use by the fleet of American Express trucks, on trolleys where there were no power lines, to operate floating buoys' flashing lights in harbors, for lighting systems on yachts, for the New York subway system's signals, in rural homes far from power stations, as well as on farms and for lighting submarines as they sailed underwater. The battery was but one of nearly eleven hundred Edison patents.

"That does it, sir," Halverton could hear from one of the trees. "Would you like to throw the switch and see if she works?"

Edison smiled and shook his head. The system had been tested countless times before.

The focal point of the campsite, the center of activity shared by all the campers, was the dining tent. Its support pole was a birch tree stripped of its limbs. The canvas was attached to a metal ring hoisted over and secured to the treetop and draped out like a skirt, where ropes and stakes conformed its perimeter into four-foot walls. Its height at the center was twelve feet above a circular table that had been fitted around the smooth white bark of the tree's trunk. There was room in the tent for a sit-down dinner for eighteen. The tent could take advantage of breezes by opening on two sides. It was designed by Edison and assembled at the Trenton Canvas Company.

The trip had been tiring. Cooks began setting out hams, with a tub of potato salad and a cauldron of beans. The weary campers served themselves, eating in shifts in the dining tent or finding room on stools and canvas chairs. Halverton and Margarete leaned their backs against a tree trunk, holding their plates over their laps. Edison passed up the conventional meal and filled himself instead with a large slice of apple pie and a handful of cookies washed down with two cups of coffee heaped with sugar. Taking note of the dinner, Halverton recalled an admonishment he used to receive at meals as a child. "An unbalanced meal makes for an unbalanced boy." But he wouldn't dream of suggesting such a thing to Edison, living disproof of the childhood warning.

Halverton began stowing his things away in his quarters. He shared a tent with three other bachelors, and Margarete's tent housed two of their fiancés. He and Margarete drew some stares because of the differences in their ages, but mainly because no one in camp really knew who they were. Everyone took them for a respectable couple, and they slept in separate tents. Halverton was a good sport about accepting the restriction. He and Margarete could always steal away for an hour or two alone, and he had every intention of doing just that. But the campground was divided into men's and women's quarters. Even married couples were split apart. Halverton wondered whose idea it was. The only pairs who enjoyed the privacy of their own tents were the Edisons, the Fords and the Firestones.

Ford and Firestone meandered through the camp after eating in order to meet people they didn't know. They were genuinely friendly, more like neighbors than anything else. "What's your name? Where are you from?"

"Sidney Halverton, sir. I'm from Texas originally, but I've lived in Trenton about four years. This is Margarete Fabry."

Ford shook his hand, and Halverton saw something in the man's expression, or within the face itself, a wildness or intensity about the eyes that put him on edge. He released his grasp, and Ford bounded ahead two steps and leaped, latching on to a tree limb where he began to rapidly chin himself.

"I'll take on any man in camp," he said without straining. "Forty-yard dash, hundred-yard dash, a mile overland. I don't care." He dropped to the ground. "Any takers?" He looked at Halverton. "You seem in pretty good shape."

"No thanks," Halverton said. He felt conspicuous, not knowing whether he could joke along with Henry Ford or to take the challenge seriously.

"Lucky for you," Ford said before going his way.

Just as Halverton made himself comfortable on the ground again, he had to stand to shake Firestone's hand. "Sit back down," Firestone said, joining them in the grass. "You're here at Al's invitation, is that right?"

"Yes sir," Halverton said. "My company, or should I say, the company I work for, made some of the newer tents for the trip."

"Oh, then you're the one who knows Morse Code. Al certainly got a kick out of that. I really like that dining tent," Firestone told him. "We'll get out money's worth out of it, I'm sure."

"This is such a beautiful place," Margarete said. "How did you ever discover it?"

"That was Mister Edison's doing too," Firestone said. "And 'discovered' is the right word in this case. He has some government maps, and they point us in the general direction. He writes us, giving us the route. Then he writes us again, changing to another route. And when we actually start, he usually selects a third. We don't ever know where we're going. I don't think he does either. You saw how we got here."

Margarete took a drink of water she had poured. Firestone had scarcely taken his eyes off of her while he was talking. She had had that effect on men since about the age of fifteen, and it was something she took for granted now. Something about the delicacy of her features contrasting with her black hair made one think of Asia. She could be Indian, Spanish, Oriental, Mexican, anything exotic.

"When do you expect the President?" she asked.

"Late tomorrow sometime," Firestone answered. "We don't know for sure. I'm sending a man back into that last town we passed through. He's to join the presidential party and guide it here. They're a pretty good-sized group them-selves. Did you two get enough to eat? There's plenty left if you're still hungry. Don't be bashful."

"None for me, thanks," Halverton said.

Margarete shook her head.

"Well, enjoy yourselves," Firestone said. "Come to me if

you have any complaints." He shook their hands as they stood. Then he walked to the next cluster of people.

"It's funny meeting someone famous," Halverton said over their food.

"How do you mean?" Margarete asked.

"Well, their faces are already so familiar from years of exposure in magazines and papers and newsreels. It's like you already know them. How strange it must be for them to see that look of recognition in every stranger's eyes."

"It must make them quite cautious, I would think."

"Maybe so, but they're so outgoing that they put you at ease. They seem genuinely friendly."

When the sun was about to set, the lights around the perimeter of the camp began to glow, and the tents with their lights within looked like a cluster of Japanese lanterns. A fire burned in the center of the site, and when it had been reduced to a pillow of coals, the lights were extinguished one by one.

From his cot, Halverton could see out the flap of his tent across the way to the dining tent. Seated alone at the table was the only person to have brought along any books. Edison was reading Robert Burns. He placed the book on the table and sat for a long time, his gaze upward, either in contemplation of the poetry he had just read or in fascination with the light bulb. Halverton watched for a few minutes, his eyes blinking slowly and heavily. With the image of Edison seated at the table, he began to sleep soundly.

6

ALTHOUGH HE SUPERVISED THEIR CONSTRUCTION by the dozen, Halverton had not slept in a tent since his

basic training at the Great Lakes naval station during the World War. He had vowed he would never again put himself in the confines of one. Not that they were so uncomfortable. His dislike of them stemmed from the regimentation of basic training. He enjoyed the outdoors, and birds had awakened him for the first time in ages. The morning was cool. Halverton wondered how formal he was expected to dress and decided against wearing a tie.

Opening the tent flap, he saw across the site a table set up with metal basins of water where several men stood, leaning over, splashing the sleep from their faces. There was a sour taste in his mouth. He heard a whirring sound to his side and looked in its direction. A man with a cap stood behind a movie camera mounted atop a tripod, his arm moving in a circular pattern as he cranked the film through.

"Stop staring at the camera or get on out of the way," the newsreel cameraman said, waving Halverton away with his free hand.

Halverton moved to the dining tent to find some coffee. Firestone greeted him as he stepped inside. "What'll you have?" he asked. "We have oranges, fresh huckleberries, bananas, cereal, toast, sausage, biscuits, flapjacks. Whatever you want."

"Some coffee would be nice," Halverton answered. "I might have some fruit later."

"Here you are," Firestone said as he poured. "There's cream and sugar, or if you prefer, there's honey next to the ice box."

"Thank you," Halverton said. "I really feel pampered."

"You're the guest," Firestone said. Halverton liked Firestone. He couldn't imagine anyone being more accomodating than he was. And it was plain that he enjoyed playing the part of the host. "Miss Fabry is across the way over there," he pointed. "Mister Edison's being interviewed, and I think she's listening in."

Edison sat in a chair, one leg crossed over the other,

opposite someone writing in a notebook. He leaned forward to hear the writer clearly and rocked back when he gave his answers. Margarete stood behind them among three or four bystanders. She saw Halverton approach sipping his coffee and waved nonchalantly to him. Edison was smoking a cigar.

"Sir," the writer asked. "Is there an overriding philosophy of life you adhere to, some line of thought that has maintained your genius?"

Edison pulled the cigar from his mouth and made a face. "I'm not too fond of that word, 'genius'. I just do whatever I have to do, to the best of my ability. My philosophy of life is work. Discovering secrets of Nature and applying them to the happiness of man. That is my task. It's not a bad service to render in the short time we are here, is it?"

"I would like to talk more about electricity. The recent rise in the costs of coal and gasoline means electricity will be more expensive too. What's the solution to keep it affordable?"

"Well, that's a very good question," Edison said. "You hit it squarely there. At present, the transmission of electricity is not very exorbitant. What we need is greater economy in the use of coal. This country is using up its natural resources at an awful rate. It's alarming. Mining promoters are mining coal, not for humanity's sake, but for making money. The general transportation of coal should be forbidden. The miners should be compelled by law, since they would not do it on their own, to turn the coal into electricity at the pit's mouth. They could then sell the electricity. We can act before the resource situation is critical, but we probably won't. I leave the prophesizing to H.G. Welles and Jules Verne and the oratory to the politicians. But I do believe that the day is coming when all the water power in the country will be used to make electricity. It ought to be.

"The cities will benefit most by electricity. I think in

twenty or thirty years, storage batteries will be common-place. You won't find a horse truck in any city. Electricity will be so cheap, it won't pay to use any other form of power. The five thousand-horsepower dynamos I put in at the West Orange plant were replaced a number of years ago. I found I could buy the current cheaper from a company in Newark."

"What about the wireless transmission of electricity I've read about?"

Edison shook his head. "I cannot conceive of much being done in that line for some time. I don't want to say it can't be done. The great difficulty with it is to find a way to channelize the Hertzian waves. I have never worked on it. But getting back to water power, I think in the centuries to come, even the waves and tides of the seas will be harnessed to make electricity. As long as we can secure coal and other fuels cheaply enough, we will continue to use them. But when they begin to disappear, we shall find it cheaper to get power in other ways. It's all a matter of price."

"What about the future of electricity in the household?"

Edison smiled and tapped the journalist's leg as if sharing a joke with him. "A few years ago, when Mrs. Edison was approached about buying an automatic washer, she was hesitant. The salesman said that was fine, he'd just leave it for her to use for a month to see how she liked it. Well, he hooked it up, and in a month's time, he was back. Said he'd come to retrieve his washer if she didn't want it anymore. You'd have thought he was asking for her firstborn. She wouldn't hear of it. Now our entire kitchen is operated by electricity. But then, you wouldn't expect otherwise, would you?" Edison laughed, tilting back in his chair as he sur-veyed the campground. "Well, I see my friend Mister Ford has returned from his hike. Would you excuse me, please? We'll continue this later if you like."

Edison abruptly stood and joined his comrade Ford in the dining tent. Ford had been gone for over an hour on his walk. Swinging from trees like Tarzan, Halverton imagined.

"How did you sleep?" Halverton asked Margarete, but she was too dumbfounded to answer. She had watched Edison walk away and was still looking at him from the distance.

"Did you sleep all right?" Halverton repeated.

She looked at him now. "He answered questions on every subject that was posed to him," she said. "I thought his knowledge would be in scientific areas only. But he commented with authority on music, art, literature, world history, everything. He must know everything there is to know. It wouldn't surprise me in the least. Thomas Edison ought to be President of the United States."

In Martinsburg, young boys clung to tree limbs to catch a glimpse of the presidential train as it entered the town. Others laid pennies on the track to be flattened for souvenirs of the visit. Once the sun was a good angle off the horizon, the heat arrived like a tide. Men were in shirtsleeves, and ladies shaded themselves with parasols. It was a smaller crowd than expected.

The *Superb* rolled into the station. Already, local officials were waiting on the platform, having thoroughly tested the public address system and the patience of the audience in a recitation of the Pledge of Allegiance and a wallowing version of the National Anthem. The *Superb* pulled to a halt, the steam brakes making clouds. Everyone in the crowd seemed to be fanning themselves, even as they stood on tiptoe for a better view. A brass band struck up a tune as Harding and the Duchess stepped out onto the train's rear platform in the midst of the familiar introductory tuba snorts of *Yes, We Have No Bananas*. From a distance, the President looked hearty, vibrant, but the spectators close to the train couldn't overlook Harding's utterly drained appearance, his cheeks and eyes sagging, his complexion jaundiced. His grey suit, neatly tailored and pressed, was too heavy for such a warm and humid day. But his smiles to the crowd and for the photographers were genuine. He reached to outstretched hands and shook them for five minutes before retreating to the podium. His was not a style of speech that relied on amplification, but the President's speech was being broadcast coast to coast by radio. The cluster of microphones was threatening to him, like cobras. Harding would be unable to emphasize statements with arm gestures, would out of necessity restrain his style — a style that, in the words of H.L. Mencken, was, "pressure, ardency, effortcy, gasping, a high grunting. It is a style that rolls and groans, struggles and complains. It is the style of a rhinoceros liberating himself by main strength from a lake of boiling molasses." Out of fairness to Harding, Mencken held a view of Harding's audience completely compatible with such a three-ring urgency. To Mencken, they were, "the yokelry of the hinterland, naive, agape, thirsty for the prodigious, and eager to yell. If a phrase has punch it does not ask that it also have a meaning. If a sentence ends with a roar, it does not inquire how it began. If a word stings, that is enough."

Harding cleared his throat to his side, putting a fist to his lips. He leaned toward the microphones. "When I was a candidate, and not your President, I opposed with all my vigor the League of Nations or any involvement in Old World controversies. I admit now that there were rudiments of good in both the League and the Hague Tribunal. There are those senators, whose numbers are few, who presently maintain that America should revert to a hermit nation. Let me assure you and reassure you that we needn't be hermits in this world, nor must we enter the League by back door, side door or cellar door."

Harding took a drink, pausing for expected applause at this point. In the campground, the speech was being heard by a group clustered about a radio. It was the first radio broadcast of a Presidential speech, ever.

"I have worked with Secretary of State Hughes on a modification of the Court, the World Court whose function, to make war illegal for now and forevermore, is the highest priority of this administration. I shall not restrict my appeal to your reason. I shall call upon your patriotism. I shall invoke your Christianity. I shall reach to the very depths of your love for your fellow countrymen of whatever race or creed throughout the world. I shall speak, as I now speak, with all the earnestness and power, with all the sincerity that is within me, and in perfect faith that God will keep clear and perceptive your understanding.

"I could not do otherwise. My soul yearns for peace. My heart is anguished by the sufferings of war. My spirit is eager to serve. My passion is for justice over force. My hope is in the great court. My mind is made up. My resolution is fixed."

The President's lips were chapped and blue. His sweat stung his eyes as he spoke. The crowd consisted of townspeople and farmers from hundreds of miles around. They cared more about corn prices than the lack of a World Court. They had passed out pennies to their children, giving them an extra one for their own train-flattened keepsake of the day. At first, they didn't know Harding's speech had ended. When it did dawn on them, they clapped and clapped.

Harding and his wife remained on the platform as the train began to move. The air rushing about him was refreshing. "Was I all right?" he asked the Duchess as he waved. "Do you think they liked me?"

"Wurr'n, you were fine," Florence Harding said. "It was a fine speech, and you don't have to make another one for days. Your friend Mister Firestone and the others will be a great relaxation for both of us. Then you can face St. Louis with renewed strength. But Wurr'n, there was one thing."

"What's that?"

"You said, 'your fellow countrymen throughout the world.' That doesn't makes sense."

Harding opened the door to the car and held it for the First Lady. "It's the thought that counts," he said.

7

THE HARDING FACTION WOULD NEARLY DOUBLE THE size of the camping party. Most of those on board the train would accompany the President to the campsite, and preparations were already being made for their arrival. Additional tents were being pitched, and food that could be fixed in advance was being attended to by the cooks. But it was not all work. The player piano had been turned on, horseshoes were being played and many of the party had scattered to explore the countryside.

The stopover in camp of the Presidential entourage was a combination of goodwill and image-building. One did not go wrong in the public eye with Edison on your side. Still, the Republicans had lost a great number of seats in Congress in the 1922 elections, and that usually meant a dissatisfaction with the White House. To regain support among the people, Harding's trip was an elaborate 1500 mile, two-month speaking tour. There were with him Secret Service agents, journalists, photographers, newsreel cameramen and various aides and guests of the President.

Halverton and Margarete had planned to take a walk in the woods after lunch, but the excitement of the President's arrival had kept them in camp. Firestone, as official host, remained there to welcome Harding, but Ford had driven away with Edison. The two had been away for hours. Edison's fears had been confirmed. Mountain people and city dwellers alike were "happening upon" the campsite with regularity. They were not turned away, neither were they welcomed with open arms. Usually, the passerby would remain until hunger forced him out of camp. Edison had begun to grumble about the many new guests and had been promised that the campsite would be moved farther out of reach as soon as the President had left.

Lunch consisted of broiled chicken in pineapple sauce, with rice, asparagus and boiled carrots. Halverton and Margarete waited until nearly everyone had eaten before serving themselves, and they had the dining tent to themselves as they sat down for the meal. Then Mrs. Edison entered. She had been holding off on lunch until her husband returned to camp but could not contain her hunger any longer. Halverton stood as she walked in, plate in hand, and he pulled a chair out for her at the table. She was much younger than Edison, perhaps fifty years old.

"Thank you, sir," she said to Halverton.

"You're Mrs. Edison, aren't you?" Margarete asked her.

"I'm proud to say yes," she answered. "And who might you two be? I've seen you in camp."

"I am Margarete Fabry, and this is Sidney Halverton."

Halverton nodded politely. He was swallowing a bite of food.

"I heard you husband speaking today," Margarete went on. "I cannot get over the expanse of his knowledge."

"It's the way he reads," Mrs. Edison said. "He reads as though he would devour every book that was ever printed. Most of us read words. He reads whole sentences at a time, several sentences if they're short ones. I've never seen anyone concentrate as he does. His deafness has something to do with it, but I've a feeling he could do it if he could hear perfectly. He's a devout believer in concentration. He thinks you can get anything you want if you know how to concentrate. He's never played bridge or cards of any kind since the children were little, and golf, never. In fact, he has little interest in sports."

"Margarete," Halverton said. "Let Mrs. Edison eat her dinner before it gets cold."

"Oh, I can talk and eat at the same time," Mina Miller Edison said. "I don't mind talking about Mister Edison."

Margarete ignored Halverton's suggestion. "What is it like living with him?" she asked.

"We always try at home to give him rest and quiet after his long hours in the laboratory. We guard him against any noise or confusion or interruption. Sometimes he stays down at the laboratory for twenty hours at a stretch and longer without sleep. When he does come home, he will lie down and fall asleep as easily as a child and perhaps sleep twenty hours straight through without waking. He has no regular habits, no regular time for rising, no regular diet. He is quite fond of apple pie. He's on his feet all day long, so he' seldom does any walking out of doors. He loves his garden, and motoring is his favorite recreation. We have our rides together almost every evening for two hours before supper-time. He looks forward to them with a great deal of pleasure. He's out with Mister Ford somewhere at this moment.

"His pursuit in the recent past has been rubber. Everything has turned to rubber in our family. We talk rubber, think rubber, dream rubber. Mister Edison refuses to let us do anything else. It's because he feels his work is unfinished. Really, that is what pulled him through his illness earlier this year. He had to get to his work. If you think of one living in the highest state of exhilaration, seeing nothing, hearing nothing, doing nothing except what has a vital bearing on the task at hand, then you have a perfect photograph of Mister Edison at such times that he is working."

"I never believed I would meet your husband," Halverton said. "Like everyone, I've heard about him since I was a small child. He's a legend."

"He ought to be President of the United States," Margarete said for the second time that day, causing Mrs. Edison to burst into laughter.

"Goodness no," she said. "He's never given more than one or two speeches in his life, and he'd sooner meet his Maker than give another one."

A rumble of automobiles interrupted the conversation. Through the tent flaps, Halverton, Margarete and Mrs. Edison could see a procession approaching. The lead car was a 1922 Pierce Arrow, brought by rail for the purpose of shuttling the President from the *Superb* to his various speaking engagements across the country. Flags waved from the front fenders. Harvey Firestone could be seen drying his hands on an apron he was removing as he walked to where the car was parking. The wake of a cloud of dust raised by the entourage floated ahead of the cars now. Firestone opened the Pierce Arrow's door, and Florence Harding reached out for his hand, stepping onto the ground and surveying the campsite as if it were a mine disaster.

Mrs. Edison craned her neck to see out of the tent. "I've never met this president before," she said. "We'd better eat up before everyone gets a case of the handshakes."

Next out of the car was Laddie Boy, Harding's Airedale. A leash ran from his collar to the confines of the automobile. Then a leg appeared, the pants rising to expose the President's garters. Firestone patted Laddie Boy's head, then reached inside the car. The wind began to gust, and a cloud of dust and leaves obscured the view for a moment. When it was clear again, the three inside the dining tent had their first view of President Warren Gamaliel Harding, his dog running in circles around him and Firestone as they shook hands.

"There he is," Mrs. Edison said. "He's just as handsome as his pictures, isn't he?"

Halverton quickly looked about inside the tent. Other campers were streaming in, and the President's arrival had their complete attention. Some were smiling, others obviously nervous as they stood uneasily. They seemed to shift their weight from one foot to the other, and they bit the inside of their cheeks. Margarete looked grim at the sight of the President, and Halverton thought she might be ill. She looked at the crowd of people beginning to surround the Hardings. It was like a depot. Men were carrying suitcases and satchels of work. Others toted heavy equipment — radio and camera gear, portable furniture.

"Feel all right?" Halverton asked Margarete.

"I'm fine," she said. There was a firmness to her voice. For what reason, he didn't know. Determination or resignation. He really knew so little about her. "Just fine."

From nowhere, Laddie Boy bounded into the tent and leaped, his front feet landing on the edge of Halverton's plate, flipping food across his shirt and onto the floor. The dog had taken a chicken leg and scooted to a corner. Halverton grabbed his collar. "No, bad dog," he scolded, tugging at the piece of chicken, the dog's lips curling and drooling as he held on to his catch.

"Laddie Boy!" a voice boomed behind them. "Heel!"

The dog cowered and walked on his belly to the President's side, leaving the chicken in the corner. Halverton stood, wiping at his shirt and hands.

"Thank you, young man," Harding told him. Firestone was at the President's side now.

"Mister President," Firestone said. "Sidney Halverton."

Harding walked past the others and pumped Halverton's hand.

"Halverton?" he said. "I met a Halverton about ten years ago in Texas. He wouldn't be your father, would he? He was a fire chief in Houston, I think."

"He sure was," a surprised Halverton said. "He's the city land commissioner now."

"I have friends in Texas," Harding said. "My buddy Scobey and I went for a cruise in the Gulf of Mexico with Mayor Campbell. I met a few other officials. We had a fine day of sailing. I was Lieutenant Governor of Ohio at the time. Perhaps your father mentioned it?"

"Dad's a Democrat," Halverton explained. "If you and he belonged to the same party, I'm sure I'd never hear the end of it. You being a Republican, though...well..."

Harding chuckled. "Well, thank you again for getting the chicken away from Laddie. Those bones can puncture a dog's stomach."

"I know," Halverton said.

"Let me show you your tent, sir," Firestone told the President. "I'm sure you'll want to freshen up after that drive."

"Yes," he said. "Yes, all right."

Then Harding saw Margarete for the first time. He stopped in his tracks and looked at her face. A smile just touched her lips. He glanced to her breasts, her slim waist and returned to her eyes.

"Wurr'n?" he could hear from outside. "Oh, Wurr'n?"

Harding and Firestone walked away.

"He must have a way with names," Halverton said to Margarete. "Remembering my father like that was something. Dad never told me he met him."

Margarete took a sip of water. She set the glass down, folded her linen napkin and placed it beside her plate. "It wasn't a very important meeting probably," she said.

8

THE DUCHESS HAD BEEN CALLING HARDING TO inform him that she was preparing to bed down for an afternoon nap, though she might be unable to sleep a wink, because the forest was, in her words, "full of allergics."

Harding was then free to demonstrate to everyone in camp that he was just one of the boys. He passed cigars out all around and shook everyone's hand at least once. He gamely chopped wood and stacked it and helped in building a fire in the already blazing summer heat.

Excess folds of skin bulged over the confinement of his stiff collar. He stood before the fire, panting, but smiling in rolled-sleeve informality as the flames climbed from the kindling to the larger logs. He looked like a turtle that a child might hold in the air, pretending it was able to stand on its hind legs. As the heat increased, Harding edged away from the fire, retreating to a canvas chair. He felt like keeling over from the exertion, but for appearance's sake, began whittling on a stick with trembling hands. Firestone picked out a chair at the President's side. With one look, he was concerned that Harding would lose a finger as he nervously made toothpicks of the small limb he was carving. The coffee pot was refilled constantly, and Firestone retrieved a cup for Harding so that he would have something to occupy his hands.

"It's been too long, Harvey," Harding said on Firestone's return. "A man shouldn't have to go to so much trouble just to bloviate among his friends."

"That's a good word," Firestone said. "What does it mean?"

"What, bloviate?" Harding said. "To loaf around. As an old newspaper editor, I had the opportunity to run into all kinds of archaic words. And as President, I'm able to help keep them from becoming extinct merely by using them. Things I say get written down."

Harding paused a moment and sipped his coffee. "Take a look around us here," he said. "You would think I could leave the White House and come and do this any time I wanted. No sir. I've got a flock of Secret Service boys to protect me from the populace, secretaries, secretaries to secretaries and the entire State Department on call at the other end of that radio over there. Secretary Hughes is sitting on the lid while I'm out of the Capitol."

"I thought Mister Coolidge would be," Firestone said.

Harding snorted. "Then we really would be in trouble," he said. "No, we can thank God that there is such a man as Charles Evans Hughes. He knows so much more than I do, which isn't saying much, I know. But in this postwar transition we're in, no one could be more eminently qualified for the job. He's a fine man."

Harding had calmed considerably since sitting with Firestone. It was as if, until that moment, he was still aboard the *Superb*, driving himself every minute to meet the schedule.

"I hope you won't consider this campout to be work," Firestone said. "I know a President cannot escape the job entirely, but I hope you'll be *able* to bloviate here."

"No, this isn't work," Harding said. "I've looked forward with anticipation to meeting Mister Edison and even to seeing Mister Ford again. From what I hear, I may have to face Ford as the Democratic nominee next year."

"I don't think so," Firestone said, shaking his head.

"He's very popular right now," Harding said. "Still, I wouldn't encourage anyone to seek the Presidency. Not in this day and age. It's such a shame that our nation has advanced to a point where the President is not allowed to be among the people who elected him anymore. He has to have this troop of advisors and protectors if he wants to so much as take a walk across the street. Look at McKinley. The poor s.o.b. was trying to shake the hand of the man who shot him. I'll tell you one thing. I wouldn't take Colonel Starling's job if it were handed to me on a silver platter. Look at him over there."

Colonel Edmund Starling was head of the White House detail of the Secret Service. He had coordinated the route of the trip across the country with advance men in every city where the President would speak or pass through. Security protection for a group of sixty was part of his assignment, and he knew who Harding would admit as a visitor. At the moment, Starling was testing the radio key with one hand and swatting flies with the other.

"He's got a tough task," Firestone said.

"Tough, hell," Harding said. "Next to impossible. He doesn't even have a life of his own. He's my shadow. Keeps my golf score, doles out the liquor and even stays outside the door when I'm on the crapper. He gets jumpy if there's even a freight train on a side track. There could be a madman in every empty boxcar we pass. And he's right, damn it. There might be. I'd have a bouquet of ulcers if I were him. Now, Barber over there, he's the wife's agent. She runs him ragged spying on the maids and the cooks and doing her errands. She even has him keeping tabs on me."

"Has she caught you?" Firestone asked jokingly.

"Once," Harding said. "Starling helped me give her the slip, and just in time too." Harding gulped at the coffee and stared at the treetops. "She makes life hell for me," he said.

Halverton had changed shirts since the episode with Laddie Boy, and he now returned to the dining tent for coffee with Margarete. "Get your boots on," he said to her. "We can explore these hills."

"I'd rather not today," she said. "It's getting late. We could do it in the morning when there's plenty of daylight, and we can take our time. I wouldn't want to get just outside of our little city and have to turn around again."

"All right," Halverton said. "That's a good idea."

"We could take a lunch," she added, stirring her coffee absently while watching Harding and Firestone. She was too far to hear what they were saying but had scarcely taken her eyes from them.

Ford drove into camp now, Edison in the passenger seat,

arm out the window and a smile across his face. The vehicle stopped, and as Ford set the brake, Edison shoved open his door. Mrs. Edison walked to the car at its arrival, and Edison presented her with a handful of wild violets, clumps of dirt still clinging to their uprooted stems.

"There was a field of them, Mother," Halverton could hear him tell her. "I wish you had been there to see it."

She wiped the hair from her husband's eyes and clutched the flowers gently. "They're beautiful," she said.

Ford's wife greeted him, locking an arm in his, and he marched with her at his side to greet the President. They shook hands and seemed the greatest of friends, which they were, as far as Henry Ford was concerned. Ford backed whoever happened to be in the Oval Office at a given time. He cared not a whit whether the nation's president was a Republican or a Democrat, so long as his actions served the interest of Ford Motor Company.

Edison entered the dining tent and shook the coffee pot, pouring himself a cup and sitting at the table. "'Afternoon," he said to Halverton.

"Hello, sir," Halverton said. "How was your ride?"

"Most pleasant," Edison said. "Mister Ford was able to identify two new species he'd never seen before. So it was an unqualified success of a day for him. He's a birdwatcher, you know, one of the most knowledgeable in the country."

"I didn't know that," Halverton said.

Edison leaned over and sipped at the coffee, pretending to ignore the approach of Harding, who was walking toward the tent with Firestone and Ford on either side. The three stepped inside.

"Al," Firestone said. "I'd like you to meet our President. Mister President, Thomas Edison."

Edison didn't stand and offered only a limp hand in greeting.

"It's my pleasure," Harding said. "I'd be honored if you would take one of my cigars."

Harding held the cigar forward, but Edison waved it away. "I don't smoke," he said. "I chew. It looks like a mighty fine cigar, but you keep it just the same. Now, if you'll excuse me, I'd like to see what kind of radio equipment the government is using nowadays. If it's all the same to you, that is."

Edison stood, turned on one heel, and left the others inside the tent. It was uncertain whether Harding or Firestone was the more embarrassed.

"What did I say?" Harding asked. "If I insulted him in any way, gentlemen, convey my apologies, please."

The three walked outdoors again, seeing Edison stroll toward the Secret Service tent. "Mister Harding," Firestone explained as they walked, "there is something you should know about Mister Edison. He's as stubborn as a tooth you want to pull. He does smoke a great deal, but he had the idea, I supose, that he was not going to take a cigar just because the President offered him one. Mister Edison does not take to everyone at first, and does not pretend to."

Harding thought for a moment. "Then I admire his frank honesty and bold forthrighteousness." He was never one to retreat in his assault on the language.

"I don't know why he did it," Ford said.

"It's nothing," Harding said. "It's quite all right."

Inside the dining tent, Mrs. Edison spoke to Halverton and Margarete. "I could wring his neck sometimes," she said, then broke into a forgiving smile as she stepped outside.

9

HALVERTON HAD LINGERED IN THE DINING TENT with Margarete, and other campers were constantly passing through it. A few of them were seated at the table. They talked of the wilderness they were invading and about their work and home towns. The First Lady interrupted their visit, dominating and filling the tent with her very presence. "As I live and breathe," she declared, singling Halverton out. "The very image of my departed son Pete, Pete DeWolfe." The Duchess sat near Halverton and studied his face closely.

"Excuse me?" he said, turning slowly in Margarete's direction, as if he would bolt and run given the chance.

"My poor dead boy," she continued. "You could be his twin. Please," she said to the others. "Please allow me to have some time alone with one who stirs such memories."

The campers began to vacate the tent, standing and shuffling self-consciously out into the open. Margarete started to leave, and Halverton grabbed her forearm. "Wait a minute," he told her, then turned to Mrs. Harding and repeated. "Wait a minute."

"It's perfectly all right," the Duchess said. "I should detain you no longer than a few moments."

"I'll go see if I can help with anything," Margarete said, leaving him alone with Mrs. Harding.

"You're very kind," Florence Harding said. She leaned closer to Halverton and asked, "Who *are* you?"

"S.M. Halverton, and I'm very sorry to hear about your son. I wasn't aware you and the President had any children. So many people lost children in the war, and in the influenza epidem —"

"He wasn't *Wurr'n's*," she said. "Don't you know anything about your own President? Pete was my son from my first marriage. Yes, I was married previously. Mister DeWolfe was a *beast* of a man, an absolute beast. And while my father never approved of the union, he was *deadly* opposed to our separation. A divorced daughter on his hands, that's what he was thinking. Well, I was not on his hands for long. I gave piano lessons and supported myself while Father just ignored me as if I'd blown away. He always wanted another son."

Halverton was very ill at ease. He had seen facial expressions like the Duchess's once before — on a man he was working with who had gone mad from heatstroke. The man had pulled out half his hair before his hands could be restrained, and he ranted about such a variety of subjects that he was incoherent. Mrs. Harding looked the same way to him.

"Pete was a wayward boy, not unlike his father," the Duchess went on. "He was always in trouble, and I couldn't rely on *him* to help influence Pete in the right direction. It was about this time that my former husband and some of his gang attempted to rob a passenger on the Marion to Colombus train. That's in rural Ohio, you know. Even though we were divorced, that was a great embarrassment for my family."

"Mrs. Harding," Halverton said as politely as he could. "My resemblance to your son is no more than a coincidence. I work in a canvas factory. I don't have the advice you might be look —"

"Don't you interrupt me," she cut in, blinking rapidly. "People have suggested that I was not a good mother to Pete, that I didn't have his welfare in mind when I sent him away to live with Father, who wanted another son anyway. I'll have you know it *was* in Pete's best interest. It *was*. To get him away from me when I couldn't stand to set eyes on him was an act of *char*ity, which is a virtue. And Wurr'n was a saint to Pete, an absolute saint. Whenever Pete was in need of money, Wurr'n opened his heart and his wallet. Not every time, but more often than not. Wurr'n had the paper to run, the Marion *Star*. So of course, I was unable to dote on Pete when I had to organize an entire newspaper. You may have heard that I used to spank the paperboys, the carriers. Well, *some*one had to keep them in line. They were squandering time and being sloppy, and in business, time is money. You didn't suppose Wurr'n was up to straightening them out, did you? Well, *did* you?"

"I didn't know anything about it," Halverton said defensively. He didn't want to hear any more about Pete, or absolute beasts or absolute saints. He only wanted out of the tent.

"And who do you think has Wurr'n's best interests at heart every minute of the day? That's right. *I* do. I knew *all* along the presidency was not suited for him, and I discouraged him in every way a wife could." The Duchess drew closer to Halverton now, looking out one flap of the tent, then the other, as if to draw him into her confidence. She began to speak in a lowered voice. "I consulted a seer, a Madam Marcia, even before the nominating convention had gotten under way. Mind you, I gave the woman not so much as my name, and she predicted that my husband would be elected President. *And*," she whispered. "That he would *not* live out his term in office."

Halverton said nothing. He was waiting the eternity until someone had to use the tent, with his hands folded limply in his lap.

"Well," she continued. "Once I knew it was written in the stars that Wurr'n would be President, I opposed it no longer. Perhaps my opposition had been selfish, I told myself. Oh, I have not had an *easy* life. Far from it. Even now, I must be on my guard. The White House staff is a pack of thieves. And Grace Coolidge thinks she is above me — *me*, the President's wife. Just who does she think she is? The *vice* president's wife, that's who she is. To think of the stately mansion they live in, whose upkeep and grounds are paid for by the government...well, it rankles, I'll tell you. A hotel apartment is *plenty* fine for the likes of them. I'll let you in on another little secret, Pete. Most of Wurr'n's companions laugh at him behind his back. You'll notice that Nicholas Longworth and his Alice are eager poker players at my husband's get-togethers, but that Alice Longworth, who wouldn't be *any*body if her daddy hadn't been the Rough Rider, *she* calls Wurr'n a slob. *Just* a slob, she says. And who is she, the Miss Nobody? I have seen the looks she gives Wurr'n when his back is turned. I fix them scrambled eggs if the party lasts until the wee hours, and she has nerve enough to complain about the food."

Halverton was hesitant to say anything at all. He nodded in sympathy to the First Lady's tirade.

"And the Attorney General is a self-righteous fellow," she proclaimed. "Where would Harry Daugherty be without my husband's connections? Oh, he professes true friendship, but only because he hasn't any *real* friends. Everyone wants the President for something. The farmers want higher prices for their crops, industry wants this, labor wants that. And Wurr'n tries to accommodate them all."

Laddie Boy scurried by the tent opening, sniffing the ground as he followed a trail. The Duchess caught a glimpse of him, interrupting her discourse. "Filthy little animal," she said. "No one appreciates the hard work I've put in all my life, Pete, not even you." One of the cooks entered now with a pot he placed on the table. "Who are you?" the Duchess asked. "Why have you come here?"

"The evening meal, Madam," the cook explained. "We'll be serving it soon."

She watched him leave and turned again to Halverton. "I used to think they would try to poison Wurr'n," he said. "But they're *much* too crafty for that."

"Mrs. Harding," Halverton said. "I would like to wash up for supper now."

"Well, go *ahead*," she said, irritated. "Who's stopping you?"

Halverton stood, pressed his lips together while he nodded one time in an affirmative gesture, but she seized his wrist before he could go away.

"I leave you with a word of caution," she said in a whisper. "There are *spies*. I overheard them aboard the train."

Halverton nodded again. "Get some rest," he said and walked toward his tent. Margarete was admiring a woman's needlepoint as he passed her, and she excused herself to be at his side. He sat on his cot just as she caught up with him.

"What's the matter, Sid?"

"Don't leave me alone with that woman again," he said, lighting a cigarette. "She'd be better off talking with Doctor Freud instead of me."

There was a new cluster of tents to house the President's security. It was a more relaxed atmosphere than the agents were accustomed to, but their routine was unchanged from the normal shift work. The Secret Service might appear to be off the job in a game of horseshoes or eating pie, but an agent was never far from Harding. In addition to keeping the President in sight, Secret Service placed sentries on the road in and out of camp. Others meandered in the woods near the campsite. They also operated the radio, which was in touch with the Presidential train. From the train, messages from the State Department were relayed to the camp.

Edison remained in the radio tent, delighting himself as he listened with an extra pair of earphones to the messages streaming in. He preferred holding one earpiece of the head-set to his better ear and jotting on paper with his free hand.

"In my Western Union days," he told the agent during a transmission lull, "I was always better at receiving than sending. It's been a while since I've done this, but I would think it hasn't changed much."

"Still the same old dots and dashes," the agent said. "As far as the actual operation goes, we sometimes work in pairs.

I prefer doing it alone. Better control that way."

The signal started again, and both men stopped speaking, each of them beginning to write in block letters.

BEACON INDICATOR STEAMER KNIT BOGGED TRANSLATOR COMMUNAL ENTRAP. BEAR ACTION BLUE NEGATE.

The message was nonsense to Edison. "I assume that's in code," he said. "Either that, or I've lost my touch more than I figured."

"Let's see," the agent said, glancing at Edison's note pad. "No, you've got it right. They'll want an answer right away. Would you like to try your hand at it? I can tell you the words, or you can refer to the codebook."

"No, you go ahead," Edison told him.

The agent tapped a quick reply, speaking as he worked the transmitter. "After a few weeks, this nonsense begins to make sense. I hardly use the code book any more. Beacon is the President. Bear is Attorney General Daugherty. The Attorney General is simply conveying his congratulations on the President's speech."

"I'll be darned," Edison said. "You know who would get a kick out of this? There's a fellow in camp. He used to be a radio operator in the Navy. First thing he ever said to me was in Morse, inside a noisy factory."

"Bring him over," the agent said. "These are not high-priority messages, as you can tell. We just have to stay in code in case something does arise."

"I understand," Edison said.

Mrs. Edison stood at the entrance to the radio tent. "It's time for dinner, dear," she said. "You want to get ready?"

"I'm not hungry," Edison replied. "I ate some candy bars earlier."

"I know you're not hungry. But the meal is planned just for us, the Firestones, the Fords, the President and his wife and Bishop Anderson. You should come sit with us at least."

"All right," Edison said, his face showing a grimace. He stood and shook the agent's hand. "I'll be back later in the evening."

"Bring that man by any time," the agent told him. "You can plug four sets of earphones into this thing."

"Fine," Edison said. "Sometime tonight, then."

It was the kind of gathering one finds recorded in historical footnotes. The Henry Ford Museum in Dearborn, Michigan has no fewer than a dozen photographs taken at the dinner. They are sharp images, highlighted by the ring of electric lights in the wilderness of West Virginia. An inspection of one picture reveals: President Harding, black eyebrows in contrast to his grey-white hair, looking more like a president than any president before or since; the Firestones, sitting erect and attentive (Harvey Firestone's moustache trimmed as neatly as the hair he parted straight down the middle of his head); Henry Ford reaching across and serving his wife a fresh salad; the bishop and his wife (marked "unidentified" in the photo's caption); Mrs. Edison heaping vegetables on her plate with a smile as wide as the silver spoon; Mrs. Harding, unaware of the camera as she looked closely at a glass; and Edison, plumped down before a cup of coffee, his dishes otherwise clean.

Extra tables had been set up in the clearing within the semicircle of sleeping tents, and the remainder of the campers dined there beneath the trees. It was grander living than they had at home. The meals were luxurious. All the dishes, from spinach souffles to baked pastries, were prepared on Ford's gasoline stove. The results were works of art. And best of all for the campers, all clean-up chores were performed by helpers, some of whom were hired only for the camping trip. Edison had accurately referred to the expedition as their "little Waldorf on wheels."

Halverton was aware that the dignitaries in the dining tent

were light years out of his league, but he nonetheless felt like a child seated at a table separate from the grown-ups. He watched them begin to leave the tent following their meal. They walked like a family after a Christmas dinner, rubbing their bellies, smoking cigars. The lights in the camp had been turned on, and they glowed more brightly as the sun met the horizon. Birds in the trees were more quiet. Halverton stood and pulled out Margarete's chair for her as Firestone and Edison stopped beside them to watch a couple of the helpers stretching a white tarp between two trees, its corners roped and pulled tautly. A projector was uncased and set on a recently vacated table. The portable chairs were being carried and arranged in rows and clusters in front of the screen.

"What's on the bill tonight?" Firestone asked.

"You can just about take your pick," Edison said. "We brought a couple of Mary Pickfords, Douglas Fairbanks as Zorro, the Gish sisters. And there's Vilma Banke."

Edison spit tobacco juice on the ground.

"The President should appreciate the movies," Firestone told him.

"Mister Harding's all right," Edison conceded. "Any man who chews tobacco's all right."

One of the cooks had started making popcorn on an open fire, which he would sack and place in rows on a table. There was lemonade, too, and sodas and cider. Just about the whole camp turned out for the movies. Harding sat as close to the screen as he could, eating the popcorn with a flair and reading the titles so loudly that one would think he was leading a cheer.

Edison ran the first reel of *Orphans of the Storm* himself to ensure that things were running to his satisfaction. He had control of the camp's lights from that position as well. He threw some lighting on the screen while rewinding the first segment. Mrs. Harding stood in the audience and edged her way toward Edison. She had been sitting beside the President, but could contain herself no longer.

"I don't see why we have to put up with that Lillian and Dorothy Gish," she told Edison. "And I for one refuse to. We had them in the White House for a viewing of that very same film last year, and they seemed to me to be nothing more than a couple of tarts."

Edison's deafness made him misunderstand the Duchess. He thought that she was raving in favor of the film.

"Yes," Edison answered her. "Yes, they have promoted the arts."

Halverton and Margarete were sharing a tangerine in chairs near the projector. Overhearing the exchange, Halverton let out a laugh into his fist. Edison, pleased to see Halverton having such a good time, smiled at him while dimming the lights once more. The Duchess retired to her tent.

Edison focused the new reel and bent at Halverton's side. "I want you to see the radio set the Secret Service has," he said. "We'll be back in a few minutes."

"Go ahead," Margarete said. "I'll wait for you."

Edison seized Halverton's arm, and they retreated in the darkness to the tent where the same agent sat before the radio, wearing a headset and finishing a plate of food.

"Here's that fellow I mentioned to you earlier," Edison said to the agent. "His name's Halverton."

"Sid," Halverton said as he shook the agent's hand.

"Pleased to meet you," the man replied. "I'm John Chambers. You two can plug in right on the side of this thing. Right there. Here, pull that cot up to sit on."

Edison and Halverton scooted forward, resting their elbows on the radio's table. Halverton slipped the speakers on like earmuffs, whereas Edison chose to hold his to his head with one hand.

"There's nothing coming over the set right now," Chambers explained. "There's another guy aboard the train doing the same thing I am. Only I'm sure he didn't have as nice a meal."

"You get plenty to eat?" Edison inquired.

"Yes sir, sure did," the agent said. "It was just excellent."

"Good," Edison said.

They sat and waited for a signal, but all that was picked up was the time check between the agents every fifteen minutes, the purpose of which was to make certain that neither of them fell asleep. Halverton found his eyes wandering back to the movie screen, but he was content where he was. He just wanted to hear something on the radio.

"You two can take over if you like," Chambers suggested. "It's time I stretched my legs anyway."

No sooner had Chambers spoken than the radio signals began to arrive.

"Sit back down," Halverton said. "Something's coming in."

The agent resumed his seat as Edison and Halverton seized their pencils.

REMAIN ST. LOUIS UNTIL CARGO SHIPPED FOR NIAGARA.

There was a pause, during which Edison and Halverton compared notes. They had copied the same message. Edison was about to cut in and ask for an explanation. Obviously, this wasn't the signal from aboard Harding's train car. But an answer to the message arrived instead. It was a different operator. The signal came slowly, as if the person at the key were consulting a Morse Code chart. The three men in the tent were listening in on a party line.

HOW LONG IN ST. LOU was the reply.

"This isn't for us," agent Chambers told them. "I don't know how we're picking it up, but it isn't ours."

Edison placed a finger over his lips and cocked his head, squinting his eyes as if to improve his hearing. "We're getting another frequency," he said. "These two fellows are talking to each other."

EXPECT TWO DAYS MAX. THEN ACCOMPANY CARGO. UNDERSTOOD?

"Well, *I* don't understand," Halverton said. "How could we suddenly start receiving the middle of their message?"

"They sound like salesmen," Edison suggested. "Like they're working on some sort of deadline. I'll wager their frequency is mixed in with ours. They get scrambled in the ionosphere sometimes."

Yes, whatever that means, Halverton thought.

"That's one of the drawbacks to radio," Edison went on. "You never will have the clarity in a signal or the undisturbed voice that you will find in a phonograph. And with a phonograph, you can choose what and who you will hear. You are not at the mercy of the fickle nature of the atmosphere. For communications to remote areas such as this, radio wins out, of course. But for entertainment, make mine the phonograph. As for music, on a radio, it is distorted and not enjoyable."

"I understand that the radio set is outselling the phonograph these days," the agent said without an ounce of tact.

If Edison heard the man, he did not answer.

IF CARGO MISES BOAT? the slow signaller, a poor speller, said.

THEN NIAGARA WILL NOTIFY YOU. UNDERSTOOD?

A few more beeps were received. If it was an answer to the last message, the three in the tent were unable to read it. Static and noise washed out the signal as suddenly as it had appeared. Then in clearly defined dots and dashes, the agent aboard the *Superb* tapped out the time of the evening.

Chambers grabbed the key. BILL — DID YOU READ PREVIOUS TRANSMISSION? — CHAMBERS.

The reply was negative.

DISREGARD, Chambers tapped. "We get a lot of long

distance signals at night. Music sometimes, too. They really come in clear, then drift out again. I don't know where or what this Niagara is, but it wasn't for us."

"It's a waterfall in upper state New York," Edison said, and the three of them laughed.

Halverton heard nothing more over the radio during the next hour, and he grew restless. When he noticed a new movie beginning, he thanked Edison and the agent, and excused himself. He wandered back to the seats, but found a fat man sitting in his chair. Margarete was gone too. The light was not at all clear. He walked up and down the rows and finally caught sight of her. She was in the chair next to Harding. Harding leaned in her direction once and whispered, and Halverton could hear her laugh. He turned away without her seeing him and walked across the campground to his tent. After listening to the Duchess in the afternoon, Halverton sympathized with the President completely. He didn't blame him for seeking out the company of other women. Harding was probably a very lonely man. Still, it nagged him that it was Margarete whom he chose.

10

WHEN HALVERTON AWOKE IN THE MORNING, HE WAS still dressed in his clothes from the previous evening. He had slept heavily, like an animal under the ground, and when he began to move about in the early light, he was sluggish and tired. He straightened his shirt, then slipped on a vest. But before he left his tent, he removed them both, stripping to an undershirt.

He changed pants, put on a fresh shirt and collar, and

walked toward a tree with his shaving cup and razor. A mirror had been hung on the bark, and there was a portable canvas washstand nearby. While most of the camp was still sleeping, he shaved, seeing President Harding in the background beyond the reflection of his own face. He was reading a newspaper at a table. Halverton didn't know where Margarete was.

He put away his shaving kit, buttoning his collar as he went to the dining tent. While he poured some coffee, one of the cooks asked what he would like for breakfast.

"I'll have the same thing as the President," Halverton declared. "And if it's not too much trouble, I'd like a couple of sack lunches for later in the day."

The cook had been wiping a place on the table, but at Halverton's order, had laid the towel over his arm like a waiter. "Will the gentleman be taking his meal inside?" he asked. "Or would he like a seat on the veranda?"

"Out there will be just fine," Halverton pointed.

With his coffee, he found a table set up, making himself comfortable under the trees, not at all sure if the cook's sarcasm would prevent his being served. But he didn't normally take breakfast, and sitting outside in the cool and quiet of the morning with a cup of coffee was a pleasant enough way to start the day for him.

Ford and Edison had left camp early, before daylight. Firestone and his wife joined Harding while Halverton awaited his food. When it did come, he almost gagged at the sight of it. For a moment he thought it was the cook's practical joke. A waffle, so large that its edges drooped over the plate, was piled high with chipped beef and drenched in brown gravy. The cook smirked as he placed the plate on the table, and Halverton felt like wrestling him to the ground because of the cocky expression. He studied the waffle, then slowly pushed it away from him. He could clearly hear the Firestones with Harding, and he listened while drinking the coffee.

"What's new in the world today?" Firestone asked the President.

Harding folded the paper crisply into fourths, sharply creasing the edges. "Listen to this," he read aloud. "Sixty people fainted yesterday when Ricardo Thannaro carried an open can of ether onto a Manhattan subway train. He said it was to cure his cold."

"My gosh," Firestone said.

"And in Bayonne, France," Harding went on. "During a bullfight, one of the bulls tossed his head, knocking the sword from the matador's hand and into the grandstand, where it pierced the heart of a wealthy Cuban spectator, who died."

"The poor man," Mrs. Firestone said, and they all nodded their heads in agreement. "And all the way from Cuba, too."

"Anything earthshaking on the domestic front?" Firestone asked.

"Well, let's see," Harding said, opening the paper again to thumb through its pages. "Says here the President made a speech in West Virginia. We know about that already. Here's something. Operators of the New England Telephone and Telegraph went on strike. It's the first labor strike by women."

Harding turned the pages, almost speaking to himself. "Unions aren't all bad," he said. His face lit up. "I'll be darned. It says here that there were 12,000 holes in one made on American golf courses last year. Kind of makes you want to keep trying, doesn't it? And here's another thing. A man calling himself Mister Zero sold jobless men on the Boston Common yesterday. He will continue to do so, he says, in an effort to ease unemployment. Why, unemployment's down to 2 percent already. What does he want? It was six times that rate when I took office."

"Does it say what jobless men are selling for nowadays?" Firestone asked, and the President smiled, shaking his head.

"I saw a newsreel recently," Mrs. Firestone said. "I think

the man in it was Mister Zero too. He climbed up the side of
a building blindfolded, then did a little tapdance on a ledge
when he made it to the top. I don't think he was supporting
a cause."

This was the sort of news Harding loved. As one-time
editor of the Marion *Star*, he had relied heavily on the wire
services. The remote and incidental, the odd and unusual
were often front-page stories. Harding had not lost his devo-
tion to the commonplace. As President, he spent hours each
evening answering correspondence from anyone who wrote
to him, even the crackpots. And he was open to the public
for thirty minutes to an hour every day before lunch. Harding was the handshakingest man ever to occupy the White
House.

"A tap dance blindfolded?" he said. "Really?"

"And on *top* of a building," Mrs. Firestone emphasized.

Halverton decided to taste a bite of the waffle. He swallowed, and had another. It was not as dreadful as he had
imagined, but he didn't like the way it sat there on the plate
as if it had been dropped from a great height. He considered
slicing up the creation into pieces for Laddie Boy, but was
afraid it might kill the dog.

Margarete walked to a chair at Halverton's side. Her hair
was pulled back tightly and tied. She was wearing a man's
shirt, baggy pleated pants and sturdy looking shoes. It
looked like a riding outfit, only more comfortable. The material was coarse and unrefined.

"Good morning," she said. "Do you think anyone will
object to me dressing in pants?"

"Would you put on a dress if they did?" Halverton asked.
"How about some coffee or breakfast?"

"No, I've already had some fruit," she said. She noticed
his preoccupation, as if he would prefer to be doing something else — reading a newspaper, taking a nap. "Are you
angry?" she asked him.

"No," he said, and then paused. "I was just curious how

you came to be sitting next to Mr. Harding last night."

"He asked me to," Margarete answered. "And I didn't see any reason to refuse him. I enjoyed his company. I've never met European royalty, and I didn't expect to meet a president. He wants very much to be liked. You shouldn't be curious."

"I guess I'm jealous. Someone like Harding can offer you things I can only dream about. That makes me feel a little desperate, I suppose."

"Do you think I'm someone who is easily swept off her feet?"

"No, of course not."

"No one, not a president or a king, could offer me more than you already have. You have given me your heart, and I accept it gratefully. It is Harding who should be jealous. Of the two, I choose you. Do you still feel desperate and abandoned?"

Halverton reached over and wrapped his fingers in hers.

One of the newspaper people had joined Harding while Margarete and Halverton were talking. The reporter was asking about the President's re-election strategy. He asked whether the entire train trip, Harding's Voyage of Understanding, was no more than a two-month campaign tour.

"It has been my philosophy all along," Harding said. "That if the present administration makes good, there cannot possibly be any doubt of renomination. If it does not make good, there ought to be no renomination."

"Then you are announcing your candidacy."

"I think it would be improper to say at this time, in these surroundings."

"The Attorney General, who was your campaign director at one time, has already said, and I quote, 'The President will be a candidate for re-election. He will be renominated and re-elected because the people will demand it.' That sounds like an announcement."

Harding drew back in his chair. "I want to speak now as

your President, on this day and on every day that I am in office. That is without condition. Without the condition that I will run again, and with no guarantee of the future other than hope. I hope for a better understanding of the issues by the country and a better understanding by me of the American people."

The reporter seemed confused.

Halverton had overheard the exchange with the President. He was still in awe of the man for who he was. The very notion of the Presidency brought to mind Lincoln, Theodore Roosevelt and Wilson. Even Harding, in his speeches, came across as a statesman at the very least. Still, it was a little disheartening to imagine that the man seated in the canvas chair a few steps away was the same man who was at the helm of the armed forces of the country. There were no visible heroic dimensions to Harding. He was a glad-hander. And look what he had for breakfast. If anything, he seemed average, not such a bad thing in itself. But did we want just an average man to lead the country? With Wilson, you knew you were in good hands. Or so it seemed. Or had the country's leaders always been less than they appeared, propped up by a grand, false image for the public? Halverton doubted it. He had not voted for Harding, and he certainly wasn't won over yet for his support in a second term.

He and Margarete stood to leave. Halverton drew her close to him by the arm, as if to whisper something to her. As she paused to listen, he bit her sharply on the ear lobe. She let out a scream that could be heard across the camp. Then she laughed at sounding such an alarm while Halverton feigned innocence.

She meandered in the direction of the automobiles, and he approached the cook near the dining tent. "How was your waffle?" the cook asked. "Come hell or high water, the President has one just like it every morning."

"It reminded me of hell and high water," Halverton

answered. "What sort of nightmare have you concocted for lunch?"

"Two ham sandwiches on rye bread, a couple of apples and a Mason jar of cider."

"That sounds very good," Halverton said, peering into the sack suspiciously. "Thank you."

Margarete returned with the blanket and a basket for the food. She held his arm, and they took to the road. It was a dry day, and little cakes of dust fell from their heels as the camp noises diminished and faded in the distance. A quarter of a mile away, and the trees swallowed all sight and sound of civilization.

"Smell the trees," she said. "It's like the Black Forest here."

"In Germany?"

"Yes. A beautiful place, and this is just as tranquil. America, from what I know of it, is like a dozen countries. It has the climate and geography of almost every place on Earth."

"When were you in Germany?"

"They're very small countries over there," she said. "Your Texas is larger than most of them." She paused. "You know, Sid, most men would question me about everywhere I've ever been. They would want to know every man I have known. You aren't like that. I have a feeling that someone's past doesn't influence you at all."

Halverton waited before speaking. "It's not that I don't care about your past," he said. "The past is what has shaped you into the person you are, the good experiences and the bad. I wonder about your family, what kind of life you have had, what you plan to do. I worry about the future sometimes, whether I will be a part of yours."

"It's working out fine," Margarete said. "You and I are probably more compatible than we realize."

"I hope so," Halverton said.

There was a man in the road ahead, and as they came

closer to him, they recognized him as one of the Secret Service agents.

"'Morning," the agent said. "Nice day for the outdoors."

"It surely is," Halverton said. "Would you like a shot of cider?"

"I don't mind if I do," the agent answered. "Here, I already have a cup."

Halverton poured him a drink. "We might be gone all day from camp."

"All right. Will you be coming back this way?"

"I don't know. Unless we cut through the woods we probably will."

"How long will the President be in camp?" Margarete asked the agent.

"We leave in the morning after services by Bishop Anderson. We'll be in St. Louis tomorrow night."

Halverton nodded without taking a step in either direction. Margarete thought he might get started in a long conversation with the agent and began to pull on his arm to lead him away.

"I hope you like the cider," she said as they began to walk again.

They could hear water. It was the creek that ran through the campsite, but they were nearly a mile upstream of there. With the agent now gone from view, they continued down the road until it bridged the creek. The water was only five feet wide, and narrower in places, but it was swift, clear and noisy. It flowed around the base of the highest piece of land for miles in any direction. Bickle Knob was over four thousand feet high, and the terrain leading from the creek to its side was almost mountainous. For Halverton it was. He had grown up in the swampy marsh area of the Texas Gulf coast.

They left the road and followed a trail on the banks of the creek. Fallen trees were scattered here and there, but the going wasn't rough. They ducked under limbs and held hands where there was a high or wide step to take, but there wasn't any snagging underbrush scratching at their legs. They walked that way for an hour. The sun had come out, and they thought of stopping for cider. The water raced toward the ocean in stretches and was a mere trickle in places. Their path began to curve. They pushed a little farther, and a pool came into view. It was perhaps ten feet wide and twice that long. The water was deeper than they had thus far seen.

"Look, you can see the bottom," Margarete said. "It would be perfect for swimming."

Halverton stepped onto a flat rock at the water's edge, then walked beneath a tree. He kicked up a pile of pine needles and lay the blanket over it. He set the basket on the ground, pulling out his shirttail at the same time. He heard a splash and turned toward the pool. He saw Margarete's clothes folded on the bank. She glided across the surface of the water, breaking the glare of the sun into chandeliers of light. When she stood in the creek, the water lapping at her hips, her hair embraced her back and shoulders like a dark paint.

"It's cold," she called out.

It was almost unreal to Halverton, like a dream. They stayed in the water together, holding each other closely, then splashing and playing, but always finding each other's arms again. When it became too cold, they dried with the blanket and lay nude in the sun.

They returned to the creek again, floating leisurely in the pool's open water. He moved to a rocky ledge on the bank. She joined him, pushing her back against his stomach, pressing the palms of her hands hard against his thighs. Halverton kissed the side of her neck, coiling his arms around Margarete's waist. She drew a breath sharply and held it. He stood, lifting her out of the water. He placed her on her feet and led her by the fingertips in the direction of the blanket. Her hair was draped about her breasts, her nipples pronounced by the cold water and by her own arousal. Lying on the blanket, her hair to one side, she curled her toes as she reached out for him, guiding him into her.

When they were sitting again having lunch, Margarete mentioned that she should have brought a bar of soap. "The camp doesn't have the privacy for a bath. You know what I'd really like?"

"What's that?" Halverton said.

"A nice, hot shower," she said. "I'd let it run until the water turned cold. But I suppose I'll have to wait until we get to the Falls for that kind of luxury."

"What do you mean?" he asked.

"What?"

"You said 'The Falls.'"

"I *did*?" She flashed a quick smile. "I don't know why. I guess I was thinking about the shower, and all that water had me confused. You know I can't even see straight after making love. I meant to say I can't wait to get home to take a real bath. Didn't you mention Niagara Falls to me?"

"Yes," Halverton said. "I did earlier in the day."

It was almost dark when they walked into camp. They sat on a couple of stools. Everyone had returned from their various outings. In one view, they could see Thomas Edison, Henry Ford, Harvey Firestone and the President of the United States.

"You know the big distinction this campout has?" Halverton asked her. "It's that there are extraordinary men here, but they're doing very ordinary things. You don't expect them to be just normal, but they are. Of course, there's not much getting back to Nature here. I've taken trips with my father and brother where we didn't see another living soul for days. We didn't have movies and radios."

Margarete placed her hand on his. "Believe me when I tell

you that I'm very happy with you right now. This has been a wonderful day with you, with many more to come. I'll never forget today, Sid."

11

IN THE MORNING, THE HELPERS BEGAN BREAKING down the camp, re-coiling the wire from the lighting system, lowering and flattening tents and loading cots and bedding onto the trucks. The camp chairs were being arranged for services by Bishop Anderson. Still standing was the dining tent, where members of the party passed through in their morning rituals.

Henry Ford stood near the tent at the gasoline stove. He was wearing a billowing chef's hat, scarf and boots, denim pants and a pistol strapped to his side. He was flipping and stacking pancakes onto plates. Edison sat a few feet away inside the tent, his maps spread before him on the dining table. Whenever he would look up from what he was doing and catch a glimpse of Ford in his outfit, he would laugh. A photographer was trying to capture it all, but Ford wouldn't stand still long enough.

Halverton had carried his things to his car after his tent was collapsed. He looked in the direction of Margarete's tent, but it was already gone. He went for some coffee, and it seemed to him that everyone he greeted looked into his face a moment longer than normal, as if he were not only the doer of something vile or something daring, but seven feet tall as well. He stepped into the cavernous dining tent. Edison, sitting before his own coffee, grinned at him. "You like pancakes?" he asked.

"Yes I do," Halverton said.

"We have a guest chef today," Edison told him. "Mister Tom Mix himself has honored us with his specialty, ranch style sourdough flapjacks."

Halverton looked out the flap of the far side of the tent. He saw Henry Ford throwing pancakes high into the air, where they flipped twice before landing perfectly on the griddle again. Edison scooted closer to Halverton.

"You want to get his goat?" he asked. "Go out there and ask Henry for doughnuts. Tell him, 'Mister Mix, I have a powerful hankerin' for doughnuts. Can you whip me up a dozen or so?'"

"He might get mad," Halverton said.

Edison shook his head. "Go ask Henry for doughnuts," he urged. "And call him Tom Mix."

Halverton carried his coffee out of the tent. Edison cupped his hand behind his ear.

"Good morning, Mister Tom Mix," Halverton said. "Those are mighty fine looking pancakes."

"And mighty fine tasting too," Ford said. He had a piece of straw in his mouth.

"It's a shame I'm not in the mood for pancakes. What I'd like is a batch of doughnuts, if you don't mind fixing them too much, Mister Mix."

Halverton glanced over his shoulder. Edison was giggling into his fist. Ford nodded his head, using the spatula to stack one pancake on the next until they were high and ready for the syrup. He pushed the dishes he'd been using out of the way, and reached for a large wooden plate. He wiped it clean with a fresh towel, sizing Halverton up, holding the new wooden dish as he turned to see what part Edison had played in this.

Quickly, Ford lifted the pancakes onto the plate, then extended the stack toward Halverton.

"No, thank you sir," Halverton said. "I ordered doughnuts, and doughnuts is what I want."

Ford smiled. "So you did," he said.

He set the plate on the ground between his feet and Halverton's, drew the pistol, and fired a shot through the pancakes, the plate, and a half of foot of the earth beneath it. The hills resounded and roared the sound of the shot back at them. Halverton stooped over and picked up the plate, fingering the hold in the wood and losing not a drop of coffee in the process.

"These doughnuts will do just fine," he said, and Edison burst out laughing as he carried them into the tent.

He sat down to eat the pancakes, powder burns and all, when Colonel Starling dashed into the tent, two other agents at his heels. "No cause for alarm, gents," Edison told them. "Someone complained about the chef's cooking, and you just don't do that. We had to shoot him."

Ford replaced his gun in the holster, and the gesture seemed to satisfy the agents, whose job allowed little room for a grandiose appreciation of humor. They stopped beyond the tent, one of them looking back over his shoulder at Halverton. He couldn't hear their words, but felt by their attention that they were speaking about him. He wondered why.

Ford entered the tent now with a fresh batch of pancakes, and he placed them before Halverton. "You're a good sport," he said and patted him on the back.

Halverton took a couple of bites. They were very good pancakes, and he told Henry Ford so. "Where did you learn to make them?"

"Oh, here and there. You pick up a few skills in a lifetime. Skills you might not be called upon to use but once every few years. But they're good to fall back on when the need arises."

"Well, they're certainly good pancakes," Halverton said. "I like them, and I'm not just saying that because you're wearing a gun." He paused and drank some of his coffee.

"By the way, I was wondering where Margarete was. It looks like they've taken down her tent. Have you seen her?"

"She was in camp a couple of hours ago," Edison told him. "I saw her around daybreak."

"What was she doing?" Halverton asked.

Edison didn't want to say. He looked to Ford for help.

"I lent the President a car," he said. "He and Miss Fabry have taken a ride together."

"I knew a Professor Fabry once," Edison interjected. "From Paris, France."

Halverton laid down his fork. "They were alone?" he said. "The two of them, no Secret Service?"

"They took his dog," Ford said. "Mister Harding was insistent about being unguarded, but as a precaution, Colonel Starling ordered them followed in another automobile. Don't worry, son. They'll be back in camp soon enough. Would I be dressed like a cowboy if anything was the matter?"

Halverton was overwhelmed with a sense of dread, the feeling washing over and isolating him until it was as if he were completely alone in the tent. He felt as though a wave had taken him away from friends on a beach and pulled him out to sea. Margarete's past, which he had so lightly dismissed the previous day, seemed very important to him now. Why would she do such a thing? And what, for that matter, was she doing? She had told him that she found Harding's company enjoyable at the films, that she had not seen a reason to refuse him. Had Harding made advances to her, and were they too much a temptation? Were the advances hers? Were there any advances at all? Whatever had happened, the thought of her with Harding at that moment was a painful thing for Halverton.

He heard a car driving into the compound. Ford threw open the tentflap and looked outside. It was the Secret Service car that had followed the President, and as the agents opened the doors, Laddie Boy bounded out of the vehicle and ran to the creek, cooling himself in belly-deep water before gulping a drink. Halverton looked farther down the road, but no other automobiles were in sight. Colonel Starling was alongside the car now listening to his men. His expression was serious. He remained there a few more moments, then looked at Halverton standing in the opening of the dining tent. He tapped the car door once with his fist and began walking toward Halverton with resignation. Henry Ford removed his chef's hat.

"I need to ask you some questions in private," Starling told Halverton. "Mister Edison, may we use your quarters?"

Edison nodded. He stood with Ford, watching Starling lead Halverton away. Halverton was confused. He momentarily thought of breaking away and running and wondered if the action would earn him a bullet in the back. He was lost, knowing for certain that he would never hear Margarete's voice again.

They opened the flaps to Edison's tent, and Starling tied them closed from the inside. Halverton looked around the tent. It was comfortable, with a wooden floor added, electrical outlets, a reading lamp and a chest of drawers. Halverton faced Harding's agent.

"How long have you known Margarete Fabry?"

"A few months," Halverton said. "Three or four months."

"Has she ever in that time expressed to you any political beliefs or ideas that could be construed as treasonous?"

"No, not at all," Halverton answered.

"Do you know for a fact that she is who she says she is?"

"I don't understand."

"Have you heard her answer to any name other than her own, or have you seen any correspondence in her possession that was not addressed to her?"

"No."

"Has she spoken to you specifically about the President?"

"Only her impression of him on meeting him here."

"Which was?"

"She felt that Mr. Harding wants to be liked. That he seems lonely, maybe. I don't remember exactly."

Starling stared into Halverton's face, studying his features, memorizing them for comparison to his reaction to the following question. "Are you her accomplice?"

"Her accomplice in what?" Halverton said without blinking. "What has she done?"

"Two hours ago, two and a half by now," Starling told him. "Mr. Firestone drove many of the ladies on a truck ride north of camp. Mrs. Firestone accompanied him, as well as Mrs. Edison and the First Lady. The President complained of a stomach pain and remained behind to rest. Shortly thereafter, however, Mr. Harding said he was feeling better, that he would join Mr. Firestone with the loan of an automobile. He requested that Miss Fabry join him, and they drove south out of camp. I had a car following at a discrete distance. A little too discrete. It lost visual contact completely. The President's car flat got away from us. We were able to locate where it pulled off the road once, and not far away they found the President's dog. The President would never abandon that dog in the countryside like that."

"Maybe the dog got away from them," Halverton suggested. "They could be looking for him."

"They wouldn't have vanished completely if that were the case," Starling said. "And we can eliminate the possibility that they have fallen victims to a third party. Not another single tire track was in the area. Now, under what conditions did you meet Miss Fabry? Who introduced her to you?"

Halverton felt the muscles in his throat begin to tighten, constricting his air passage to such an extent that he feared for a moment that he could not breathe, let alone speak with Colonel Starling. He swallowed and took in a lungful of air. "We met in a park," he said. "In Trenton. I saw her in the park, and we began to speak. No one introduced us."

"And this was three or four months ago. Had you already been invited on the camping trip at that time?"

"Yes, a few days earlier, by Mr. Edison. I didn't know Margarete at the time at all."

"And what occurred between the day you were invited to the campout and the day you met Miss Fabry?"

"Nothing," Halverton said. "I worked my shift and stayed home in the evenings. I met Mr. Edison at work, then it was mentioned in the paper the following day, and..." The realization suddenly hit him. It was if he had just been informed of a death in the family. His chief feeling was one of astonishment and denial that anyone could be so manipulative and premeditated as to enter a person's heart, only to tear her way out with razors. "I was in the paper. My name and photograph."

"Then she probably sought you out," Starling said. "She used you as a way to get at the President."

"Good God, I walked right into it," Halverton said, shaking his head in disbelief. "What an idiot. And to think she had me begging her to come with me here."

"Is there anything you can tell me, anything at all that might be of help? Time is very important right now."

Halverton shook his head. "I'm sorry," he said. "But nothing comes to mind. She told me she was Dutch, but that could have been idle chatter."

Starling drew open the tent flap and took a step outside, looking in at Halverton. "That might be something we can follow up on," he said. "But it isn't likely. At any rate, you'd best remain in camp. I may want to question you more later on."

Halverton stayed in Edison's tent. He felt a falling sensation and lay on his side to think. He could see two cars belonging to the Secret Service, three men in each, start their engines and race southward out of camp. Other agents were running around like poultry at feeding time. Halverton rolled onto his back and closed his eyes. When Edison entered the tent, he sat up.

"Keep your seat," he told Halverton, sitting across from him on the other bed. Edison gazed outside at the stools and chairs in formation, the bishop standing before them going over some notes, while all around him the commotion with the agents continued. "It's a source of continual perplexity," he observed.

"What is?" Halverton said.

Edison gestured toward Bishop Anderson. "I cannot see that creeds amount to anything," he said. "And personally, I am amazed that apparently sound minds set such great store in them."

"I'm in trouble," Halverton said. "We all are — the whole country — if the Secret Service's fears are confirmed."

Edison said nothing, waiting for Halverton to speak.

"They think the President has been kidnapped by Margarete."

The words sent a jolt through Edison. He opened his eyes wide. "What do you think?" he asked.

"I really don't know. Maybe she has done such a thing. She deceived me completely, or somebody has."

"Who?"

"I don't know. Perhaps the Secret Service. Mrs. Harding spoke to me of spies. I thought it was a delusion. If that's the case, then they're right among the President's staff, perhaps even some of his advisors. I'm not sure we can trust anyone at this point."

"It's an unprecedented crisis," Edison said. "Whichever way you look at it. Certainly though, it would be a heap worse if someone in government is involved."

They sat, facing each other in silence, thinking for a long time. Finally, Halverton spoke up.

"I know where she might have taken him," he said. "It's hardly anything, but it's all I can think of."

"Well, what is it?" Edison said.

"Canada," Halverton said. "Canada, by way of Niagara Falls. Remember that radio message we picked up the other night?"

"Sure," Edison said. "Those salesmen."

"I don't think they were salesmen at all," Halverton said. "They mentioned St. Louis and Niagara. St. Louis is where the President was scheduled to be today. And yesterday, Margarete made a slip of the tongue. Said she was looking forward to a bath, but expected she'd have to wait until 'The Falls' to take one. That's twice I heard of Niagara in as many days, and I think it's more than coincidence."

"And you think the radio messages were sent by people involved in this thing?" Edison frowned. "Damnation, it goes against my grain to have to rely on supposition. Under the circumstances, we have no other choice. We'll have to regard what we know as solid proof if we're to make any headway at all."

"What should we do?" Halverton asked him. "Don't forget. That was the Secret Service radio we heard that on."

"Well, we're privy to some confidential information here, that's sure. I think Colonel Starling and his boys are on our side, but we cannot afford to take the chance if they're not. Not when the republic itself could be at stake. Let's wait till Harvey gets back, then you and me and him and Henry ought to light out for Niagara Falls. What do you say?"

"Can we do that?" Halverton said. "Look at all the magazine and newspaper people here."

"You leave them to me. I'll just have a tantrum for my privacy, and we can slip away as if nothing has happened. We were moving the campsite anyway as soon as the President left. Whatever we do, one thing is certain. We'll do *some*thing. We shall make a brilliant success of it, or a brilliant failure. We'll get Mister Harding back. We'll get there ahead of him." Edison stood and clapped Halverton solidly on the back. "Yes sir, we're going to Niagara."

12

IT WAS EDISON'S DECISION THAT THEY TRAVEL IN the truck for reasons of anonymity, or as close to anonymity as he, Henry Ford and Harvey Firestone could expect. The truck carried provisions of food, a small stove fed on gasoline from the tank, the camp's spare storage battery and a pair of tents with mattresses. Its unique construction, including nickel plating, was hand made under Ford's direct supervision. The truck was practical and handy. All storage compartments could be reached from the ground. Its cab had not one, but two, passenger seats. The four riders could be accomodated in relative luxury, independent of any outside conveniences. The only thing a hotel or tourist cabin could offer them which they did not already carry was running water, and Ford was working on a solution to that.

There had been a brief huddle when Firestone returned to camp with the ladies. He was told the situation with Harding and of Edison's proposed journey to Niagara Falls. He agreed immediately, and within five minutes of his arrival in camp, he had embraced his wife and thrown a suitcase onto the truck. He sat in the back seat of the cab beside Halverton, the two watching Ford and Edison speak to their wives. Firestone turned toward the younger man, saying quickly but without panic in his voice, "You realize, of course, this may be the death of us all." Halverton did not answer.

And for the benefit of everyone in shouting distance, Edi-

son had his tantrum, pulling away from his wife and screaming that his vacation had become no more than a traveling
circus, that his every move and word were being recorded for
posterity. The lack of privacy was tiresome, he said. "Me,
Henry and Harvey are going so deep into the woods that you
won't find us till we want to be found. I don't suggest you
follow." Edison marched into his tent for effect, and his wife
was now at the side of the truck to see them off.

"You won't let him come to any harm, will you Harvey?"
she asked. "Mister Halverton, you will look out for him. He's
not a young man." Tears formed in her eyes. She rested her
hand on the door, and Halverton touched her for reassur-
ance.

"No harm will come to any of us," he told her.

"How can you be certain?" she asked.

It was Firestone who answered. "Because we're right," he
stated. "And I might add we're good, and the good always
win out over their adversaries.

Ford and Edison were at the truck now. Ford held the
elder man's arm as he climbed into the front seat, then
walked around the hood of the vehicle himself. He was still
dressed in his Western attire. He climbed behind the wheel,
started the engine, his wife comforting Mrs. Edison as she
backed away from the truck. The motor idled a moment,
then, as they began to move, Halverton leaned forward in his
seat, looking out for a last view of the campsite as it folded
in upon itself. None of the tents remained standing, and piles
of canvas and bedding littered the ground. He saw Bishop
Anderson, looking bewildered, still standing before the
assembled chairs. Up ahead, in the President's Pierce Arrow,
Agents Starling and Barber could be seen talking with Mrs.
Harding. She seemed not to be listening as the truck drove
past her. She rocked forward and back in her seat, catching
Halverton's eyes momentarily before he rode out of camp.

Some of the cars would come their way, but would scatter

and seek their own directions before finding them. As unconvincing and out of character as Edison's tantrum had been, one thing was certain: With the exit of him, Ford and Firestone, the vacation — the campout — had come to an end.

Halverton pushed back against his seat again, watching the pattern of tree limbs above him contrast with the scene in the side mirror over Ford's shoulder as the truck moved down the dirt road. The Monongahela Forest was one of the most isolated areas in the United States, and it would be hours, perhaps a day, before they reached a paved road. Each man was absorbed in his own thoughts, and Edison was the first to break the silence by voicing his. "We sure ain't no *de*tectives," he said. "Not one solid clue, and we go traipsing off across three states in hope of what?"

"It's all we have, Al," Firestone said.

"It doesn't have to be," Ford said. "We could get help. We could hire Wyatt Earp or somebody like that. Bat Masterson maybe."

Firestone barked a laugh. "Masterson writes a newspaper column, and Wyatt Earp, if he is alive, is in an old folk's home."

"What'd you say?" Edison asked, turning in his seat and tilting his ear toward Firestone.

"An old folk's home," Firestone shouted. "I said Wyatt Earp's in an old folk's home."

"I didn't know he was still alive," Edison said.

"Neither did I," Halverton said.

Firestone grew exasperated. "Let's not distract ourselves from the task at hand," he said. "I agree that Niagara is our only hint and must be our most likely target. But if that is the case, only one thing bothers me."

"What is that?" Ford said as he drove.

"Why did they take the road south out of camp?"

"That's not so hard to understand," Henry Ford

answered. "To throw us off the track. We must assume that we are correct, and anything contradictory is either irrelevant or put there purposely to confuse us. I have my own theory about this entire rotten scheme."

Ford became quiet. He was waiting for someone to ask his explanation or was allowing the silence to build interest in what he had to say. Edison kept his hand at his ear.

"International Jewish banking power," Ford said. "Its aim is the destruction of Christian civilization by world revolt and war. The Jews want to gain control of politics, and commerce and finance. You see, most of them, they're traders who don't want to produce anything on their own but want to make something off of what somebody else produces. Intemperance, high rents, decline in morals, both private and public, short skirts, vulgar Broadway shows, flashy jewelry, night clubs, scarlet literature — these are all results of the international Jew."

"Go get 'em, Henry!" Edison hooted, his voice excited and shrill. "But where is the logic in that? If we could corner the trade in short skirts and Broadway shows, I'd have had the patent on them long ago, and you, my friend, would be cranking them out on the assembly line right alongside the Model T."

Firestone and Halverton were forced to smile.

"Well, you know what I mean. An incident like Harding's disappearance has international implications. It could precipitate another war, or even revolution. The Bolsheviks would love to get a foot in the door."

Halverton turned his attention to the forest. It was so thick that the sunlight was unable to penetrate its denser areas. As the light flickered through the limbs, he began to think of Margarete, Sundays in oceanside cottages and time flying by in evenings on the porch of Mrs. Meek's rooming house. He could not believe that her interest in him had been solely as a means to an end, for he could see that her pleasure in his company was real, her enthusiasm genuine. He felt a strong sense of anger and betrayal over her part in the President's abduction. He was in love with Margarete, and loved her still. But even love had its limits. If he could find her again, there was no question in his mind whose side he would choose in a confrontation.

The truck bolted at a bump in the road, and all four men grabbed something to hold. It was a poor road, with winding curves and deep ruts.

"If we had the time," Firestone told Ford, "I'd like to go back and hit that hole again without these balloon tires. You'd see a difference, Henry. The balloon tire is the tire of the future. It didn't explode, did it? And it has handled every road condition we've encountered."

Ford looked to Edison for a reaction.

"He's right as rain," Edison said. "Safest thing in the world, the balloon tire. And soon, we shall produce the rubber for them ourselves — loosen the stranglehold the British Empire has on the rubber supplies in Africa."

"Bullets won't bounce off of them, sharp objects can puncture them," Firestone said. "But they are reasonably safe, more than the old-fashioned tires. They're economical. You, of all people, should know the value in reducing a good's costs."

"I do, Harvey," Ford said. "No doubt about that. My whole aim has been to make cars cheaper and cheaper. And make them simpler as well — turn them out like needles and pins. We've only just started. I'll tell you what. Just as soon as we complete this mission of ours to save the world, I'll give you an answer on the balloon tires. I have been thinking about them. I don't want you to think I haven't."

"Well, I'd appreciate some more thought in the right direction," Firestone said, rearranging himself in the seat.

Halverton nudged him. "I have balloon tires on my car, Mister Firestone," he said. "They haven't given me an ounce of trouble."

"Hear that, Henry?" Firestone chuckled. "Another satisfied customer."

Edison could hear none of the bantering. He was as much a lip reader as anything, and if something held his attention, what little of his hearing that remained, faded, and nothing else existed for him. His maps of the countryside were spread across his lap, and he studied them silently. Occasionally, he made a marking on them with a stubby pencil he kept tucked behind his ear. "We ought to be about even with the Maryland state line right about now," he announced. "East of here, two, two and a half miles. We're out of the Alleghenies now. But some of these foothills are nothing to sneeze at."

"We'll avoid the cities, won't we Henry?" Firestone asked. "Surely you and Al would be recognized almost anywhere."

"That's the truth," Ford said. "But that handicap is shared by Mister Harding. That's something in our favor. I would not be surprised if she moves him under the cover of darkness, holing up somewhere in the daylight hours."

The truck made twenty-five miles an hour in some of the straightaways, but the smooth stretches were not long ones, and the passengers fairly crept a majority of the time. The same creek whose banks had held their tents crisscrossed the road a dozen times by early afternoon. It was never a great distance away from the road and often ran alongside their northward route. They habitually looked up and down the stream each time they encountered it, and at one such crossing, something caught Edison's eye. He seized Ford's arm and called out, "Stop this thing. Stop the truck."

Ford hit the brakes, and Edison bounded off the running board before the truck had completely stopped, scooting out of sight into the underbrush. "What is it?" Firestone asked, climbing out of his seat in back. "What did he see?"

Ford shrugged, and the three men began to follow Edison to discover the source of his distraction. They found him inspecting an old unused grist mill, with an oaken overshot waterwheel at least twelve feet in diameter. Some slats of the wheel were missing. Gravel and mud were banked against its bottom, anchoring it in place as if it was set in cement. Water uselessly trickled through the wheel and around the walls of the small stone mill house.

"Such a fine piece of handwork to go to so great a waste." Edison lamented as the three others joined him. "Look, Henry, Harvey. Enough potential power here to operate a household."

"It's a shame," Ford admitted. "Put a wheel like that every ten yards along this creek, and you'd have a power station."

"Get the camera," Firestone suggested. "It's a good picture."

Ford retrieved the camera from the truck, and Halverton offered to photograph them. Edison climbed to the wheel's axle, resting a hand on its rim above his head. Ford squatted on the uppermost slat, his shoes together, knees spread far apart and hooked under his elbows. Firestone squeezed between the mill house and the wheel, perched on the other side of the axle. He was trying to hold himself steady and barely hanging on, making a genuine smile for the camera. Halverton found them in the frame of the box camera and set off the shutter. He hoped the picture would come out all right, since he considered himself to be in enough trouble without an irate Henry Ford charging after him in an imagined rage over a blurry picture. As it turned out, the photograph was perfect, becoming part of the collection in the Henry Ford Museum in Dearborn, Michigan.

"How about me taking another one."

"You know how to advance the film?" Ford called out.

"That's it," Edison declared, climbing down from his position on the wheel. "Let's get on our way."

Halverton closed the camera into its case and returned it to Ford. He walked back to the truck at Firestone's side.

"Mister Edison likes riding in automobiles, as you've

guessed," Firestone said. "That is, as long as he rides in the front seat. He has no use for any other part of a car."

"What's the name of that creek?" Halverton asked in the truck, and no one knew. Firestone repeated the question in a shout to Edison, who consulted his map.

"Cheat Creek," he announced. "That's Cheat Creek, the State of West Virginia."

"Shit Creek is more like it," Ford said at the wheel. "If anyone was ever up Shit Creek, its us."

Halverton wondered what had become of the builders of the wheel, whether they or their descendants still owned the land. Perhaps they were victims of the influenza epidemic of 1918 or had been routed over half a century earlier by the armies of the South. He had no idea how old the wheel was.

Two hours passed. They crossed Cheat Creek one final time a few miles out of Pennsylvania, where it was as wide as a river. They were hungry. Edison was exhilarated by their headway and suggested stopping to eat. Ford wheeled the truck down an inviting lane. A weathered barn was ahead, looking as ancient and neglected as the grist mill. One of its double doors had fallen to the ground, and the other was pushed open against the planked front of the structure.

They climbed out and inspected the site, Ford opening the rear of the truck and laying out bread, ham and a jug of cider. Halverton helped him with the sandwiches, making three. Edison had begged off, producing a chocolate bar from a bag he had packed. Just as they were comfortable and preparing to eat, a hay wagon came into view. It was driven by a man in overalls standing on the wagon's seat. The man seemed to be kissing the mountain air to coax his two white mules forward. He constantly smacked his lips while he drove. At his side a girl, twelve or thirteen, also in overalls, pushed the hair back from her eyes. She could have been the man's daughter or sister, or even his wife. In the mountains, it was hard to say.

The man pulled up on the reins, stopping his animals just

short of the truck with a groaning "whoa." He squinted his face and studied the strangers blocking his access to the barn. The two parties stared at each other for nearly a full minute, and Henry Ford, feeling confronted, called out. "Excuse me, do you object to us having our lunch here?"

"Yes," the man said bluntly.

"Do you own this property?"

"Belongs to my grandmother."

"Then tell us how much damage we're doing, and I'll pay you."

The man and girl looked at each other in disbelief, as if Ford was speaking Italian.

"I don't rightly know," the man answered. "This load is pretty heavy. My mules is wore out."

"Can you wait twenty minutes for five dollars?" Edison said.

Again, the two on the wagon were incredulous. The girl spoke up this time. "Mister, we'll wait all day and half the night for five dollars."

Ford reached into his pocket and flipped the girl a gold piece. She caught the coin with both hands. "Just look at it," she exclaimed to her companion. "It ain't no bigger than a nickel."

"I seen one before," the man told her. "Don't you go losin' it now. We'll give it to Grandma." He climbed out of the wagon, then lifted the girl onto the ground. "Stamp's the name," he said, extending a hand to Ford.

"I'm Henry Ford. This is H.S. Firestone, Sid Halverton and the gentleman in the shade over there is Mister Thomas Edison. Will you join us for some cider?"

Edison nodded at the introduction. Stamp looked at each of their faces. "By God, I believe you are. I should have knowed, seein' that fancy autotruck there." He pointed to Edison. "Honey," he said. "Do you know who that man is?"

" 'Course I do," she said proudly. "That's Mister Phono-graph."

The two joined the travelers for lunch, contributing a pail of crisp apples themselves and refusing payment for them when Ford offered. The girl had joined Edison on a log, and the two were getting along like old friends. Edison had spread his maps on the ground.

"How far is it to Elkins?" he asked her. "We started out just north of there this morning."

She looked to the treetops and gestured the distance with a flair. "Ever and ever, so many miles," was her answer.

Edison asked if she lived nearby. He was sure that she did.

"Yes, sir. But I went to Fairmont once. That's forty miles. I been on a train five times."

"A world traveler," Edison said.

Stamp talked about his crops with Ford and Firestone, themselves farm boys. He said they could stand some rain. "And we had that freeze on the second of June. A real cold snap one night. Nothin' we could do but plant again."

As soon as they finished eating, Ford packed away the extra food, and they were on their way again. "Can we give either of you a lift?" he offered.

"Thank you, no sir," Stamp said. "I got to work this hay."

"You could take me," the girl said. "Just around the bend to Grandma's."

"Go ahead," Stamp told her. "It's all right by me."

She rode in front seated between Edison and Ford, point-ing out the home from the road. The truck halted, and she ran the fifty feet uphill to a cabin surrounded by sweet peas. A hound greeted her lazily on the porch. They watched her disappear momentarily inside, then she was on the porch again, pulling an aged woman by the hand. The old woman looked down at the five dollar gold piece in her palm, then shaded her eyes from the sun. She looked in the direction of the road. Everyone inside the truck waved at the two mountain women, then continued down the road.

13

EDISON KEPT A BOTTLE OF WATER BESIDE HIM ON the front seat. He uncorked it and took a swallow, wiped his mouth on his sleeve and said, "If any of us becomes separated from the others, lost or somehow left behind, let's meet or leave word at the main post office in Niagara."

Everyone nodded in agreement.

"And we should get a newspaper as soon as possible. We might find some help there. For all we know, the situation may be resolved by now."

"I think we should contact the Niagara Falls authorities," Ford suggested. "Let the police know what we know."

Halverton was about to speak. He leaned forward, then let it pass.

"What were you going to say?" Firestone asked him.

"I don't think calling the police up there is a very good idea," he answered.

"Why not?" Ford said, looking at Halverton in the rear view mirror.

"Because if they are going into Canada, and it *is* only a theory, then they chose Niagara as the crossing point for a reason. It could very well be that some members of the police force are partners in this thing."

"That does make sense," Ford admitted. "Very well. But don't be bashful about speaking up from now on. We have to be equals in this thing."

"It isn't easy for me to think that way," Halverton told him. "My gosh, have you lost sight of who you people are?

Mr. Ford, I've read that you are worth over a billion dollars. Mr. Firestone, I know you have rubber plantations in South America and holdings in Africa. Who knows where else? And Mr. Edison, you have amazed the world for two generations. Myself, I work in a canvas factory fifty-five hours a week. I'm a common man. How can I be your equal?"

"You hold it right there," Firestone said. "Every one of us is just plain, common people. Yes, we have great wealth. Money is not a problem anymore. We rarely have to think about it, and we usually don't. I will tell you one thing. We all three deal with a great number of men, and I believe we're pretty fair judges of the human race. We talked it over before having you join us, and we agreed you're a good man. We wanted you to be our partner in this venture. If you have anything to offer, anything at all, why, speak up without hesitation."

"Very well," Halverton said. "Mr. Ford, I don't think a person in your position should say the things you did about Jews. You're too much an influence to say something so irresponsible. Mr. Edison was right to make a joke of it, because the opinion is laughable."

"I wasn't speaking about all Jews," Ford answered. "I spoke of the International Jewish banking power. May I point out that it was exactly what you said it was — an opinion. May I also point out that this is the United States of America, one of the few countries on God's green earth that allows each and every person to hold absolutely any opinion they please. And if that woman you know is successful, all we might have remaining of our liberty and democracy will be a fond memory."

"Hopefully not," Halverton said. "I suppose I lost my head over her. Do you know what it's like to lose your head over a woman?"

Ford turned around quickly in his seat. "What do you mean by that?" he demanded. "What have you heard?"

"Nothing," Halverton said. "I haven't heard anything."

Firestone reached over and squeezed Halverton's hand, putting a finger of his other hand to his lips to quiet him.

What Halverton was not aware of was that Henry Ford, billionaire industrialist, was also in love, with a woman other than his wife. The woman had given birth to Ford's son less than three months earlier. Henry Ford, at the age of sixty, was a father again, though there is not an iota of evidence to substantiate this fact in the Ford Museum in Dearborn, Michigan.

The truck gave out a loud raspy noise, the sound of metal shredding and grating on itself. It startled everyone with its suddenness. Even Edison could hear the shrill whine. Ford put on the brake and turned off the motor. He jumped onto the ground and opened up the hoodflap while the others climbed down to stick their faces into the engine heat along with his. Water trickled from the radiator until it was drained. Pieces of a rubber belt were lodged in the wiring of the distributor, and still more shreds of it were hanging here and there. To compound the problem, the fan had sheared off all four of its blades.

Ford reached inside and pulled one of the fan blades loose. "Harvey, you and Mr. Halverton there," he said curiously. "See whether you can find those other blades in the road a ways back. Looks to me like the fan came loose. Cut through the belt and punctured the radiator, not to mention tearing itself to pieces."

"She needs repairs all right," Edison commented. "That radiator needs replacing. And the fan too."

"Say, Al," Ford directed. "I have a soldering iron and a couple of electric drills back there. Hook up your battery and we'll put them to use."

"I'll grab the tool kit along with them," Edison said.

He opened the rear of the truck while Firestone and Halverton were combing the ground. They had found two of the fan's blades, but the remaining one had thrown itself farther away. They were searching in the grass by the roadside now.

Edison rummaged through the compartment. He located some spare belts tied together and tossed them onto the tailgate. The storage battery had been shoved back against the tool box, and Edison had to slide the heavy contraption toward him to gain access to the tools. He grunted and worried the thing out of the way, then set the box of tools down by the belts. One of their two strings of wiring he had packed was just like an extension cord — a heavy duty cable with a socket spliced on its end. The other was a string of lights, some sixty feet in length. Edison could find only the latter, but he poked around until he put a hand on the appropriate one. Ford appeared at the tailgate now.

"Need some help?" he asked.

"No, all of it's right there," Edison said. "As soon as I plug in, we'll have power."

Halverton walked to the front of the truck with all the missing fan blades for Ford, while Firestone helped Edison by stringing the cable toward the hood of the truck. Ford connected the soldering iron.

"Fine," he told Halverton, examining the blades. "Why don't you and Harvey see if you can flatten out the rougher edges. There should be a hammer in the box."

"Go ahead, Henry," Edison shouted. "You got juice now."

Ford felt the tip of the iron. It began to warm, and he touched a strand of solder to it, melting a globule on the end of the spool. He climbed onto the bumper, fingering the hole in the radiator, then reached in with both hands to begin plugging the hole. He had rolled up his sleeves, and it was the first time Halverton had seen him with his tie loosened. A half hour elapsed, Ford squinting throughout from the resin smoke of the burning solder. Finally, he lifted his hands. "Done," he announced. "Now, let's remove what's left of the fan."

"I'll take care of that," Edison said. He dug in with a wrench and pair of pliers and loosened the damaged piece with the gusto of a master mechanic, blackening his fingers in grease and removing the part in seconds. He lifted the fan in the air and held it sideways, examining it with one eye closed. "It don't look bent to me," he said. "What have you in mind, sewing the blades back on?"

"Exactly," Ford answered. "We'll drill holes both in the sheared off arms of the blade, and also the stubs. Then run some copper wiring I've got back there through it and set it back in place. We can replace the pin with a bolt. It ought to hold."

Edison stepped to the cab of the truck for his bottle of water. He took two good swigs from it, then toted it to the front again to watch Ford work on the fan. He offered everyone a drink in the afternoon heat, and Halverton took him up on it. He threw back his head and took in a mouthful, swishing it around in his mouth before swallowing. He smacked his lips and looked curiously at the bottle.

"What have you got in this?" he asked.

"It's water," Edison smiled. "Plain spring water."

"It tastes minty," Halverton said.

"It is minty," Edison confirmed. "I never could stand the taste of water and years ago hit upon the solution of putting a few drops of peppermint extract in what I drink."

Firestone was leaning against the fender listening. "Let me see that bottle," he said, taking a sip of it. "You never cease to amaze," he said almost to himself as he shook his head. "Peppermint."

Ford had worked the drill through the first blade, but was having difficulty in keeping the pieces lined up with each other. He was pressing his weight against the fan to steady it. It was tedious and time-consuming. "Hand me that wire," he said.

He ran the copper through the holes, pulling the knots tightly with pliers at each stitch. By the time all the blades had been reattached, another hour had passed. For good measure, Ford soldered over his stitches, and the fan was once again a solid piece of workmanship. He set the bolt in the fan, looping the belt around it, then tightening everything that had come loose. Halverton drew a bucket of water from their drinking rations and poured it into the radiator. Ford checked the dirt below. Not a drop had fallen through. "Start it up, Harvey," he said.

Firestone sat behind the wheel. The engine turned over smoothly and began to idle. He revved the motor. The fan was slightly misshapen, but there was not a thing wrong with its function. It spun and held fast.

Edison disconnected the storage battery, and all four men packed things away. They were dirty and hot and had lost an hour and a half driving time. But Ford had made a major repair without the use of a garage and had made it look simple in the process.

"That was a fine piece of work, Mr. Ford," Halverton said.

"Sure was, Henry," Firestone agreed.

Ford nodded, closed the hood and climbed back into the truck.

"What else would you expect from the God-damnedest mechanic in the world?" he said.

Once under way, the wind rushing through the open window refreshed them, and they were not so tired. They snacked on apples, and the truck ran beautifully. It was dusk, and in the twilight Ford misjudged a waterhole in the road, didn't see it until they were already upon it. Too late to apply the brakes, he gunned the engine and tried making it through. They skidded sideways and slid to a halt with the motor racing. He threw it into reverse, but the truck did not move. It was up to its axles.

"Damn!" Ford said and slapped the steering wheel.

The only thing the four men accomplished in the next quarter hour was covering themselves in mud. They could see dry ground in the headlights not thirty feet in the distance, but they were frozen in place.

"I'll walk on ahead," Halverton said. "There was a house not too far up there. I saw it from that last ridge. They might have a pair of mules."

"I'll come with you," Ford said.

The house was a pitiful sight. Even the chickens looked starved. A family was seated at a table inside an open door, and a woman stepped out in the bare yard when Ford called out, "Hello to the house!" He explained their problem and asked if they could borrow a mule or an ox if they had one. The man at the table stayed inside, hunched over a bowl of stew he was spooning into his mouth. Most of it seemed to dribble down over a week-old beard. Halverton saw a child at the table with him.

"If your husband would like to make sure his mule won't be harmed, he's welcome to have a look," Ford said. "We'll do all the work."

"We got a milk cow," the woman said. " 'Fraid that's all I can offer. The husband got to stay here. He's got bad lungs from working the mines. Tires hisself out just moving around the house."

"Who's out there, Mama?" the child asked.

"Just two men," the woman called. She turned back to Ford. "I got me a man that tires hisself and a boy that can't walk. Doctor says he needs an operation." She laughed tiredly. "I'll fetch the cow directly."

With the cow straining on the end of the rope, and Ford, Firestone and Halverton pushing as Edison guided, the vehicle edged out of the low spot and found a footing on solid ground. Edison couldn't drive and slammed the brakes hard to keep from hitting the cow. Ford reached in and took over.

"We got us a pump in front of the house," the woman said. "Drive on up there and clean yourselves if you like."

"Thank you, ma'am," Ford said. "We are greatly indebted to you."

They washed themselves as best they could in the headlights. By the time the woman caught up with them they
were at least feeling more refreshed, if not a little cleaner.
Ford asked the woman her name and told her who he was.

"I want your boy to have that operation so he can take
care of you someday," he told her. "You offered us all you
had tonight, and I'd like to do this for you."

He reached for his wallet and pressed money into her
palm. It was a stack of hundreds.

"Let me know where a letter can reach you," Ford said.
"When I return home, I'll make arrangements for your boy.
I've got a couple of boys myself, and it would hurt greatly
not to be in the position to help them. Don't worry about the
cost. I'll see to it that all the expenses are taken care of."

Firestone copied down the address she gave in a shaky
voice, then the woman broke down and began to weep,
turning her back on them and walking inside.

14

HALVERTON HAD NEVER MET ANYONE WHO EXUDED
the degree of enthusiasm and cheerfulness that Edison did. A
smile was as much a part of his features as his high forehead
and unruly hair. Little wonder he was able to transform a
staff of both highly educated scientists and workers into an
"isomnia squad." To match his own level of energy was
challenge enough to work beyond the physical capacity to
which one was accustomed. Then the body and its weak-
nesses could be put aside. Edison himself remarked on the
trip that his own body was nothing more than something to
carry about his brains.

It was an hour or two after meeting the mudhole. Everyone was fairly uncomfortable, with dirt caked onto clothing. And the constant bouncing in the truck did not allow anyone to sleep.

"Let's pull over for a spell," Edison suggested, "Rest up, fix a little grub. You fellows look hungry."

Ford wiped his eyes and maneuvered the vehicle to the side of the road. "We have some steaks back there in the ice box," He said. "Let's fix them the way Burroughs liked them."

"The only way you'll eat them," Firestone said.

Ford started a campfire and cut some green branches from a tree to skewer the meat. Until their companion, the late naturalist and writer John Burroughs, had showed them this method, Ford had sworn off all meat. Perhaps it was because of the cut of beef or the fact that the feast marked the end to a long and determined attempt at vegetarianism. Food had never tasted better to him. The only way Ford would now eat a steak was seared simply over an open fire, cooked rare.

"There's a bin full of vegetables back there," he said. "You want to make a fresh salad out of them? There's squash and potatoes, a few cukes."

Halverton carried out plates for the supper. "Raw potatoes?" he questioned.

"Raw vegetables is about all I eat," Ford answered.

"Better boil them," Edison cautioned. "Boil them at least fifteen minutes to drive out the typhus spores. You shouldn't eat anything that hasn't been boiled or baked. Don't you know anything?"

"What about salads?" Ford asked him.

"I don't eat salads," Edison said.

"Not a thing wrong with good, clean vegetables," Ford said, draping the meat over the flames. "Now, chicken, that's another matter."

Halverton squatted beside the fire. "What's wrong with chicken?" he asked.

"Chicken meat is only good for feeding hawks," Ford said. "Look at what a chicken eats. Look at the sallow color of its flesh. I don't touch it, and you have to admit, at sixty years of age, my physical condition could match your own. How old are you?"

"Thirty-one today."

"Happy birthday to you," Ford said. "Don't you agree?"

"Yes sir, I do," Halverton told him. "You're about my father's age, and he looks much older than you."

"Any man can live to the age of 125 or 150," Ford said, turning the meat as Firestone put a pot of squash in the fire. "Just as long as he keeps the carbon out of his system, that is. I know I'll live to a hundred."

"Better boil those vegetables a good, long time," Edison warned again. "Typhus."

They sat on the ground holding the tin plates in their laps. Even Edison had a steak and a mound of sliced squash. When they had finished, Ford collected the dishes and rubbed dirt around in them to soak up the juices, clapping them clean over the fire. They all stretched out on the ground.

Edison picked at some food in his teeth. "Americans do the work of three-horsepower engines," he said. "But they consume enough fuel to operate a fifty-horsepower engine. They could cut down on their food intake by two thirds. They drug their systems with too much sleep and wear their clothes too tight. None of that is beneficial to a healthy and hardy body."

Halverton found a seat on the end of a log. He rolled a cigarette from a pouch of tobacco and lit it with a burning stick. "How did you three ever start these camping trips?" he wanted to know. "When did you first go?"

"My first campout?" Edison said. "That's an easy one. It was my first vacation. I was about your age. The year was 18 and 78. Menlo Park had been established, and I had recently come up with the phonograph. Well, that really drew the crowds. They haven't slowed since, but I wasn't accustomed to it yet, so I went out west. Ever since I was a boy, the West had fascinated me, seeing those prairie schooners stop in my hometown for supplies. They would leave Milan, Ohio and seemed to stretch to the horizon, heading west. That was a temptation for an inquisitive boy, hearing about fields of gold and land, land, land.

"Well, it took me a while. Like I say, in the summer of '78, I had my chance and I took it. I had done some business with Jay Gould, the railroad man, and as a result, was given a few privileges on the train. They allowed me to ride on the cowcatcher on front of the locomotive, and I rode that way, nothing ahead but those two rails, the wind rushing in my face and not a sound. Not that I could hear, at any rate. It was like being a bird. Had a close call on that cattle catcher. The train hit a bear in the tracks and hurled the animal upward. It struck just under the headlight. I ducked and probably saved my life.

"It astounded me to discover that even out there I was quite well known. Cowboys would ride hundreds of miles across the plains to meet me. They had bronco-busting for my benefit and fast gun displays. You ever hear of a fellow by the name of Texas Jack? He was out there. He got to drinking and feeling rowdy and shot up a sign in front of a dry-goods store. Then we traveled out into Ute country. Saw some Indians. Mind you, this was about two years after Custer's demise."

"But the trip had a scientific purpose," Ford pointed out.

"Sure," Edison said. "Wyoming had a total eclipse of the sun that summer. Scientists from all over the world descended on the place. I tested my tasimeter, which proved to be too sensitive. It could measure down to a millionth of a degree Fahrenheit. The heat from the corona of the sun was far too great for the capacity of the instrument. I watched the scientists as they took their calculations. They first set up their instruments to determine their exact location on the earth in relation to the sun. I was amazed at the immense amount of mathematics and preserved one of their sheets. It looked like a timetable of a Chinese railroad. They were not in error of more than a hundred feet. It was a revelation to me that the astronomers and physicists could be so precise. I had always been fascinated when I read of the great distances between the planets and the vastness of our solar system. The margin of error of one hundred feet was nothing.

"After the eclipse I went on to Sacramento Valley. The only time I was forced to desert my post on the cowcatcher was when we passed through the snowshed on the summit of the Sierras in the Rocky Mountains. All told, I was gone from Menlo Park for two months. That was my first camping trip."

Edison poked a stick into the fire and stirred up the coals. Sparks exploded into the air, and, lifted by the heat, swarmed toward the treetops as they died out. "Ought to see some shooting stars tonight," he said. "Been seeing 'em all during the trip. They'll be common until mid-August. It's their time of year."

"The idea of us taking these trips together had its birth in 1915," Firestone said, propped on his side. "It was the World's Fair in San Francisco. Mr. Ford had come out in his train car, and Mr. Edison had come out in another car for the celebration of Edison Day at the fair."

"That's right," Edison said.

"After an electric dinner that had been given in his honor, we looked about for a bit of something to do to pass the time. The electric dinner, by the way, was not a banquet of wires and sockets and switches, but a banquet at which all the food was cooked by electricity. Electrical cooking was still something of a novelty at the time."

"It was too much food," Edison said. "I can remember that."

"We decided to visit Luther Burbank at Santa Rosa and ran up there in the private car. Just as Mr. Edison had made great strides in the field of electricity, so, too, Burbank has worked wonders in the field of horticulture."

"You should have seen the peas," Ford interrupted. "Acres of them, all of the same size so they could be more easily harvested by machinery. Excuse me Harvey, go ahead."

"Well, Mr. Ford and Mr. Edison were due in Los Angeles and were to go on from there to an exposition being held in San Diego. But they thought they were being commercialized and wanted to get away from the crowds that threatened to prevent us from moving at all. We abandoned the private car and continued by automobile. We ended up touring a motion picture studio, seeing how films were made. Then the head of the concern asked Mr. Edison to lay the cornerstone of a building, which he did. But we were not prepared for the brass band that came out of thin air to escort us to the site five hundred feet away.

"The school children, the next day, wanted to see Mr. Edison. They lined the road and threw flowers. And it pleased him. He agreed to tour the schools the following day, as long as he din't have to make a speech. Eventually we reached San Diego. The crowds were enormous for their Edison Day, even though the guest of honor didn't show up until four in the afternoon. He gave a reception on the exposition grounds to the school children, and as they passed him, each tossed a bunch of flowers to him, until at the end, he was waist-high in a drift of flowers. I was so moved that I burst into tears. Well, we had such a good time that we decided to take time off the following summer to spend time together away from the crowds. That first campout was 1916. It consisted of Mr. Edison, Burroughs, myself with my two sons and a crew. Mr. Ford was called away on business at the last minute, but hasn't missed another one. We've gone every year since."

Firestone paused a moment, thinking back over the trips. "You'd have liked Burroughs, Sid. He could look at a bird and tell you its species in Latin, identify any bush, tree or flower and tell you the age of the rocks beneath your feet. Nothing in Nature was a secret to him. I sorely miss the gentleman."

Halverton covered his mouth to yawn. It was nearly ten o'clock. Ford happened to be looking at him and began to yawn with him.

"None of that, now," Edison cautioned. "We had better push on. Have a cup of coffee perhaps and get back in the truck."

"Wait a minute," Firestone said. "What's this I heard about how you used to keep your men in the labs going all night?"

"You mean when I played the organ and sang? That was surely enough to awaken the dead."

"I heard you made them fight each other," Firestone said.

"Oh, poppycock," Edison chuckled. "Sometimes we had a few rounds of boxing, that's all. We had a chemist who was a very good boxer."

"I've got some gloves in the truck," Ford said. "Two pairs. Let's do it."

"No," Halverton said. "It's too dark. Somebody's going to hurt themselves."

"We'll string up the lights," Edison suggested. "Make a ring out of them."

"I don't like the idea of it," Halverton repeated.

"Well, why not?" Ford challenged him.

"This kind of thing always happened to us enlisted men in the Navy. Mr. Ford, I appreciate the fact that you're as strong as a man half your age. You can do a lot of chin ups, and you chop wood real well. But the fact is, I'm the only one here who *is* half your age. Surely you don't want to hit Mr. Edison in the face, do you? Or your friend Mr. Firestone.

I can't believe you're even considering it when we have so much to do."

"That was an astute observation," Ford said. "Al, you be in his corner, and I'll take Harvey in mine. I'll go get the gloves."

"Wait," Halverton pleaded. "We really don't have the time."

"Nonsense," Ford said. "It will only take a few minutes." And that was that.

The string of lights defined the boxing ring, one corner formed at the storage battery on the tailgate, the other junctures tied to available tree limbs. What they ended up with wasn't square, but it created an open space more than suitable for their purposes. The naked bulbs were spaced three feet apart and hung about chest-high. Moths were flying about the sources of light. Ford was digging in one of the truck's many compartments and sang out when he located the gloves. "Here they are," he shouted.

Halverton had been hoping he would never find them, for the last thing he was aiming for as one of his life's goals was to face Henry Ford in a boxing match. What was it in Ford's nature that was so unreasonably competitive? Was this attitude responsible for the man's success? What possible difference would it make if Ford could bloody Halverton's nose or outdistance him in a footrace? Halverton guessed that Ford was challenged by Halverton's youth. By conquering a younger man, Ford in a way denied his mortality. Well, he wasn't about to take a beating just to humor his opponent in the ring. Edison walked up to Halverton with the gloves Ford had tossed down. "Take off your shirt," he said. "Let me tie these things on you."

Halverton unbuttoned and removed his collar, then began unfastening his shirt. Ford was doing the same, handing his clothing to Firestone. Halverton turned his back on his opponent while Edison laced him up. "I don't want him to get hurt," he said. "So I'll try not to hit him. I'll just jab and miss, maybe tap him a few times. I really feel funny about this. Do you have any advice for me?"

Edison finished lacing the gloves, and began rubbing Halverton's shoulders. An unlit cigar was in his mouth. "Stay away from his right," he warned.

"What about his left?" Halverton wanted to know.

Edison paused and considered the question. "Well, stay away from his left too. Incidentally, did you fight in the Navy?"

Halverton looked over warily at Ford. "Yeah, I got knocked out both times."

"Pretty big fellows, your opponents?"

"Not particularly," Halverton said. "No."

Firestone approached them now carrying a bucket. "Here," he said. "This is to sit on between rounds. Henry's idea."

"Fine," Edison said. "This is Sid's corner by the truck. Set it down for me, will you? Is your man about ready?"

Firestone scratched his head, looking back over his shoulder. "I believe he is," he said.

"All right, let's get the combatants to the center of the ring."

Edison lifted the wire for Halverton to duck beneath. He was still carrying Halverton's shirt over one arm, and picked up a jug of water that he placed near the bucket. Ford met them in the ring. He made fists and danced from one foot to another, tapping his gloves together every few seconds. He was still wearing cowboy boots.

"I want to see a clean fight," Edison said. "No hitting below the belt, no eye-gouging, no biting and no kicking. Rounds will last three minutes, except in the event of a knockdown, in which case the round will end. When I say to break, I want to see a clean break. I shall clap my hands together twice at the start and the end of each round. Do you both understand the rules?"

Halverton and Ford nodded.

"Good. Now shake hands, retire to your corners and come out fighting when I give the signal. The fight's a three-rounder."

Halverton retreated to his corner with his back to the ring. It was a moonless night, and the wind was stirring lightly, the glare of the lights behind him creating an eerie sensation. Bushes and trees looked like pencil drawings. He imagined it was all a dream. Edison clapped his hands.

He turned, and Ford was on him in a second, landing three quick jabs to his right eye before he had even raised his own hands. Halverton ducked out of the way and protected his face. Ford's blows landed twice on Halverton's gloves and missed altogether another time. Halverton danced out of his reach, then made two slow and deliberate shots at Ford, just enough to keep his opponent on his toes, but nothing that he was unable to dodge. It backed Ford to the center of the ring.

"Keep that left up!" Edison shouted. "Don't let him get away!"

"Come on, Henry," Firestone urged.

Neither man connected with a solid blow by the end of the first round. Halverton sat on his bucket, and Edison fanned him with his shirt.

"I wasn't ready for him. He came out so fast."

"You're doing all right," Edison told him. "But instead of aiming at his head, try leading him. Henry dodges to his left almost every time."

"I'll try to remember that."

"Need some water? It's there at your side."

Halverton rinsed out his mouth and spit on the ground. "It tastes minty. Is this your water?"

Edison nodded. He stopped fanning Halverton, leaning forward to wipe the sweat from his face with the shirt.

Halverton was ready for Ford's quick start this time. He moved steadily to the center of the ring and pursued the auto magnate into a corner. Ford would have been in trouble if Halverton was as serious about the fight as he. But Halverton didn't pin him there. Instead, he continued with his deliberate approach. Still, Ford had to be watched carefully. He missed two left jabs, then landed a right to Halverton's jaw that backed the younger man out to the center again. Solely out of defense, Halverton connected with two left jabs to the side of Ford's head.

Edison and Firestone continued to shout the things men normally do at fights. Edison held his watch to one of the light bulbs. Just as he was about to clap his hands, Ford sunk a right uppercut into Halverton's midsection, and you could hear the air rush from his lungs.

Edison clapped. "Time!" he shouted. "Time!"

"Are you hurt?" he asked Halverton in the corner.

"I'm fine," he answered, taking a swig of water, holding the jug between his gloves.

"This is the last round. If you don't want to hit him, that's your business. But don't hurt yourself in the process."

Edison clapped again, and both men rushed to the center. Ford threw a volley of five quick lefts. Halverton raised a forearm and deflected the first three and jumped away from the last two. He squinted his eyes to sqeeze the sweat out of them, keeping his fists in front of him for protection.

Ford continued hammering away, punctuating the attack this time with a right cross. It caught his ribs, and Halverton grabbed Ford's arms while he caught his breath. Ford was a good, scrappy fighter. For a man of sixty, he was phenomenal.

"Break!" Edison yelled.

Halverton turned him loose and danced out of the way, but Ford wouldn't allow his escape to be a long one. He backed Halverton against the string of lights and scored with several body shots, the kind that wear a man down. Halverton took a step forward, raising his right arm to ward off the jabs. The two men's feet were raising a fog of dust.

Ford connected with a hard right to the chest, the force of

the blow throwing Halverton against one of the light bulbs. It was like a branding iron on his right shoulder blade. Out of reflex, and intending nothing more than to keep himself from being badly burned, Halverton swung his arm wildly away from the wire.

He caught Henry Ford leaning into his roundhouse right and knocked him out cold.

15

HALVERTON WATCHED WITH MIXED FEELINGS AS Edison and Firestone attended to a prostrate Henry Ford. He hoped more than anything that Ford was uninjured. At the same time, there was relief in the fact that the fight was finished, that Ford was in no condition to say or do a thing. It may have been a hasty opinion on his part, but Halverton seemed to like Ford best when the man was unconscious. It was only then that he felt he needn't keep one eye on him. In Ford's waking hours, his uncontained bundle of energy made Halverton edgy. That exact quality in Edison, however, was stimulating, inspiring.

Firestone patted Ford's cheeks, while Edison fanned the air for him. They were both speaking to Ford as if he was a tardy child who refused to get out of bed.

"Get on up now," Firestone was urging.

"Rise and shine, Henry," Edison said. "Rise and shine."

Halverton bit at the laces of one of the boxing gloves, the string gritty and salty against the tip of his tongue. He pulled the glove off between his knees and removed the other one with his free hand. "He's coming around," he said. "Look, he's blinking."

Edison offered water. Ford took a sip and slowly sat up. A

cowlick had shaped his hair into a pointed crest on one side of his head, giving his face an off-balanced and surprised look, like a lemon drop. He stood on his own power and steadied his feet. "I went off to Hawaii there for a moment," he said.

"Mr. Ford, I do apologize," Halverton said. "I had no intention of hurting you."

"Wasn't your fault," Ford told him. "I left myself open."

Edison, seeing Ford moving about again, pronounced him fit and began tending to the string of lights. Ford drank some more water and insisted upon remaining the driver when the foursome returned to their positions in the truck. Halverton leaned gingerly back into the seat. His shoulder felt blistered from the light bulb. Firestone again sat at his side in the back seat. He looked like a man about to explode as the motor started.

"I can't stand it," he said. "I cannot think of a more likeable man than Warren G. Harding. Who in the world would wish to harm him? You know, I can't help thinking that he could have helped us find him if he'd opened up a little more back in camp. Yesterday he seemed like such a troubled man. He sat down once and held his head in his hands. He looked so forlorn I thought he would cry. I wanted to help. Know what he said when I asked him what was bothering him? He looked up from the ground, and in a voice close to tears said, 'My God, this is a hell of a job. I have no trouble with my enemies. I can take care of my enemies all right. But my friends, my God damn friends, Harvey, they're the ones keeping me walking the floor nights. They're selling me all over Washington and all over the country.'"

"He asked what I would do if I discovered someone in the upper levels of my company who had done something illegal while holding that position. Would I keep quiet and protect the name of Firestone Tire and Rubber or would I make a clean breast of it with the public and risk scandal and shame?"

Ford put the truck into gear, and they began to move into the darkness. "What did you tell him?" he asked

"I said I'd flush the rat into the open, and the people would understand."

"Good for you," Edison said.

Firestone paused and looked out of his window. "The President deserves to be treated decently," he said. "I hope he is."

Early in the day, President Harding stood on the shoulder of a road, watching. He felt numbness, like one ordered about until there was only a little feeling left. They were getting rid of the automobile. First, there had been the exhilaration of Margarete's company, driving madly out of camp with her at his side. There was the expectation of the thrill in seeing a new lover undress for the first time. He had stretched out in the back seat, anticipating the delight, removing his tie and loosening his shirt. She reached for something in her purse, and he closed his eyes. Then he felt her weight on top of him. It was no lover's grasp, but a wrestler's. She pinned him to the seat. There was a scent of hospitals, then a handkerchief clamped tightly over his mouth and nostrils. He breathed in the chloroform, her face above him losing its shape and color.

When he awoke she was standing with two men. One was young, probably not out of his twenties. He was dressed neatly like a college boy, Harding thought. He held a handsome leather case. The second man was older. He looked to Harding like a worker, someone who spent his days outdoors or in a factory. He was thin, but muscular. His face was a coarse pillow of premature wrinkles.

They were at the edge of a cornfield. A creek with a high, steep bank ran beside them. A crow eating an ear of corn turned a black eye at the humans. Harding heard their voices.

"We'll push 'er into the creek and take the Packard from here," the older one said. "That all right with you?"

Margarete ran a hand through her hair, lifting it away from her neck. She nodded her head yes.

"It's fine with me, Uncle Warner," the younger man answered.

Margarete approached the vehicle and put her face to the window. "Step out, Mr. Harding," she said. "Please hurry. We are transferring cars."

Harding complied. Anxiety had replaced the air in his lungs, and his chest heaved with every breath. He was docile. She opened his door, and he stood on the roadside watching. In a way, he was removed from the scene by his own fear. It was like seeing a motion picture instead of actually being there. He saw the car rolling in neutral, started by gravity and the steepness of the road. It was given an extra push by the uncle, landing straight down on its radiator, hesitating a moment like a tree about to fall, then flipping over, coming to rest on its roof. Water flowed through its open windows. The crow shouted and took to the air. Harding waited for further instructions and turned to Margarete.

"We haven't time," she said, and nodded in the direction of the second automobile.

The President understood and climbed into the back seat. Margarete followed and reached across Harding to lock his door. They drove away. The two men were in front, the older one behind the wheel, his nephew resting on his knees facing the back seat.

"Never seen me a president up close before," he said "We were all set to see your speech down in St. Louis. Had our sights on you, you might say."

Harding ignored him and gazed out the window.

"I'm talking to you, Mister," the young man said. "You

got that speech already memorized? I want to hear it. Right now."

Margarete sat forward quickly and backhanded him across the face. She gritted her teeth and spoke to the driver. "If you have no control over him, we can leave him in the creek too. I was assured that your behavior would be professional, and I expect and demand that much."

The driver turned to his companion and touched his shoulder with the back of his hand. "Turn around, Reed," he said. "Just face forward and be civilized. Reed, do you hear me?"

Reed scowled, lowering himself in the seat as he felt his cheek. He faced the windshield and moved his hand higher up his head, massaging his forehead with the palm of his hand. Harding noticed a slight lump the size of a half dollar just below the hairline. Reed rubbed the place and brooded silently.

Margarete turned to Harding now. "Sir, could I have your attention for a few moments?" she asked. "We must take a few precautions to ensure your safety. We do have a set of handcuffs, and we could probably fashion a gag if the situation merited it. But there is no reason we cannot go through this in as comfortable and respectful a way as possible under the circumstances. Are you listening?"

Harding looked in her direction, then faced his window again.

"As difficult as this may be to understand at this time, what has happened to you, this abduction, is a positive action. Had it not occurred, you would have been murdered in St. Louis. Had I failed this morning, you would have been dead tonight. That is not our intention, and I would have greatly regretted that option. What I ask of you is very simple. Please, just remain calm and cooperate with instructions to the letter. That is all I ask. Do not attempt to escape, nor to speak with anyone we might encounter. That would put their lives in jeopardy as wells as yours. Literally months of planning have preceded this day. And we will have success with or without your good behavior. Your cooperation is only for your comfort." She paused a moment and looked at Harding's profile. "Do you have any questions?" she asked.

Harding faced her now and tried to penetrate her eyes. He was afraid and sighed deeply. "You are doomed to failure," he said. "The best thing, the only solution, would be to allow me to leave, and leave right now. Stop the automobile. If you do this now, I will make certain that no charges will be brought against any of you. I do have that power, even in my present condition."

Margarete shook her head. "You are in no position to make bargains," she said firmly. "None whatsoever." She reached into her bag and produced a flask of liquor, unscrewing the cap and extending it to Harding. "It is a long journey," she said.

Harding took the flask and shook its contents. "I made a pledge of abstinence two months ago," he said. "Not a drop has passed my lips since. But as you have already discovered, and no doubt relied upon, beauty has a greater influence on me than it should. To your health, Miss Fabry, or whoever you are."

Margarete smiled slightly, acknowledging the toast with a nod of her head. She capped the pint container and returned it to her bag. Harding licked his lips, then wiped them dry, resting his arm on the car window.

"I would never have believed this four years ago," the President said. "I was a one-term senator, a kid in a candy shop. Yes, if circumstances were slightly different, Mr. Cox or Mr. Debs might be in this seat now."

"And who are they?" Margarete asked him.

"Who are they? I defeated Cox for the presidency," Harding answered. "Where were you at the time? Debs received 4 percent of the vote as the Socialist candidate. He was serving a prison sentence at the time for being a pacifist during the war. I pardoned him. Surely you've heard of these men."

"I recognized the name Debs," Margarete said. "You see, I was not in the United States at the time of your election. I am a recent immigrant. To me, it is irrelevant who they were or who might be in your place and what might have been. You are the man we wanted, Mr. Harding."

The President chuckled. It was a bitter and disgusted laugh.

" 'We think the country's ready, for another man like Teddy. We need another Lincoln, to do the country's think-ing. Mis-ter Har-ding, you're the man for us!' That was the official Republican campaign song. Jolson wrote it. You paraphrased it beautifully." Harding rubbed the palms of his hands together and looked to the floor. "Bishop Anderson pleaded for me to abstain from liquor. He said it would make me the 'moral hero of millions of persons.' My own convictions did not lead in that direction. Could I impose on you for another shot?"

Margarete handed him the flask. The car moved steadily down the dirt road, raising a wake of chalky dust. If anyone did see them, Harding would be indistinguishable in the back seat. They drove until early afternoon, covering as much distance as possible before pulling up for a rest.

Warner, Margarete's driver, found a barn and shed just in sight of the road. He drove behind the building and parked the vehicle. Margarete told Harding that they would rest until dark. Reed, the youngest of the group, was the first one out of the Packard. He carried his leather case into the barn, made a quick inspection of the premises. When he returned to the automobile, Warner turned off the engine, and Mar-garete opened her door. She walked at the President's side into the shade of the barn. Harding seated himself on a bale of hay and watched Reed carry in his satchel and place it in the dirt and manure. He unlatched the brass catches with one hand, felt his forehead lightly with the fingertips of the other, then removed a cylinder that looked like a can for a reel of movie film. Harding was horrified when he realized what it was. Reed reached to the other side of the case and lifted the weapon like it was made of glass. He snapped the drum into place just in front of the trigger housing. It had a butt like a rifle, with two pistol grips, one in front of the cartridge cylinder and one behind it. Concentric rings graced the forward end of the barrel, and air vents riddled the very tip of the piece.

"You ever seen a Thompson submachine gun?" Reed asked Harding. "I took it out of the hands of a dead government agent."

"Take it away," Harding pleaded. "Please, it's so unnecessary.

"Do as he says," Margarete ordered. "Stand guard outside, but don't attract attention."

Reed looked to Warner, and Warner nodded his consent — as if either of them had any say in the pecking order. They both knew that Margarete was in control. Reed walked outside into the daylight, then squatted against a tree. He rested the gun across his legs.

"He's not a bad boy," Warner said. "He tries to be good, to do the right thing. He fell off of a scaffold a couple of years ago and cracked his skull. Had a metal plate put in, high up on the forehead, about right here," he pointed to his own head. "Claims he doesn't need sleep anymore since the accident, and I'll be damned if I've seen him sleep. He rests, sure. We waited three days together in St. Louis. I never saw him close his eyes."

Margarete wiped her brow with her sleeve. The air was still and hot.

"Mr. Harding, this is another reason for your cooperation," she said. "These two men were originally hired to kill you. Our employer believed I needed the help in moving you, which was true. I couldn't do it alone." She addressed Warner now. "Our chances of discovery are greatest right now. From now until dark. After that, we shall restrict our movements to nighttime."

Harding wrung his hands and looked at the rafters in the barn.

"We will not harm you," Margarete told him. "After all, I saved your life. If we had wanted you dead, it would have happened days ago, if not weeks ago. So do not despair, Mr Harding."

"It's hopeless," Harding answered.

"Things are never hopeless," she said. "You cannot change your predicament. You no longer have control of yourself or of the country. Still, you can have hope."

Harding pursed his lips. "Then I hope you will be made to pay for this outrageous act."

"Not likely," Margarete said. "You put too much faith in your countrymen, Mr. Harding. We will succeed. I assure you of that."

16

HARDING CONTEMPLATED THE IDEA OF FREEDOM AS he waited out the afternoon heat in the confinement of the barn. To exercise the simplest act of his own freedom, he would be able, without permission or hindrance, to stand and walk down the road in either direction he pleased. But the reality of the situation prevented him from considering such an action. He twisted his back against the wall of the barn to relieve an itch. To reach the barn door, he would need to pass by Margarete and Warner, both of them quite alert and apparently resolute. And outside, blurry in the waves of heat, there was Reed holding a machine gun in his lap.

The President lifted the flask to his lips and brooded. He ruminated on who might be responsible for the conspiracy, who might be the one to gain the most by his disappearance. Most likely, it was someone with both the connections and the money to accomplish it. It could be Charlie Forbes. Harding had made Forbes director of the newly formed Veterans Bureau, and Forbes had made himself a millionaire on his $10,000 salary. Rumors made the rounds that government surpluses were being sold for a tenth of their value — huge quantities of hospital linen, beds, drugs, medicinal alcohol, pajamas. Warehouses swelled with materiel and emptied overnight. Boxcars were stuffed to overflowing. Hospital building contracts regularly included the director's "handling fee." The bureau bought up more supplies than it would ever need, with kickbacks to the shippers. It acquired enough floor wax to last a century, and at twenty-five times its value.

Harding had the situation investigated, then sent for Forbes for a conference in the White House. At the same time, a confused visitor walked in on the meeting by mistake, only to find the President's hands around Forbes's throat, bouncing the director's head against the wall in a volley of threats. "You yellow rat!" Harding had bellowed. "You double-crossing bastard! You wheedling honey-fugler!"

It might be Forbes, but Harding doubted that Forbes had the guts.

There was Jess Smith, who had shared a house with Attorney General Daugherty. Smith had found more pies than he had fingers to put in them, from whiskey and gambling to graft involving millions of dollars. The situation grew more complicated, culminating in a distraught Jess Smith putting a bullet in his brain, the second suicide associated with the three-year-old Harding administration. Perhaps friends of Smith felt Harding was responsible or could have at least helped out.

Harding dismissed the idea that his wife could be involved. There was so little feeling left between him and the Duchess that such an elaborate scheme seemed unwarranted and pointless.

And what of Secretary of the Interior Albert Fall? Forbes's betrayal of Harding had been profound, but surely some of his appointments were above suspicion. Harding remembered asking Fall about the rumor of a questionable loan, the size of which he had not heard. And something about naval oil leases in California's Elk Hills and Wyoming's Teapot Dome reserves. But rumors flew about Washington like paper in ticker tape parades. Fall reassured the President that nothing had occurred that was not completely ethical and legal. Harry Sinclair, of Sinclair Oil, had loaned Fall the down payment for a ranch in New Mexico he intended to buy, and that was the extent of it. Fall's word was good enough for Harding. Those appointments he considered beyond reproach were Commerce Secretary Herbert Hoover, Secretary of State Charles Evans Hughes, Chief Justice of the Supreme Court William Howard Taft, Treasury Secretary Andrew Mellon and Secretary of the Interior Albert Fall. Harding could rule those five out of the kidnapping completely. He opened the flask and spoke aloud before taking a sip. "None of them would ever dream of giving me an ounce of trouble."

The stillness of the afternoon made it slow and heavy, making Harding feel like he could barely pull himself out of a hard sleep. Margarete and Warner offered the President some slices of canned meat, which he ate with the remnants of the whiskey. His stomach burned as the shadows lengthened, and the western sky began to turn pink. When Reed stood in the barn door, holding the gun like an extension of his arm, he was nothing but a silhouette, and

Harding knew they would be moving again soon. He was placed once more at Margarete's side in the Packard. When they continued on their way, Harding tried to determine their direction, but the road took so many turns and curves that the aurora of the setting sun was first on one side of the car, then the other, behind them, and, finally, a soft glow in their faces as it died and became dark again.

"Just what are your plans?" Harding asked. "Any demands? Is there a particular destination?"

"Wouldn't it be rather unwise to say?" Margarete told him.

"Why?" the President said. "If you are successful, I will know eventually. If you're not, well, it would hardly matter."

"But that knowledge adds to our advantage," she answered. "Don't you see? We may need all the advantages we have, should something alter our plans. I will tell you this, Mister Harding. Our most difficult task has already been performed. For nearly twelve hours, this country has been without a president, in effect. Let's say that there are no demands and no destination. I for one am curious to see the reaction thus far. We should read some interesting newspapers in the morning."

"Yes," Harding conceded. "I should think you will."

The President felt the dulling effects of the liquor on his system combine with the steady jostling of the automobile. The Packard's seats were soft and luxurious, and he grew weary. He leaned against the car door, bundling his coat into a pillow. He felt that if they moved out of the isolation of the forest and began to encounter towns and cities, a chance of rescue or escape was inevitable. He knew that his very presence must affect his captors in some way, make them nervous, perhaps too cautious or too daring. That could help him. For now, entrapped in the back seat of the moving automobile, he could afford to wait. He closed his eyes and slept.

At some point during the night, Harding began to stir. He

had no idea how long he had slept, but his head was throbbing, and his bladder was full. He rubbed the back of his neck and tapped Reed in the seat in front of him. "Please pull over when you can," he said. "I need to relieve myself."

Warner heard the President and veered the Packard into an open field, driving down a path along a row of hedges.

"Not too far," Margarete advised. "Stay close to the road."

The headlights picked up a rabbit in the plowed field running ahead of the car. The animal felt confined and in his blindness from the lights, couldn't find its way into the hedgerow. It ran in the area flooded by the light, darted in one direction, then the other. Warner braked the vehicle and shut off the headlights, and the rabbit vanished in the darkness.

"I will stay with the automobile," Margarete told Reed. "You go with him. Don't be long."

Reed stepped out of the car with his gun, carrying it freely and comfortably in both hands. He had opened Harding's door for him, then followed a step or two behind the President as he walked to the modest camouflage of the hedgerow.

"That's about far enough," Reed told him. "Do your business."

Harding unbuttoned his pants, a light, refreshing breeze in his face. He began to wet the ground in front of him, the muted trickling in the soft earth the only sound in the night.

"How does a young man get himself mixed up in such a mess?" Harding asked him.

"Easy," Reed answered. "This is the land of opportunity. The land of milk and honey. Nothing can stop you if you try."

"That's right," Harding said. "Nothing can stop a man without a conscience. Nothing can hinder a man without a trace of patriotism."

"What's patriotism got to do with this?"

"It's got everything to do with this," the President told

him. "Patriotism is the soul of nationality and the energy of civilization."

"Just shut your mouth," Reed said. "Don't say another thing. I'm not interested in listening to your speeches, and I'm already disappointed I didn't get a shot at you in Saint Louie, so don't tempt me out here. I might slip and shoot off your balls."

A branch snapped on the far side of the hedgerow. Reed looked past the row of bushes, but the moon was so small that he could scarcely see a thing. He placed a hand sharply on Harding's shoulder, the President instinctively taking a step back, and Reed craned his neck to make out a shape as his vision adjusted to the night. It was a pair of eyes just past the hedgerow. Then another, and another, now four pairs in all. Harding saw them too.

"Who's out there?" Reed called out. "Answer me now, who's there?"

No answer came. Reed threw Harding to the ground and opened fire into the bushes. Harding had landed solidly on his back and now clamped his hands tightly over his ears. The noise directly above him was deafening. A flame blurted thunder out of the barrel. Spent, heated cartridges rained down on the President as he trembled and shouted for Reed to stop. As he lay in the dirt, the shots seemed to ring for minutes as Reed sprayed the area from side to side, with no more expression on his face than a gardener watering his lawn. Finally, he stopped, the last blasts echoing against a bluff in the far distance. Small trees and bushes were shredded as if they'd been hit by artillery. Margarete and Warner had run to the area. Warner had a pistol drawn, and they were shouting to each other all at the same time.

"Well, what did you see?" Warner demanded.

Reed was still holding the gun at the bushes, and it became evident that it was not his imagination that something had been there. The light wind carried the smell of blood, and the stillness of the night was broken now by a gurgling bawl and the clanging of a cow bell.

Margarete pushed her way into the hedgerow, and beyond. All around her lay dead and dying cows and calves, horns broken, one with a snapped spine, but still moving about on two legs, another bewildered, its intestines and stomachs trailing for yards behind it. Those left living possessed an unnatural calm, standing in place, eyeing Margarete as if she had come to milk them. She stepped over and around them and called for Warner."Kill the wounded ones so we can leave as soon as possible." she said. She turned her back on the scene to speak with Reed. "It was not your fault," she told him. "We have to be cautious. We have to be." Isolated and muffled pistol shots began firing behind her.

Harding was still on the ground, but he had been able to see what had happened. Had it been daylight, they could see that his face had been drained of its color. The incident had shaken him to the bone. Margarete stood before him while awaiting her partners.

"When I was a boy," Harding said, wiping his mouth dry, "I had a dog who bothered my uncle's sheep. It was a friendly dog whose idea of play was a little rough. But it was a good dog. One day I saw Uncle Perry reach down and take my dog by the hind legs, one in each hand. Then he whirled the terrified animal about his head and dashed its head against the side of the corn crib. I can feel the horror of it yet, can still see that terrified, awful look in my dog's face." He stood now beside Margarete, gesturing to the row of bushes where the gunshots still rang out. "If that had been a farmer and his family walking to their house, I have the feeling it wouldn't make any difference to you in the slightest." The President brushed off his trousers and arms as Margarete led him to the car. "You are a pack of butchers and nothing more. Who are you, really? What is your name? Who are you?"

They faced each other in the plowed field, and her lips parted. She smiled widely, and said, "Not even those two cow-hunters know that, and it would be best to keep it that way."

At that moment, near the horizon, a meteor, so bright and clear that it left behind a train, flared brilliantly in the night sky. It was a vivid green. Harding watched it burn and fade.

Ford and Firestone were asleep in the back seat, and Halverton had taken over temporarily as driver. Edison pointed to the shooting star.

"I saw it," Halverton told him. "That was really a good one."

"Yes it was," Edison answered. "If any of it survived all the way to the earth, I believe you'd find a little copper, a little nickel in it perhaps. That is what would give it such a clear green appearance as it burned."

"Is that right?" Halverton said.

Edison nodded. "Yep, copper and nickel. And maybe some iron."

17

HALVERTON WAS IN A RARE POSITION. HE WAS AWARE that it was literally the opportunity of a lifetime to share the company of Thomas Edison for hours on end. It was an opportunity he would not waste. The sighting of the shooting star began the discussion, and Halverton, though limited in his own education and experience, wanted to cover vast subjects — space, afterlife, science, and even Edison the man. He sought Edison's opinions on such matters, and posed some questions for him while guiding the truck on its ever northward route.

"I guess no one knows how long that meteor has been flying through the heavens, do they?"

"Einstein might," Edison said as he lit a cigar. "I am interested in Einstein, but I can't understand a thing he says. I am out of my depth when it comes to mathematics. I don't have to moan over the fact anymore. Not since I found out through my questionaire that professors at Harvard and Yale are as ignorant as I am. I got along all right with Steinmetz. Are you familiar with Steinmetz?"

"Of the General Electric Laboratories, isn't he?"

"That's right," Edison said. "But we got along fine because he never mentioned mathematics when he talked to me. He knew I didn't know anything about it, so he forgot all about it when he was with me. I'll tell you one thing. I am in a position where I needn't understand mathematics. I can always hire a mathematician, for all the good that does."

Halverton smiled and nodded.

"Mathematicians can be impractical," Edison went on. "As soon as we developed and began producing the incandescent bulb, I found it necessary to determine the volume of a particular bulb. And I posed the problem to a couple of mathematicians. Well, the irregular shape of the thing made a real challenge for them, and they spent the better part of a day trying to agree upon an answer. They finally brought to me what they considered a workable equation for the problem. All this, mind you, to find out how much space is inside a light bulb. I checked the figures, and the work was impressive. But there was a margin of error of 2 percent. That 2 percent adds up when you're talking in terms of millions of bulbs, so I set out to find my own answer and gave it to them in five minutes or so. And the margin of error was zero. Know how I came to the answer?"

Halverton downshifted the truck for a steep incline. "Let

me think a minute," he said as he drove. He was stumped for a moment. Then he considered the bulb abstractly, not as a light at all, but as a container of air. Now the problem was easy. "You could remove the socket and fill the bulb with water," Halverton said. "Then pour the water into a measured cup, and take your reading."

"That's exactly right," Edison smiled. "Those two mathematicians spent eighteen hours on the problem and couldn't arrive at a compatible solution. Now, that is the difference between education and practicality. You are a practical man. You have a practical job. You follow designs and plans and fit your material to specifications. The dining tent from your company showed that. Not everyone can follow a set of plans. It's as great a talent as fine wood-working."

"I don't know about that," Halverton said.

"You're far too modest," Edison said. "Just like John Kreusi. You probably haven't even heard his name before."

"Not that I know of."

"And yet he is the man who built the first phonograph. He never considered himself the possessor of any great talent. I could show him a rough sketch, and he would make a model to exact specifications. When I gave him the sketch for the phonograph, he took one look at the drawing and asked what the thing did. Said it looked like a sausage grinder. I said, 'It doesn't grind meat, John. It talks.' The point is, Kreusi made the thing without even knowing what it was."

"I saw an interview in a magazine with you once," Halverton said. "You said that the phonograph was your greatest invention. Do you still believe that?"

"Of course," said Edison. "Sure. And that is becasue the phonograph was without precedent. The motion picture camera first required the still camera. Many people were working on the incandescent light simultaneously. The arc lamp pointed the way. The same is true of the telephone. Bell came out with the first one, but today's model is a combination of his and mine. My carbon transmitter enabled his telephone to operate. But no one had even suggested a thing like the phonograph. I was never so taken aback in my life as when I first heard my voice coming from the machine. I was always afraid of things that worked the first time, as did the phonograph. When the news broke, everyone considered it a hoax. 'Edison has invented a machine that talks,' the papers said. I had done more than that, as things turned out. I had established a reputation. Those were fine days in Menlo Park."

"Did you have an exact purpose in mind there?" Halverton asked. "Did you know how things would develop?"

"The purpose of Menlo Park," Edison asked. "Was to put out a minor invention every ten days and a major one every six months or so. There was no independent study, just as in West Orange. My daily written instructions have always been the plans of attack. It has worked out well."

"What do you consider a minor invention?"

"Oh, paraffin paper, say," Edison answered. "Preserves and jellies have always been sealed with paraffin. I thought, why not coat a piece of paper with wax for the same purpose. Today, pastry shops throughout the world use waxed paper, and it's in almost every household. That reminds me. I know we're trying to keep a low profile, but as soon as we come to a town, do you think we could stop at a bakery and pick up an apple pie or two?"

"That's fine with me," Halverton said. "I could run errands since no one knows my face. I hope you don't mind all these questions."

"Not at all," Edison said. "Go on, please."

Without realizing it, Halverton had steadily increased the loudness of his voice to accomodate Edison's deafness. Now he was fairly shouting. "How does the idea of an invention come to you?"

"I go at it various ways. It would take all night to explain. A real new thing, like a beautiful melody, is pulled out of space, a fact that is inexplicable. Stored up experience is the principal thing, but the key to successful methods comes unsolicited, right out of the air. Patient observation in experiments is priceless. The storage battery took five years to develop. Some fifty thousand experiments, so many we lost count. Some may call it genius, but I say genius is about 98 percent perspiration and 2 percent inspiration."

"Will science ever be able to create life?"

"No, I think not."

"How can crime be stopped?"

"The Baumes Law seems valid. Crime will diminish if it don't pay."

"Do you believe in the five-day work week?"

"For myself, no. But as the introduction of automatic machinery becomes more general, it will become compulsory to prevent overproduction and all its problems. Then, too, excessive leisure time will have to be dealt with. I believe our cities will become even more crowded, and as cars become more affordable, streets may become impassable at certain times of the day. But the five-day work week is an idea whose time has come. The people deserve it. They have earned it."

"Is television possible?"

"Possible, yes," Edison said, tapping a cigar ash out the window. "But of very little general value. It is a stunt."

"Why is it that some people are more intelligent than others? I guess what I mean is, what is intelligence, and for that matter, what is consciousness?"

"They are one and the same," Edison answered. "That which is not organized high enough to function with a trace of intelligence is only matter. I am convinced that the human body is made up of entities that are intelligent and are directed by a higher power. When one cuts his finger, I believe it is the intelligence of these entities that heals the wound. When one is sick, it is the intelligence of the entities that brings convalescence. You know that there are living cells in the body so tiny that the microscope cannot find them at all. The entities that give life and soul to the human body are finer still and lie infinitely beyond the reach of our finest scientific instruments. When these entities leave the body, the body is like a ship without a rudder — deserted, motionless and dead. To me, it seems that every atom is in possession of intelligence. Look at the thousands of ways that atoms of hydrogen can combine with those of other elements to form the most diverse substances. Do you mean to say that they do this without intelligence? I believe that the great majority of man's intelligent entities reside in the brain, to dictate the body's functions. Upon death, they disperse, only to be picked up by others. A more intelligent man possesses a greater amount of the entities. I set out to prove their existence, but failed to do so."

"Is there anything you wish to accomplish that you haven't been able to?"

"Many things," Edison said. "For instance, aside from developing a cheap synthetic rubber, I would like to record Beethoven's Ninth Symphony with an orchestra of seventy-five musicians. Things I have left purposely unfinished also, with the expectation that someone will pick up where I left off. In 1914 I developed a motion picture with sound. The sound and picture were not synchronized well, and I couldn't afford the time to perfect it. I am certain it will come to pass. Just as in the recent introduction of the helicopter. I built one in 1885, twenty years before the Wright brothers flew at Kitty Hawk. I used guncotton made from stock-ticker paper, which was fed into the cylinder of the engine and exploded with a spark. I got good results, but burned one of my men pretty badly, and burned some of my own hair and decided that the experiments were too dangerous at the time. It was like playing with dynamite. But I became assured that the solution to aerial navigation was only a matter of experiment. When an engine could be developed that would weigh only three or four pounds to the horsepower, the problem of the air would be solved. I never changed my mind, but I had to wait twenty years to be proved right."

"Mr. Edison, do you ever plan to retire?"

Edison smiled and drew deeply on his cigar. "Yes I do," he said. "The day before my funeral."

The sky was getting light out the right window of the truck. Suddenly, the bouncing and jolting that had been constant since leaving the campsite nearly a day earlier abruptly ceased. Halverton shifted the truck into its highest gear and increased their speed.

Their progress had taken them to a paved road.

18

THEY WERE WELL INTO PENNSYLVANIA NOW. IN another ten years, the National Highway Act would crisscross the countryside with mountain roads; but in 1923, pavement was a luxury rarely found outside of cities and towns. They had passed through a dozen small communities in the night. For all the activity they showed, they could have been ghost towns. At Edison's direction, Halverton steered clear of the large cities. Pittsburg had passed to the west some forty miles away, Johnstown to the east. Their rural route was inconspicuous, but slow. As the sun began to rise, Halverton drove the truck over the brick streets of a town by the name of Black Lick. It was all Edison could stand.

"We have to find a newspaper," he said. "I'm lost without my paper."

Halverton nodded and parked the truck facing in at the curb at the side of an ice truck. There was a grocery store and a bakery in view, and Halverton imagined as he stepped down from the cab that one of them would have a newspaper. He walked inside the grocery first. The clerk was busy helping a woman.

This was in the days when you told the clerk everything you needed at the front counter, and he would bring them to you an item or two at a time, all the while keeping up a conversation about things in general, about nothing in particular.

He was surprised that they weren't speaking about the President's disappearance. With radio, they ought to have known of it by now. He waited for a lull in the conversation.

"What's the news in this part of the world?" he interrupted.

The clerk was bagging the woman's food.

"Pretty awful accident," the man said. "The sheriff said there wasn't a thing anyone could do for the young man found in the wreckage."

"What happened?" Halverton asked. "Car run off the road?"

"A plane crashed yesterday evening, right on the main road outside of Homer City. Sheriff said it was a lucky thing there wasn't any more people on board, or they'd all be dead too. The plane had eight seats in it."

"What caused the crash?"

"They think he was just flying too low, and he went into the side of a mountain."

"Have you heard anything about the President's trip to Alaska?"

"No. He's going clear across the country. That's all I know."

Halverton bought a quart of milk and walked out to the

sun on the sidewalk. He was almost giddy from a lack of sleep, but it felt marvelous to stretch his legs after a day and night of riding in the truck. He entered the bakery, standing aside as the ice man shouldered his way in with a block on his back.

"'Morning, stranger," the baker greeted Halverton. "What'll you have this morning?"

"How's your apple pie?"

"I have to say it's excellent."

"Good," Halverton said, taking in the aroma of the bakery. "I'd like two of them."

The baker turned and pulled the pies from a cooling rack. He began to wrap them in waxed paper, and Halverton asked him where he might find a newspaper.

"You'll have to go to Indiana."

"Indiana?"

"Indiana, Pennsylvania. It's a few miles up the road. You might ask Jack if he has one before you leave. He came out of Indiana this morning." The baker made a package of the pies and set them on the counter. "Jack's the ice man yonder."

Another block of ice moved past Halverton to the cooler in the back of the store. As the receipt for the ice was being signed, Halverton asked if he had a newspaper.

"I sure do," the ice man answered. "I've read all I want of it. Say, did you hear about the plane crash?"

"Yes," Halverton said. "Yes, I did."

Halverton paid for the pie. He followed Jack to his truck, and the ice man threw his tongs onto the floorboard, jumped in and started his engine, reaching for the newspaper on the seat beside him. It was a Ford truck, resting on Firestone tires, with a battery developed by Edison.

"What do I owe you?"

Jack shook his head, pulled a cap tightly down on his forehead. He gave Halverton the paper and backed the truck into the street. Halverton watched the ice truck turn a corner and disappear as it continued its route to the next town. He tucked the paper under his arm, holding the bottle of milk in one hand, balancing the pies in the other. Ford was awake now with a change of clothes. He was in the driver's seat. Firestone opened the back door, taking the items from Halverton one by one before he climbed in.

"Smell that apple pie!" Edison cried.

"A plane crashed up the road a piece," Halverton said. "That's all they're talking about here. Nobody said a thing about Harding. Not a thing."

Ford took the paper and removed the front section of it. "They have wire service," he said. "If there was anything to print, they'd have it." He opened the paper and shuffled quickly through the back pages. "Well, here's something. It says the President has postponed his progress to Alaska to further relax with his friends, Misters Edison, Firestone and Ford. It says he might stay another three days with them."

"Then it's been hushed," Firestone said.

"And a good thing, too," Ford commented. "Think of the pandemonium that news would stir up. I, for one, am glad the story hasn't broken. Three days, they say. Not much time."

"Let's see that paper," Edison said, spreading it on his lap. "Now hand me the pie."

Edison placed the pie on one leg and folded the paper back over the other one, lodging the milk bottle between his knees. He removed the bottle cap and broke off a piece of pie, arching his eyebrows at the newspaper as he began to read. Without removing his gaze from the paper, he said, "Shake a leg, Henry. You've had your beauty sleep. Now it's time to move on."

The slaughter of the cattle and the noise of the gunfire had, at first, terrified the President. But when he had time to consider the shooting, it only brought out his anger. When the group was on the road again, Harding spoke with sarcasm.

"Are we ready so soon?" he said. "You're quite sure you're done? If we scouted the area, I'm sure you could find a flock of chickens to maim. Or how about goats? I understand they're great sport."

"I didn't know they were cows," Reed said from the front seat. "You think I'd waste my rounds and risk being caught for a bunch of cows?"

Margarete interrupted. "Mr. Harding," she said. "You must be aware that the three of us here have a very great deal at stake. We know the risks, and we have to take precautions.

Harding was pleased with the reaction. His captors were defensive, and that reassured him that there might be a weakness. Probably not an Achilles heel, but it showed that they were vulnerable, and he was heartened. Margarete was still a mystery to him. He was still somewhat frightened by her, and more than slightly in awe. In Warner, he saw a certain strength. But he knew it was easy to misinterpret a quiet man. Reed, the President was convinced, was trash.

"From the way you act around cattle," Harding continued, "I now see there's no reason to believe you'll be successful in your plan. You're already tripping over your own feet."

Reed turned around in his seat. "That's mighty bold talk to make in the company of white folks," he said. "Oh, I'm not saying you're *all* nigger, Mr. Harding, sir. What are you? A sixteenth? An eighth? Are you an octoroon, or what?"

"Settle down, son," Warner told him.

"No, let him speak," Harding said. "I've lived with that putrid rumor all my life, and I expect to take it to my grave. It only makes the accuser look like a damned idiot, so I don't mind."

"Do you deny it?" Reed asked.

"I deny nothing," Harding said. "Who among us can say? Maybe an ancestor did jump the fence way back when. It's not important."

"President Warren Sambo Harding has spoken," Reed said.

"Stop it," Margarete shouted. "These blunt little barbs you are throwing at each other are childish. Keep in mind that we have a job to do, and that job is not child's play."

Harding was feeling much better. He crossed his legs, pulled out a plug of tobacco from his coat, and bit off a chew. "United we stand," he told Margarete. "Isn't that right?"

"Something to that effect," Margarete said. "You know, as close as our quarters are, one can expect certain disagreements. If we had a very great distance to travel, I would choose better accomodations."

"How far *are* we going?" Harding asked.

"Hopefully, by morning light, we will have arrived," she said. "Can we expect to stay on schedule, Warner?"

"As nearly as I can tell," the driver said. "There are four fields as possible rendezvous sites. Just like when your car and ours met up. If we aren't at the first site, he will fly over to the next, then the next, and the last one if he has to. All we have to do is wait for him. He can find us."

Harding had a sinking sensation. His vision seemed to blur. Suddenly lightheaded, his pulse throbbed in his ears like a drum. He wanted to call for Doctor Sawyer. He wondered where his physician was. Back at the campsite? Waiting aboard the *Superb*? How could one roadblock the very sky? "It sounds as if you're talking about an airplane."

"Yes," Margarete said.

"And our destination?"

"I shall inform you of that after we are in the air," she told him.

Harding ceased chewing the tobacco. He swished the juice

around in his mouth a moment, then spit the whole wad out the window. His new optimism had been shattered. He looked outside and realized that he could distinguish trees and horizons. There was a chill in the morning air, and Harding welcomed the new day by drawing his coat closer and rolling his window up to cut the wind.

They parked on a bluff hidden by a cluster of trees. Warner raised the hood of the car, and as the other three stepped out of the Packard, the heat of the engine warmed the air around them. "It ran fine," Warner said. "It ran just fine. I sort of hate to have to leave it behind here."

"Would you rather drive all the way?" Margarete asked him. Warner smiled and shook his head no.

As the sun began to rise, it lit up miles and miles of farmland below the bluff, like a huge sheet being lifted to expose a panoramic canvas. In the distance, a river cut through the valley. Tractor rows plotted huge squares of topsoil, and colors changed by the minute as the day brightened. President Harding strolled away from the automobile, and Margarete followed. Reed, with his ever-present weapon, remained with his uncle at the Packard.

"This is a beautiful, beautiful land," Harding said to her. "I wouldn't trade it for all the empires in Europe."

"Europe is beautiful too," Margarete said. "I was born in Holland. I know the continent well."

"The wife and I made a trip to Europe a few years ago," the President said. "We took in the sights, saw the antiquities."

"And what was your impression of the people?"

"I viewed the people with American eyes. Understand?"

"I'm beginning to."

"So that when I saw incredible injustice, overcrowding and unspeakable poverty, it made me realize just how ignorant Europeans must be."

"In what way?"

"Why, too stupid to come to America," Harding told her.

"This is truly the land of unlimited freedom, unbridled ambition and quite simply, the last bastion of heaven on Earth. No, thank you, madam. You can have your Holland and its windmills and tulips. You can keep the Eiffel Tower and the sewage canals of Venice. Give me the freedom of the United States of America."

Margarete paused before speaking. "Perhaps we both see inequalities that the other is blind to," she said, speaking slowly and deliberately, a trace of an accent surfacing as she articulated her thoughts. "You paint a warm and wonderful picture of your country, but you hide the flaws. There is a violent tendency in America that does not allow dissent. Labor strikes are settled with dynamite and shootings. Negroes are hanged with no more reaction from the populace than if they were decorations on a Christmas tree. This problem has no geographic boundary in this country. It's horrible."

Harding twisted his back. "You're a fine one to lecture on violence in America," he said. "But you have a point. Democracy in America is somewhat of a lie, and will remain so until there is educational and economic equality for all."

Margarete's eyes were set on the horizon. She glanced now and then at the sky when an object caught her attention, an object that invariably proved to be a swooping bird. "I would like you to know that I have searched my conscience and believe in the rightness of what I am doing," she said. "I have to believe that. Otherwise, I could not have acted. I am also happy that we have succeeded in not spilling a drop of human blood. Still, even if we had killed, we would be right."

"You will be held responsible for whatever happens to me," Harding told her, "whether it's actually your fault or not. If, say, I catch pneumonia, you will be held accountable."

"I know that," she said.

"Then do the right thing," Harding pleaded. "It still isn't too late."

"I told you that I believe I am right," she answered. "I won't be persuaded by emotion."

"Emotion, you say? There's a joke."

"It's no joke," Margarete said. "You are a very attractive man."

"I'm a flabby, grey, fifty-seven year old politician," Harding said, shaking his head. "What is so alluring in that?"

"You're President of the United States," Margarete answered quickly.

Harding turned away from her. He could see Warner's feet protruding from beneath the Packard. Reed was squatted beside him, poking his face under a fender too.

"How did you meet up with those two birds?" Harding gestured.

"It was arranged," she said. "I'm accustomed to working alone, but the scope of what we are doing called for more than one person. The driver is fine. I don't expect any trouble from him. The younger one is a bit temperamental. He is, well, he's temperamental, that's all. I wouldn't have chosen him, but he's here."

"You talk as if you've done this kind of thing before."

"Not this exactly," Margarete answered. "I've gained the confidence of certain people to gather information before, but never anything like an abduction."

"It just occurred to me that you're a spy," Harding said. "You're no common criminal like that boy with the gun. What country has employed you?"

Margarete laughed lightly, tracing her wrist with the tip of her index finger. She touched the tattoo, running her finger from the snake's head, around and under along its body, then reversed again at the head. It was an inconspicuous tattoo, and now was the first time Harding had noticed it.

When looking at such an attractive woman, the wrists tended to be overlooked.

"That's too romantic a term for what I do," she smiled.

"Was the young man in camp with you part of your plans?"

"Insofar as I used him to get to you, yes."

"How can you do that?" Harding asked. "You work like some kind of pickpocket with people's feelings."

"And I rely on that," Margarete said. "Sid is a fine man. I was fortunate to find him, and extremely fortunate that the difference in our ages didn't matter to him. I have feelings too. But I cannot do what I am doing forever. You, for example, would you have left the campground with me had I been seventy? I think you know the answer."

"How old are you?" Harding asked.

"Not so much younger than you," she said. "I am forty-six. I know I appear to be younger. Diet and exercise is the key to health and if I may be immodest, to beauty."

"What will you do when all of this is over?" he said. "That is, after you deliver my head on a silver platter."

"I haven't given it much thought," she said. "I would like to see for myself if the mystique of the Latin man is valid. Perhaps I will travel South.

"What will you do if the plane doesn't show up?"

"Oh, it will show," she assured him. "Still, we have the automobile if it doesn't."

"And do you plan to starve me in the meantime?" Harding said. "How about some breakfast?"

"I think there is some canned meat left," Margarete said. "Also, bread and some peanut butter."

Harding frowned as Warner approached the two of them. His hands were covered with grease and oil. Margarete and Harding had made themselves comfortable on the ground, and she stood now to speak with Warner.

"Good thing we aren't traveling any farther by car," the

driver said. "There's a leak in the oil pan. Not a bad one, but she's dripped a pretty good puddle since we stopped."

"Would it help to keep putting oil in it?" Margarete asked.

"Yes, that would hold it for awhile. I wouldn't want to drive it for hundreds of miles, though. It will get worse."

"Well, let's wait here until evening," she told him. "In the meantime, you may want to service the automobile. Fill it with petrol, and buy some oil for the trip."

"Where do you suppose Bill is with the plane?"

"He could be checking the other landing strips." she said. "He could have engine trouble. I don't know. If he hasn't shown by evening, we shall leave without him. The plane was a convenience, not a necessity."

Reed joined the group, picking up a rock and tossing it off the edge of the bluff.

"I think in that case we should get another car," Warner said. "Do you have the cash to cover the cost of one? We only have about twenty between us."

Margarete shook her head, keeping an eye on Reed as he threw a steady volley of rocks out in the air, listening to them land in the bushes below. "Let's steal us a car," he said.

Harding got to his feet and brushed off the seat of his trousers. He touched Margarete on the shoulder and asked with a smile, "Do you ever get the feeling you're losing control?"

19

EDISON WAS EXAMINING HIS MAPS OF THE AREA, measuring off inches with the span of his fingers and calculating the distance in miles. The warm air was blowing hair into his face, but the old man didn't bother pushing it away.

"How far have we come?" Halverton asked from the back seat.

Edison cupped his hand behind his ear, and the question had to be repeated for him.

"As near as I can tell, two hundred and fifty miles or so. That's after twenty-three hours of steady driving — except for our stops. We're making good time."

"Do you suppose we should have caught a train?" Firestone said. "Surely we could cover a greater distance in that amount of time."

Ford pivoted at the steering wheel to answer. "The train's fine for speed, Harvey. But we have other things to consider besides speed. By boarding a train, we risk disclosing our whereabouts to the Secret Service — something we should avoid. Anyway, I still believe we are ahead of that bitch and Mr. Harding." He returned his attention to the road, then as an afterthought added, "No offense, Mr. Halverton. I know you're still quite fond of her. But you have to realize that she is the enemy. Should we be fortunate enough to encounter her, we must be prepared to do battle without hesitation."

"Are you willing to kill her, Mr. Ford?" Halverton asked.

"My God," Ford exclaimed. "Don't make it sound like that's what I have in mind. But if it comes to that, we must all be willing."

It was a subject they had probably all considered, but none of them had voiced it to the others until now. They made faces and shifted in their seats. They had to think of the situation in terms of war, where killing was not murder, where extremes were excused for the cause. They knew what they had to do, but that made it no easier. Chances were slim they would even have to.

They had traveled in the truck only a few miles out from

their stop for the newspaper and pie when they came upon the crash site. A dozen men with rakes were standing about in a huge blackened area that stretched from the shoulder of the road some hundred yards into the densely wooded countryside. It looked as if the plane had tried setting down on the pavement, then exploded on impact. A firetruck was parked nearby, and hoses watered down the steaming wreckage. A man on the side of the road directed Ford's truck to pass by, and Ford drove slowly in a low gear, the transmission whining as the truck climbed the hillside.

"Almost unbelievable destruction," Edison commented.

"I've never flown," Ford said. "And I never expect to."

"Pull over to the side," Edison said. "Let's take a quick look about. We could learn something."

Halverton was the last of the four to leave the truck. None of the men in the woods seemed to notice the famed trio who had stopped by. Halverton saw a man with Edison he assumed to be the sheriff. If the sheriff recognized him, he gave no sign of it. There was no hearty handshake or excited introduction. Edison poked the ground with a stick, the sheriff standing with crossed arms, both men shaking their heads as they spoke. Behind them, higher on the hill, a portion of the plane's fuselage was still attached to the charred tail section. The rest was debris. Halverton didn't see how anyone could guess at the number of passengers. So much was nothing more than ashes. He returned to the truck and awaited the others. When they joined him, Firestone handed over a small book, the outer edges of the paper burned away.

"What's this?"

"Mr. Edison found it on the ground," Eirestone explained.

Halverton opened the cover. It was a Morse code dictionary with letters and words broken down to dots and dashes, an aid to a novice operator.

"They found remnants of a radio set, some tubes and

such," Firestone went on. "It's just speculation, mind you, but this plane might have figured in with Mr. Harding. We have no way of telling."

"Did you mention that to the authorities here?"

"No, I didn't see a point in it."

They settled once more into their seats to continue their trip. Halverton leaned his head out the window and waved casually to the workers. He pulled himself back inside and looked over at Ford. "Do you think that the airplane will ever do away with the automobile?"

"Do you?" Ford said.

"I don't know. I just wonder about it."

"Well," Ford said. "The company keeps up with the development of aviation, though, as I mentioned earlier, I never expect to fly myself. We build machines and we keep up with the developments. We had a machine at the show in New York. Just a little thing, and it flies as well as the big machines, goes in and out, up and down just like that." Ford was waving his right hand to imitate the flight of the plane. "Airplanes can only operate when subsidized," he went on. "We're flying between Chicago and Detroit every day now, but we're subsidizing our aviation. There *is* something magic about flying, though. A plane goes overhead, and you automatically stop what you're doing and take a look. I like that."

"I'm partial to dirigibles in that respect," Edison said. "These flying ships as big as clouds, with aerial drawing rooms and sleeping compartments. They have their own generators and radios to maintain contact with the ground. I've worked with hydrogen, and guess one of these days a dirigible will explode and the great airships will cease to fly until a safer way is found. Still, that's something to catch the eye for you. A dirigible."

They were silent a moment. Then Ford spoke up. "Yes," he said, as if he'd been weighing a proposition. "Harvey, you've always been one out front with advertising. I've just thought of something bigger than any billboard, better than the side of the tallest building. How about painting up a dirigible to sell your balloon tires? See the connection? The Firestone dirigible would be as famous as the product itself."

Firestone rubbed his chin. He didn't take the suggestion lightly. He could see its possibilities. Finally, he shook his head and smiled. "Tires and blimps are two different animals," he said. "There would be no association of one with the other in the consumer's mind. It would never work. Not in a hundred years."

Halverton had been awake for a very long time. He had driven the truck all night and was still covered with the dirt picked up from pushing the truck out of the mudhole. In addition, his back stung from where he had brushed against the light bulb in the boxing match. He couldn't lean back in the seat comfortably. Now there was a sooty smell in the vehicle from their walk through the crash site. He closed his eyes, so weary that he fell asleep within seconds.

He awoke from the noise. It was tumultuous, like a speakeasy. People were shouting. Halverton opened his eyes, slightly alarmed. The view from his window was a sea of smiling faces and waving arms. Ford moved the vehicle slowly through the gathering, tapping the horn steadily to open gaps for the truck. Edison, Halverton saw, alternately tipped his hat to the crowd and glanced patiently at his fellow travelers.

"What is it?" Halverton asked. "Where are we?"

"Du Bois, Pennsylvania," Firestone told him. "It started about thirty miles back, and from then on, we've had a welcoming committee in every town."

An excited man jumped onto the moving running board, seized Edison's hand and gave it a vigorous shaking before he leaped to the street again.

"How can they know you're coming?"

"We can't outrace the telephone," Firestone answered. "Even the small towns are turning out. It's a shame, too, because we were clipping right along there for a while."

A hand reached inside and rumpled Halverton's hair. He ducked his head and pushed the arm away. They were the center of attention — a one-car parade. Children and adults who acted like children chased each other down the sidewalks and streets to keep pace with the truck.

"What can we do about it?" Halverton shouted above the crowd.

"Not a thing," Firestone said. "Other than abandoning the truck. Say, Henry, what do you say to that? Let's pick us up a car and go the rest of the way."

"You could be right," Ford said. "Let's wait it out, though. Could be this is the last crowd we'll see. Al, check the maps. We can change course slightly, and it won't be so easy to guess where we'll turn up."

Ford made a couple of turns, taking a new parallel route through the city. The onlookers were more sparse and seemed content to wave from a safe distance when they noticed the truck at all.

The countryside had been tamed. There was less forest and more farmland. Houses and barns were simple, but solid. Some were probably two hundred years old. Ford had guessed right about the crowds. With only a minor adjustment in their flexible itinerary, Du Bois apparently was populated by the last of their admirers. Once, just shy of the New York state line, a group of ragged-looking children presented the truck with a bouquet of wildflowers. They must have been farm children, because they were miles from a town, positioned at a crossroads where the truck had to make a stop. Ford pulled the vehicle onto the road's gravel shoulder, and the four men greeted the youngsters, shaking their little hands as if they were dignitaries. Edison was especially delighted by the envoys. He accepted the flowers and presented each of the children with a candy bar or a box of Cracker Jacks in return, out of his own supply. One of the children pointed to Halverton and asked Edison, "Is that your son?"

They moved down the road again, their spirits lifted by the visit and by the fact that they were only a hundred miles from Niagara Falls.

"Where *are* your sons, anyway?" Halverton asked. "I would have thought they would be camping with you."

"My son Russell's in Africa," Firestone said. "He just negotiated a ninety-nine year lease with the King of Liberia on a million acres of land to raise rubber. He did a fine job there, but he couldn't get back in time to join us. Harvey, Junior. made the voyage with him."

"My son Edsel was tied up with business too," Ford said. "I believe Mr. Edison's sons just didn't want to come. They are not fond of the attention. Isn't that right, Al?"

Edison hadn't heard anything, and when he spoke, it was a change of subject.

"I think we should get some rest," he said. "The fact of the matter is, we can make Niagara by nightfall. I propose that we take a break for a few hours in order to regenerate our strength. Perhaps even map out a strategy. We can get there by morning. You see, this way we can drive straight through Buffalo without the attention that our presence might otherwise create. We shall lose a few hours, sure. But we must understand, we must realize, that we cannot be the only four men on top of this situation. I believe in my heart that the Secret Service, and probably the Bureau of Investigation, are working themselves to the bone over Mr. Harding's and our country's unfortunate dilemma. What do you say? We'll abide by a vote."

"I'm all for driving straight through," Ford said. "We don't know how long the patched radiator will hold. We can rest later."

"I can't decide," Firestone answered. "Both sides make sense. Sid, how do you go?"

Halverton was anxious to reach Niagara, but his brief nap had done nothing to relieve his exhaustion. He hesitated a moment.

"I'm with Mr. Edison," he told them.

It boosted his spirits to have his vote count as much as the others, and he was thrilled to be in on the decision making. Ford hedged a little on the agreement, claiming he would like them to advance at least as far as New York State before calling it a day.

They stopped at an isolated bend on the Genesee River, just as beautiful a spot, Edison mentioned, as any campsite in their decade of treks into the wilderness. That placed it in the company of the Great Smoky Mountains, the Monongahela Forest, the Adirondacks and Catskills, Vermont, Massachusetts, Maryland, Tennessee and North Carolina. Steep, heavily wooded hills banked right into the river, and before they were even out of the truck, they could see ducks swimming and fish breaking water. At the moment, the whole world seemed pastoral and tame, and looking about at Nature, it was easy to forget your troubles.

Once they were parked, and had adjusted to the sudden quiet, Henry Ford busied himself with calisthenics and exercises at the side of his truck. Firestone began rummaging through their cooking utensils in the storage area to fix a pot of coffee. He asked Halverton's help in making the fire, convinced that the brew would have more taste than a pot prepared on the truck's stove. Halverton scrounged the area for kindling, while Edison sat braced against a tree trunk, fanning his reddened face with his hat. Although he would be the last to admit it, the inventor was worn out. He loved "tinkering in Nature's wondrous laboratory," as he called the camping, but he was still a man approaching eight full decades in age. He was almost as tired as the younger men.

Firestone placed the coffee pot on the edge of the flames, then took a seat a few feet from Edison on the ground.

"How are you doing, Al?" he asked. "This isn't too strenuous for you, is it?"

"Too tough for a dude, maybe," Edison said." But I ain't no dude."

Halverton thought that Edison was as fine a man as he had ever met and as fine as any he should ever hope to encounter. He wasn't sure whether he could put his finger on the exact qualities he found so admirable. Simplicity was surely one of the traits, and kindness. Firestone poured coffee for the three of them, and they passed around the sugar. Halverton posed a question.

"Mr. Firestone, how do you judge a man? What is it you see in a person you look up to?"

Firestone blew on the surface of his cup. "There's not one infallible formula," he said. "I've employed thousands of men and picked scores for promotion. Of course, sometimes I have guessed wrong. When I used to hire all my employees myself, I asked applicants a good many questions people would think irrelevant."

"Like what?"

"Oh, I'd go back to a boy's grandparents. Who and what were they? Where was he born? What did his father do? And all the time I was getting a line on his character. From his answers and the way he gave them, I learned whether he thought clearly and quickly, what his powers of reasoning and analysis were."

Halverton wondered how he would do if Firestone gave him such a test. He remembered that his grandfather's last name had been Halvorsen and that he had settled in Indiana after emigrating from Norway. Later on, the family name had been changed to Halverton. Would a recitation of these facts by Sid have provided any clues to his character?

"Anyway," Firestone said, "when I was finished with an

applicant, I had a pretty good idea whether he was energetic, straightforward and ambitious. Minor faults could be corrected, but the fundamentals were there. And while I talked with him, I watched his face and hands. I always do that. We like a man to look us straight in the eye, but there is a difference even in how men do this. Some of them do it because they are watching you. And that's all right too, unless there is some suspicion behind it. And if suspicion and distrust are part of his character, it is safe to conclude either one of two things. Either he has been fooled so often that he has come to expect it, in which case there is something wrong with him. Or, he himself is looking for the chance to get the better of you.

"Now, there is a kind of man who doesn't look you in the eye that doesn't bother me. That's the thoughtful type. And he thinks better when he can detach himself from outside influence. He is very likely to be looking down at his hands, or out a window, while you are talking. He is listening and thinking. When he brings his eyes back to your face, there is a directness that almost knocks you over."

Halverton gestured with his head toward the tree.

"Yes, like Mr. Edison," Firestone said. "Exactly. Now, the way a man uses his hands is very significant too. Suppose you are talking to an applicant for a position, and after you have explained what will be expected of him, he gives a flabby little wave of his hand and says, 'I guess I can do it.' Maybe I am wrong, but my feeling is that he is nothing but a guesser, and not a very good one at that. If he involuntarily shuts his hand hard, as if gripping some material thing, and says, 'I believe I can do it. I certainly will try!' I am inclined to think he's the type who will take off his coat and make a good job of it. These are things I look for in a prospective employee, and I've found that you can judge the man himself pretty well by them."

Halverton considered Firestone's criteria. He thought it

curious that he seemed to put everything in business terms. It wasn't exactly the answer he had expected. Still, he found he didn't know what to do with his hands or his eyes.

"You wouldn't be very happy in another kind of work, would you, Mr. Firestone?"

"You're dadblamed right, Sid. I'm a manager, and a good one too. You could take everything I have. Just leave me something to run, an organization, a company. Feed me bread and water if that's all you have, but give me something to operate, and I'd pull through."

Firestone looked satisfyingly into the fire, then seemed to dismiss the subject with a shrug as if his insight might be way off target, rather than common sense. "I'd better put some water on for Henry," he said.

Henry Ford believed that coffee was abrasive to the system, and he liked to drink a mug of hot water in place of it. Firestone called to him when the water began to boil, and Edison huddled with the others for his second cup. He carried a section of the newspaper and folded it on the ground at his side. The four of them just sat there underneath a tree by the river. It was a group who didn't feel the need to keep talking constantly in order to enjoy each other's company. Halverton sipped at his coffee and pulled out the newspaper's photogravure section. Local news dominated the paper, but there were a few pictures and paragraphs of international news.

"Look here," Halverton said. "Did you see this, Mr. Edison? They've named a boulevard after you in Buenos Aires."

Edison smiled slightly and acknowledged the honor.

"Yes, they asked me to attend several weeks ago. I thanked them, but declined the invitation. It's a shame, in a way. I don't like to disappoint people, because in general they are very kind to me. I know it must hurt them."

"You've never let anyone down, Al," Ford said.

"I have, Henry. I have indeed. I am one of the hardest persons in the world to live with, and I know that. I have had experiments with disastrous outcomes. I lost a man by exposing him to excessive doses of X-rays." Edison paused and reflected a moment. "That point was never brought so close to home as with the death of my wife Mary. There was so much time I could have devoted to her. Once that time has passed, no power or invention can ever bring it back. We honeymooned in Niagara Falls, a place so splendorous in its beauty that Mark Twain situated the Garden of Eden there when he wrote his diaries of Adam and Eve."

Ford seemed the most uncomfortable with Edison's gloominess. He helped himself to more hot water, squatting as he poured from the long-handled pan, making broad and exaggerated gestures as he did so. "Well, what are our chances of success, boys?" he shouted out. "What do we have, really?"

Edison perked up. "Our task is just like inventing," he said. "We must keep working with patient observation and hope for a streak of luck."

"What's our observation given us so far?" Firestone asked.

"The Morse book," Edison reminded them, removing the tattered pages from a pocket and tossing it to the dirt. "Not only that, but we ourselves are in the process of facing the same physical barriers of time, distance and terrain that the renegades are. I almost wish we were at war. In a war, you know who you are fighting and you have every means at your disposal."

Another silence fell on the group for perhaps a minute. Firestone was the first to speak again.

"You were in the Navy, Sid," he said. "What did you do in the Conflict?"

"The *Delaware* didn't see as much action as many of the battleships. In fact, our only contact with the enemy was when we had two torpedoes fired at us. We took an evasive action and never caught sight of the sub. We had drilled for weeks for just such an emergency, but that was the only time we really had to take battle stations. My brother and I were both assigned to the *Delaware*, so I wasn't as lonely as a lot of the boys. Even a brother wasn't much help in keeping yourself occupied, though."

"You may owe your life to Edison," Ford said. "It was one of his developments in the steering mechanisms of battle-ships that gave them such maneuverability. He improved our torpedoes too."

"Now, Henry," Edison said. "I'm sure he feels badly enough from what has developed from his Miss Fabry. Don't go making him feel like I saved his life to boot."

"But I do appreciate it," Halverton was quick to say. "Everybody owes a great debt to Mr. Edison."

Firestone listened intently, then threw his hands in the air.

"Al, did you ever get that patent mess straightened out from your naval work?"

"No, Harvey," Edison answered. "The government still maintains that as head of the Naval Advisory Board, I was their employee. As such, they feel any and all inventions in that time belong to them. I have appealed the decision, but it is still in the courts. I'm not optimistic about the outcome."

"Patent laws should be abolished," Ford suggested. "They could be replaced by gentlemanly agreements between the parties. They shouldn't be any more complicated than that."

The statement nearly doubled Edison over in laughter.

Halverton failed to see the humor in the conversation and felt that he could add very little to the discussion. What did he know about the advantages and pitfalls of the current patent laws? Edison seemed to sense his isolation, and after getting the bellylaugh out of his system, tapped Halverton on the shoulder.

"Help an old man to his feet," he told him. "Let's you and me take us a little walk."

They could hear cars on the road from where they were parked. Towns were no longer separated by a great distance, and people passed from one of them to the others, not in a constant stream, but every now and then. The wilderness was behind them now. Edison and Halverton walked away from the truck, and away from the river, in a low draw that might be a tributary in rainy weather. Halverton glanced over his shoulder at Ford and Firestone sitting beside the fire. He seemed to have Ford's full attention, even at a distance.

Edison stopped once to pick up a stone, keeping his eyes fixed on the ground they crossed. But he seemed to day-dream. He paused once and looked into the trees. "No one," he said, "has improved yet on *Evangeline* or *Les Miserables*." After a minute or so he reached down and seized another rock. Halverton didn't know what kind of minerals were in them, but it was apparent even to him that they were of identical nature. Edison wiped the dirt from them, exposing them in the dry palm of his hand.

"What have you got there?" Halverton asked him.

Edison stopped and raised an arm, pointing out the wide draw they were following that stretched before them.

"We are in the midst of a huge track," he explained. "Made not by an animal, but by a river of ice."

"A glacier?"

"Precisely," Edison said. "This gravel was produced in its path. Great boulders were lifted up, crushed and carried by its massive weight, moving inches a year. But don't worry about running into the beast. It has a ten-thousand-year head start on us. The Finger Lakes were formed in the same way. They are a few miles from us."

Halverton began to believe that Edison's knowledge had no boundaries. Outdoors, he seemed a part of Nature. In the laboratory, he astounded the world for two generations. To be in Edison's company was to remain flabbergasted.

Halverton shook his head. "How can you be such a wealth of information?" he asked.

Edison shrugged off the question and seemingly changed

the subject. "Deafness is a source of great despair for people who have perfect hearing," he said. "It is generally thought to be a terrible thing. But imagine losing your sight. Go ahead, close your eyes. But a blind man will tell you there are many things worse than that. There are ways to circumvent anything. Now, most people believe that deafness affects everything you hear. But in the case of my deafness, I can hear certain frequencies perfectly. My wife's voice, for example, is as clear as a bell. Yet I haven't heard a bird sing for sixty years. I have learned to *think* by being shut away from confusion and sound. And I have a lot more thinking I want to do before I die. If they fix up my ear, and I am told an operation, a simple one, would be successful, I'll have to learn to think all over again. I haven't the time to lose."

They stopped and leaned against a large rock covered in a slick green moss. Edison ran his hand over the vegetation while he gathered his thoughts. "I know I am different from others, and I speak of more than my deafness. Henry is different, and Harvey too. Harvey speaks of us being just common men. In ways, we are, certainly. But in many ways we are much less than that. When Mr. Ford prepared to sail to Europe in his Peace Ship before our entry into the World War, he offered me a million dollars to join him. I refused. Only a fool would make such a proposition, and it took even a bigger fool to turn the offer down. A normal person would snatch up such an opportunity. What I am trying to say is, that the three of us have all done things that make no more sense than a dog chasing its tail." Edison closed his hand on the two pebbles he still carried and raised a finger in Halverton's face. "In an emergency situation, I would rely on *you*, out of the four of us. The rest of us, we're the oddballs. We wouldn't be where we are if we were normal. Trust your *own* judgment, put your skills to the test, because in a pinch, Henry, Harvey and myself might be no more assistance than a cuckoo bird. Do you understand what I'm saying?"

"I think so," Halverton said. "I don't really agree, but I understand."

"I watched Henry's ship sail for Europe, a valiant effort that proved to be in vain. Just after he pulled away from the wharf, a man jumped into the water and had to be fished out. He told the police he had done it to ward off torpedoes from the Peace Ship. His was an action I found great respect for. It didn't do anything, but it made all the sense in the world to me. His name, he said, was Mr. Zero."

"Mr. Zero?" Halverton said. "I heard that name just the other day. I remember. It was in camp. President Harding read aloud from the paper that a man calling himself Mr. Zero was selling men on the Boston Common. Men who were out of work. It seemed to irritate the President."

Edison clapped his hands. "Good for Mr. Zero!" he cheered.

When they returned to the truck, Ford had fashioned a fishing pole and line and was trying his luck in the river. Firestone was lying on the ground reading the paper.

"Where's that pie?" Edison shouted from the truck's running board. "I had it right here on the seat."

Firestone folded the newspaper.

"I hate to tell him this," he said.

"Tell him what?" Halverton asked.

"Henry threw the pie away. He said it wasn't a fit diet for a man of Edison's age."

"He shouldn't have done that," Halverton said indignantly. "It wasn't even his. I paid for it."

"Well, he threw it in the river."

Halverton watched Ford standing on the river bank, watching his cork floating in the water. "Mr. Firestone, let's you and me go swimming in the Genesee. It looks like a fairly good spot right over there, just about where Mr. Ford is, as a matter of fact. I realize our splashing around like that will probably interfere with his fishing. He might even get wet."

Firestone liked the idea. "All right," he said. "Let's go."

They stripped to their underwear at the side of the truck.

Firestone's shorts looked like they were cut from a pair of long johns, extending almost to his knees. Halverton took out a change of clothing and placed them with a towel and a bar of soap beneath a tree. They asked Edison to join them, but he declined.

"No, I think I'll roll up right here in the back of the truck and have a nap," he said.

"Would you rather I put up one of the cots for you?" Firestone asked. "It would just take a minute."

"No, I'm fine right here," Edison said.

He looked like he couldn't be comfortable. The lid of the storage compartment was raised, and Edison sat in the chamber on a coil of wire. The string of lights was at his feet, and he was unable to stretch out completely.

Halverton was excited about disrupting Ford's fishing. In front of Edison, he told Firestone that he was feeling optimistic about their chances of catching up with the kidnappers. "I think we're on the right track. Our truck is in running order, and we have all the gas and supplies we need. I believe we've got them licked."

Halverton hoped he had spoken loud enough for Edison to hear. He knew they hadn't gotten a damn thing, but that was the way to talk.

20

MARGARETE GESTURED TO THE AUTOMOBILE AS Warner stopped the car in front of them. "Get in," she told the President.

"What about your airplane reservations?" Harding asked. "I was so looking forward to flying away."

"Please don't be difficult," Margarete requested. "There

was a problem, mechanical or otherwise. There will be no plane. So we will continue to take our chances on the ground. Please, get in the car now."

Reed poked the President in the ribs. "You heard the lady," he barked.

Warner turned off the ignition. "Let's think this thing out a minute," he suggested.

"I already have," Margarete snapped. "You stay at the wheel, and you," she pointed at Reed. "This is a final warning. You follow orders, and at no time put a strain on yourself by trying to do any independent thinking or acting. That includes any manhandling of Mr. Harding. And Mr. Harding, please get in the damn car."

"I just wanted to say," Warner said, pausing. "I bought the gas and the extra oil, but we're likely to burn up the engine if we run it all day and really work the motor."

"Which is precisely why we are leaving now without waiting for darkness to fall. Can you determine a route and keep us on it?"

"Yes," the driver said.

"Then we shall travel as far as the faulty engine and our luck will render us. Everyone, get into the car. Now."

No one said any more until they were a few miles away. Harding turned to Margarete in the back seat and complimented her in all sincerity, "You were forceful back there. It was a marvel to witness. You could have moved a battalion."

"No I couldn't," she said under her breath. "But I suppose I did want to demonstrate to you, and yes, to myself, that I was in control. The entire situation is in my hands."

"How do you feel about that?" Harding asked.

She hesitated a moment, looked out the window and smiled to herself. "I *love* it," she admitted.

Harding pulled out a plug of tobacco, taking a few short nibbles around the edge of it. Aside from his predicament, he had not felt well all morning. He told himself that it was probably indigestion or heartburn. He was not accustomed to greasy canned meat. And the constant jostling of the auto, along with the stress of his abduction, had to be a factor. He closed the package of tobacco, squeezing the juice through his teeth. Suddenly a pain so sharp and pounding that he was forced to hold his breath exploded in his chest. The President gripped his hands, closing them on air. He exhaled slowly at a measured rate.

"Please, a drink," he managed to say.

Margarete opened a pint of liquor without looking at him. "You know what Will Rogers said when we saw him on the stage in New York?" she asked, passing Harding the flask. "He said that Prohibition was better than no whiskey at all."

"No, water," the President gasped. "A drink of water."

Margarete saw him now. "Stop the car!" she said with alarm, almost in a shriek.

Harding fell forward and collapsed on the seat. When he came to, he was lying down. A wet handkerchief was pressed to his forehead. His collar had been removed, and his shirt was open to his stomach.

"You're better now?" Margarete said.

"I don't know," Harding answered. "It was the oddest sensation. I had a chest pain. Then it was as if a cloud had passed in front of the sun. A very dark cloud. I could hear your voice like it was coming from the end of a long and empty corridor."

"Is there any pain in your chest now or in your left arm?"

"No, none. I'm a bit frightened though."

"He's a God damn faker," Reed's voice said from somewhere outside the car.

"We have to continue," Margarete told Harding. "I know it's unpleasant for you, but we have no choice."

Harding took the handkerchief in his hand. "What the hell is the point of it all?" he said. "I am not worthy of the attention, believe me. I have been out of my league for years.

My element is a small newspaper office. It requires little bravery."

Harding was lying in the back seat. After he had spoken, Reed strutted to the automobile from the side of the road and cockily placed his foot on the running board beside the President's face. He rested the muzzle of his submachine gun against the side of Harding's jaw. "We haven't asked a damn thing of you," he chided. "Much less, bravery."

Margarete reached across Harding and pushed the gun away from him. "We have not had to ask anything of him," she answered for the President. "Unlike you, his behavior under the circumstances has been exemplary. Unlike you, his maturity tells him he has very much to fear here. Also unlike you, I am convinced he will reach our destination. I'm not so certain you will."

"Better listen to her," Warner cautioned his nephew.

"You're all against me!" Reed shouted. "From the moment we picked him up, I've been ordered about like a puppy. It's getting a little old, Uncle Warner. It's getting a little old, and I'm sick of it."

"Apparently you don't comprehend what we have done," Warner explained to him. "Think about it. Consider it. After we have kidnapped the President of the United States, he might have well suffered a heart attack. This is hardly the time to give you the attention you demand like a spoiled child. What do you want us to do, son? Leave you here on the roadside? Do you?"

Reed cast his eyes down on the ground and slowly shook his head. He looked like he wanted to cry. "I'll try," he promised. "I just get such bad headaches, it makes me mean. That's all it is, Uncle Warner. Honest. I'm sorry, Miss Fabry."

"He'll be all right now," Warner told her.

"It's about time," Margarete said. "Shall we get going now?"

Harding sat up gradually in a slow, painstaking motion

as his car door was shut. Years ago, when he had experienced a series of breakdowns and was treated at Dr. Kellog's sanitarium in Battle Creek, Michigan, Harding had met a young man of whom Reed reminded him a great deal. Harding had watched Reed for a couple of days now, and in all those hours of cramped close quarters, he hadn't seen him so much as nap. Doctor Kellogg's patient was much the same. He never slept, and the least antagonism brought out a flurry of temper. The President still thought of that short fuse as a weakness in the trio. And the more chances he took to rile him, it seemed to him the greater the odds of his escape during the possible subsequent pandemonium. "Young man," he called to Reed.

Reed looked over his shoulder at Harding.

"You're a God damn honey-fugling punk. That's what you are."

Reed turned around without saying a word and looked at the expanse of road before them. Harding watched the back of his head. Then, turning his attention to the driver, he could see Warner checking him in the rear view mirror. To his left, Margarete glanced at him, breaking her attention only momentarily. It was dusty and hot, and she sighed once as she wiped droplets of perspiration from her forehead. It dawned on Harding now that, with minor variation, they were three of a kind. They had reacted to his possible heart attack with all the compassion one afforded a sneeze. And they had admitted to the President already that his life was expendable, that Reed and Warner would have shot him dead in St. Louis. It was clear to Harding now that they would not hesitate to kill him yet if anything hindered them to the point of failing their mission.

He never believed that his abduction would last as long as it had. He realized that there might be only one moment when he could be liberated and sadly concluded that the moment might have to be of his own making. With effort and patience, the President waited. Hours passed. The Packard now drove on pavement. Trees were a blur as they flew past on the landscape. Small talk occupied the passengers.

"Do you like having servants and cooks and things to do everything for you?" Reed asked Harding.

"It's all right," Harding said. "It's fairly luxurious in the White House."

"Who cuts your hair?"

In the distance, he saw his chance, answering the question absently. "Oh, the wife cuts it," he said. "I never was one to go out and pay for something I could stay home and get for free."

Harding tilted his face down, appearing to watch the floorboard as he massaged his forehead with the palm of his hand. He would have liked them to think he was ill again. Over the top of his fingers, he watched a curve approaching, a tree stump directly ahead.

Margarete noticed his behavior. "Feeling sick?" she asked.

The car slowed slightly for the turn. "No, I'm fine." The President could see the bend ahead. He raised his head and twisted his back stretching his arms from side to side at eye level. Just as Warner gripped the steering wheel from below to handle the turn, Harding bolted, releasing his arm with all his strength, catching Reed just under the ear with the point of his elbow. He shoved Margarete away from him, reached over the front seat and seized the steering wheel, hoping to anchor it in position. The car squealed as the brakes were applied, then rumbled deeply as the tires left the pavement and tore past the gravel shoulder of the road. Warner tried wrestling the wheel away from Harding, and was landing blows about the President's face with his left hand. Harding winced, but never relaxed his grip as the Packard crashed into the tree stump.

Harding somersaulted into the front seat when Warner and Reed flew into the windshield. He found himself upside down, his face on the floorboard. He righted himself and quickly climbed over Reed and out the door, jumping away as if the car was a sinking ship. He began to run, ducking his head from tree limbs, feeling the underbrush slapping at his shins. He panted and heaved, never once looking over his shoulder. Out of necessity, he stalled and stopped to catch his breath, bending over with his hands on his knees. He heard a rustling in the fallen leaves. He stood and ran a couple of steps, but was tackled brutally from the rear. Warner, bleeding from a gash on his forehead, was on his chest, pinning his arms to the ground. On his back, Harding looked in the direction of the car. Margarete was standing there with her arms crossed. She looked to Harding, of all things, relieved. Neither of the captors showed the slightest anger. It was as if they had expected their prey to bolt away sooner or later, and now that he had tried, he wouldn't do it again.

Warner pulled Harding to his feet and pushed him one time gently in the direction of the road. "Nice try," he complimented him.

They found Reed at the side of the Packard, puffy-faced and confused looking. The wreck itself had popped a rather nasty blow to the middle of his face just a moment after Harding's elbow to his head. He sat on the running board feeling his nose and front teeth. Harding hadn't wanted to hurt any of them. He abhorred physical violence. And the President feared retaliatory measures for his outburst now.

"What will you do with me?" he asked them.

"We could put you in the trunk," Reed suggested, spitting in the dirt. "Except that wouldn't do any good since the car won't go any farther. Look at it, Uncle Warner. The oil's all over the ground."

Warner squatted on the ground and looked up under the fender. One glance was all it took. He stood, nonchalantly wiping the dirt from his hands. "Reed's right," he said. "We must have scraped bottom and tore open the oil pan."

Margarete thought only for a moment, "Get the cuffs.

Warner, you put them on Mr. Harding and take Reed's gun. Give Reed your pistol. There is plenty of cover in the direction the President ran. We shall wait for Reed over there."

"Where am I going?" Reed wanted to know.

"You are taking the pistol," Margarete explained to him. "Get us a car. Don't use the gun unless you absolutely must. That would attract attention. But by any means, get us a car. We will wait as long as it takes."

"We're counting on you," Warner said, handing over the revolver butt first.

Reed snapped it open automatically and checked the cartridges. "I'll wave somebody down soon enough," he said. "You won't have long to wait."

They were Reed's farewell words. After speaking, he turned his back on the group and walked briskly away on the shoulder of the road. It looked like he was out on a stroll.

The handcuffs were not as humiliating as the President had dreaded. They were cold to the touch at first, but not all that uncomfortable. Harding was marched between the two of them into the woods, behind Margarete and in front of Warner. He felt they would not harm him now, but how could he be absolutely certain? What if they became surrounded? Would they shoot him then? Harding had grown accustomed to a high level of anxiety, the surge of adrenalin seemingly as frequent as his pulse. Still, his despair did not overwhelm him, and the President surprised himself in that respect. Even now, walking through the underbrush after all he had endured, he found himself keeping his attention focused on Margarete's pleasant looking rear end just ahead of him.

Reed walked for over an hour without success. It wasn't that there was a lack of traffic. Those cars with more than two occupants he didn't bother with. And the few he did try to hail down paid him no heed. The weather was hot, and Reed was thirsty. From the peak of a small hill he saw a

river below and decided to have a drink. In a few minutes he
was at the water's edge. He splashed his face and drank from
cupped hands. He wetted the back of his neck, and thought
he heard voices. He froze, listening for them again. They
were laughing. He stepped away from the river and climbed
a few feet away. There, not a couple of hundred yards from
him, he sighted the source of the noise. He would never have
seen them had they been quiet. Two men in their undershorts were standing in knee-deep water. They were throwing water and splashing a third man on the river bank.
Nearby was a huge, magnificent and unattended truck parked
on a dirt access to the road. Its huge gas tanks assured a
nonstop trip if he could get his hands on it. The men were at
least two hundred feet from the vehicle.

Reed circled back to the road, and kept the truck between
himself and the swimmers. He walked directly up to it without even crouching. He reached up and tried the doors on
the passenger's side, but they seemed to be locked. He walked
around the truck to the driver's door, in full view now of the
three men at the river.

Halverton was laughing with Firestone in the water. He
wiped his hair from his face and squeezed the water from his
eyes. He was the first to see the figure standing beside the
truck. "We have a visitor," he said. They all saw him open
the door and climb into the seat.

"Hey, get away from there!" Ford shouted, laying down
his fishing pole.

Reed slammed the door shut and started up the engine,
revving it loudly before throwing the truck into gear.

"Al's in the back," Firestone cried.

Halverton bolted out of the water, running past Ford and
Firestone in his bare feet. Reed turned the truck around in a
tight circle, racing directly over their campfire and over
small bushes. They were all shouting at the intruder, but
even Halverton was too slow to catch up with the truck. He

managed to get within twenty feet or so of its moving rear bumper. He ran after it desperately, like a wild man. The lid of the rear storage compartment flew open, and there sat Edison, holding on tightly in the midst of dangling wires and equipment, viewing the furor in the wake of the truck. Even if he was not moving, he was too high off the ground to jump. The vehicle made a sharp entrance onto the road, and the last any of them saw of Edison was his bracing himself as he leaned into the turn.

21

THEY STOOD THERE WHEN THE DUST HAD SETTLED, separated by the distance that each of them had run toward the truck. It was a helpless feeling, and a hopeless one. There wasn't a thing any of them could do. When they regrouped, shuffling silently toward each other, Henry Ford's anger rose to the surface. Halverton could see that he was seething.

"A little frontier justice," Ford was saying. "That would put a halt to car thieves. String 'em up from the nearest light pole. Make an example of them."

"Yes, yes, Henry," Firestone told him. "But what about Al? There's no telling what will happen to him when that fellow discovers him in the back of the truck. Fortunately, I don't think he'll be visible from the inside of the cab."

"I wouldn't want to be that thief," Halverton said. "Can you imagine stealing a truck and having Thomas Edison climb out of it when you come to a stop?"

"No, I can't," Ford answered. "I find it very difficult to imagine stealing anything at all. My mind doesn't work that way."

"Now, Henry," Firestone said.

"Furthermore, I find it extremely hard to believe that President Harding has apparently disappeared from the face of the Earth. I don't suppose you could enlighten us on either situation, could you Mr. Halverton?"

"What do you mean by that?" Halverton asked.

"I mean that whenever something has come to pass on this trip, something invariably bad, you've been right in the middle of it. The woman you escorted disappears with the President. Now Al and our truck, *my* truck, get snatched right from under our noses after you so conveniently suggested we take a rest stop here."

"I suggested nothing of the kind," Halverton defended himself. "I agreed to it, but I didn't bring it up. I might point out that you haven't been far from the center ring yourself. But I don't have any ridiculous charges or suspicions of you."

Ford pushed him hard with both hands, and Firestone restrained him, pulling him by the arm. "What are your plans?" Ford asked. "Are you picking us off one at a time? That's a cowardly way to proceed."

"That's enough, Henry," Firestone said, still with a grasp on Ford. "Sid, he doesn't mean it."

"The hell I don't," Ford said. "As far as I am concerned, this little partnership of ours has been terminated."

"You want me to leave?" Halverton asked.

"The sooner the better," Ford answered.

"No, the three of us should stay together," Firestone said. "I won't hear of us breaking up when we're not two hundred miles from Niagara Falls."

"Then you go with him," Ford said. "I refuse to share his company another mile." He pleaded now and appeared close to tears. "Surely you can see, Harvey. Thomas Edison is my truest friend. When I told him of my plans with the automobile at our first meeting, he gave me encouragement when no one else would. 'There you have it.' I remember him saying. 'A car with its own portable fuel is the answer.' He pounded the table while he spoke, and this great man's excitement was the best tonic in the world.

"Need I remind you where I would be today without his help and friendship? Presidents will come and go, but there will always be but one Edison."

"He'll be fine," Firestone said, trying to calm Ford. "He'll be just fine. Sid's right. I wouldn't want to be the fellow to tangle with him when he's discovered in the truck."

"Just the same," Ford said, pointing a finger at Halverton. "I've always had my suspicions about him. I just hadn't voiced them."

"All right," Halverton said. "If my very presence is that unnerving to you, perhaps we could work better by ourselves. You could be right. Mr. Firestone, thank you for being the side of logic here. It's likely we'll see each other in Niagara Falls."

Ford turned his back and walked away. Firestone seized Halverton's hand and shook it. "Look at it this way," he said. "At least you had the good sense to take a pair of pants out of the truck."

Halverton smiled. It hadn't dawned on him until then that they were both still in their undershorts, lending very little dignity to whatever they might have to say. He put on his shirt and trousers, and was sitting down now to tie his shoes. Henry Ford was standing on the river bank facing the water. Halverton could see Ford's box camera and his pistol on the ground beside him.

Firestone clapped Halverton between the shoulder blades when he had finished dressing, and the younger man shook his hand once more. He walked up to the road, where he picked up his pace and began to trot.

With the wind standing his hair on end, Edison was perched atop the rear of the truck like a hobo on the roof of a boxcar.

The lid of the storage compartment was hinged like a trap-door, and it was his intention to sit down and close himself inside when the vehicle threatened to stop. When the engine ceased, he would let himself down.

It took only a few minutes for the truck to cover the ground that Reed had walked. Edison felt the vehicle slowing, and he ducked down out of sight. Faintly, he could hear the truck's horn as he stopped, and he raised the lid for a peek outside. Deaf though he might have been, his vision was almost perfect. What he saw astonished him. It was Margarete and a man carrying a weapon marching the President in handcuffs uphill toward the truck.

"Good Lord," Harding said at the sight of the truck.

"Where did you find this?" Margarete asked Reed. "Was there anyone near it when you took it? Any other cars?"

"Some men in a river," Reed said. "Three of them. One of them gave chase, but I left them flatfooted. They were alone."

"Did you hurt anyone?" Harding wanted to know.

"Were they camping or just passing through?" Margarete asked him. "Could you tell?"

"There was a campfire. I think they were camping. Why?"

"This truck belongs to Henry Ford," Margarete said. "It was used in the campout. Maybe they broke camp after we left."

"That's right," Harding said to her. "These trips cover hundreds of miles usually, you know. It was probably a group of helpers your henchman saw."

"I don't like all this waiting around out here in the open," Warner said nervously. "If it's safe to use this vehicle, let's get under way. If not, get it out of here and find us another one."

"Yes, you're right," Margarete said. She opened the door for the President. He hesitated when a movement caught his attention, but was hustled inside the truck, this time seated between Margarete and Warner. As Harding made himself comfortable, he decided in hindsight that what he had seen was the lid of the storage compartment closing itself from the inside.

The more territory they covered in their newly acquired truck, the more visibly distraught they appeared. As they passed through a town, Margarete and Warner practically leaned out the windows in order to obscure a pedestrian's view inside the vehicle. In actuality, their fears were not rational. From the level of the sidewalks, no one could have seen President Harding as he rode down the brick streets. The very size and custom design of the truck drew attention, and that was the basis of their anxiety. Everywhere they went, people pointed and stared, and children chased after them and waved. Also, what Margarete and her crew could not know was the fact that the truck had been sighted in cities and towns to the south. And that the citizens of those population centers had telephoned and telegraphed friends and relatives in the area to be on the lookout for Henry Ford and Thomas Edison wheeling through the countryside in a marvelous two-seated camping truck.

"I don't like it," Reed said, holding the steering wheel tightly. "All these people, all these people. They're bound to know who we have. I don't like it at all."

"Just drive normally," Warner told him. "Don't drive too fast or too slow and draw attention. We'll be fine."

It was one of those towns, an unremarkable hamlet whose residents could pinpoint their location by saying they were just east of Buffalo or exactly a hundred miles south of Rochester, a town with a name like Scottsburg, or Dalton or Dansville. Its name could have placed it not only anywhere in New York, but in any state in the country.

The truck lumbered down the main street, straining in the low gear to maintain a slow speed. Cars were parked here and there at angles along the curb. Reed had broken out in a sweat. He was jumpy. Absolutely every person he saw in the town was staring at him.

A man was sitting in a chair on the sidewalk when the truck pulled into view. He seemed to have been waiting for it, for when it was a block away, he stood and waved his arms.

"What's that fool doing?" Reed asked.

"Pay him no mind," Margarete said. She waved nonchalantly in the direction of the man.

But the man was in obvious rapture. He was simply overjoyed and ran into the street now at the vehicle's approach, taking the one opportunity in his lifetime to see firsthand one so famous as Ford and Edison. Reed panicked and stepped on the accelerator, the truck lurching forward, but still at a slow enough speed for the small-town New Yorker to run alongside and leap onto the moving running board. He stuck his face against the window of the front seat, peering at the interior.

He never had time to determine who or what was in the truck, for in his fright, Reed had seized the pistol where it had laid on the seat. Before anyone had a chance to stop him, the shot shattered the glass of the window, hitting the man in the forehead and blowing off the back of his head.

22

HALVERTON WAS SO LOST IN THOUGHT THAT CARS passed him by without even a feeble attempt on his part to flag them down. He wasn't intentionally trying to cover the great distance on foot, even though it appeared that way. One would assume that he was thinking about his present dilemma, how the recent events seemed to be snowballing. Or at least one might imagine that he was plotting a set of attack plans for Niagara Falls.

No.

As he moved briskly at the side of the road, Halverton was thinking of his father. Specifically, of an occurrence in his childhood — the horrible storm of 1900. After the hurricane had blown past Houston, Halverton's father, along with a handful of other civic leaders, volunteered his services in aiding the survivors in neighboring Galveston. His father was away from the family for three days without a word. When he returned during the night, Halverton listened for him, waiting on the stairway landing. His mother prepared his father a meal, and the worn-out man drank coffee as he began to speak. He had not slept. Halverton, eight years old, was to hear things that no child should.

At the approach of the storm, he heard his father relate, crowds gathered at the beaches to watch the waves, cresting higher and more powerfully than anyone had even seen in the Gulf. There were thousands and thousands of people.

When the tide rose, they became trapped. The entire city was swallowed by the sea, leaving only a few houses intact on the entire island. The wind howled so loudly that it muffled the screams of people as their homes, with them in them, were torn and carried away. Every last person on the beach had disappeared. Six thousand dead. The worst natural disaster ever to hit North America.

Halverton's father was conscripted for burial detail, but there being such an enormous number of bodies, the corpses were loaded onto barges and dumped at sea. The tide carried them back to Galveston, like a recurring nightmare. Halverton's father helped stack them in pyres. Many bodies, he noticed, were missing fingers and teeth, victims of looters and ghouls, cut into for anything of value. The city, once a pleasure-ground of casinos, resorts and nightclubs, was covered again now. Not by water, but by the smoke of burning flesh.

His father began to weep in the parlor, and the boy tiptoed in his nightshirt back to his own bedroom. It was such a frightening image, such a picture of hell, that he repressed the memory of it. He had not thought of those details from that day to this. Why did the nightmare come back right now? The trees around him were towering, beautiful pines, and the river flowed steadily and reassuringly in the distance. But President Harding was still missing, and now Edison had disappeared too. Halverton felt a kinship with the doomed beach strollers as they watched the magnificent, peaking waves. He felt as if the land itself could rise up and swamp him. Not literally, of course, but if Harding's capture signalled the onset of political chaos, then the lives of every American were threatened as surely as if what was now taking place were some natural catastrophe.

He began humming a tune to chase the thoughts from his head, to clear his mind in order to work on the immediate problem, which was finding transportation to Niagara Falls. The introductory notes of the song seemed to come from nowhere. He stopped humming and began to sing aloud, softly and under his breath as he walked at the roadside:

> *We have stringbeans and onions*
> *Cabbages and scallions,*
> *All kinds of fruit, and say,*
> *Yes, we have no bananas,*
> *We have no bananas today.*

He turned and waved his arms vigorously at an approaching automobile. It passed him, but veered to the shoulder and loudly applied it brakes. Halverton ran as the car door was pushed open for him.

"Jump in," the driver, a large barrel-chested man, told him. "How far are you going?"

"Up to Niagara Falls," Halverton said. "I appreciate the ride."

"You don't sound like you're from these parts," the man said, staring off down the road.

"I'm from Texas," Halverton answered.

"Well, then. You haven't much farther to go, do you?"

Halverton didn't correct the man's assumption that he had traveled the span of the country by means of his thumb. He had never hitchhiked before in his life, but had decided that being agreeable, which was part of his nature anyway, would be to his advantage.

"Yes, I'm almost there."

"I'm not going quite that far, in fact just another sixty miles or so. I've got a couple of errands on the way to take care of, so if you're in a hurry, I ought to let you out. You could find a faster car."

"I don't mind," Halverton said.

"Say, you could help me on the errands if you don't mind. It would save us both time."

"All right."

"I take orders, and when the merchandise comes in, I make the deliveries."

"You're a traveling salesman."

"No, a bootlegger," the rotund driver smiled.

Halverton happened to glance in the back seat. The area was completely taken up with small wooden crates, stacked so high that he couldn't see out the rear window.

"Aren't you afraid of the sheriff catching you?" Halverton asked him.

"There's very little crime in this neck of the woods," the man smiled again, apparently pleased to have someone to talk with. "The sheriff's only part-time, and he doesn't do much when he *is* at work. So there's very little chance of him catching up with me." He lifted the lapel of his jacket and showed Halverton a brightly polished badge pinned to his vest. "See, the reason I know all that is, I'm the sheriff."

Edison had heard the shot fired. The sound was immediately followed by a lurch in the truck, and he bumped his head hard against the wall of the storage bin. It was easy to surmise what had happened when he raised the lid for a view outside. The dead man lay in the street flat on his back. A bright crimson halo of blood surrounded his head. Bystanders began to encircle the victim, the Edison could see more than one of them pointing in the direction of the truck as it sped away.

Because the truck was seen by so many people, by at least a dozen witnesses, Edison felt that the perpetrators in the cab would soon dispose of the vehicle. It was likely that he would be discovered at that time. He sat down again in the darkness of the cubicle. They were moving so fast that wires, belts and tools were bouncing from their hangers. This was no distraction to Edison. He braced himself and considered what he might do when the struck stopped. His legendary concentration was once again at work.

Inside the truck, it was pandemonium. Immediately on firing the pistol, Reed had burst into tears and jammed the accelerator to the floor. Warner flew into the front seat and wrestled the gun from his nephew's hand, shouting all the while, "You fool! You God damned little fool!"

President Harding's face was drained of color. "He's going to get us all killed," he said softly. "Heaven help us. Heaven help us."

Margarete had looked out the window. She pulled her head inside and shouted at Reed. "Faster! Get out of this town as fast as you can!"

Reed was wiping away his tears with the sleeves of his coat. "I didn't mean to," he said. "He just jumped up there right at us, and I shot him. I didn't mean to. Lord. I've never shot a man before. You think he's dead?"

"He was dead when he hit the ground," Warner said, shaking his head. He was bewildered, disgusted. "Of all the God damned fool things. All we had to do was to keep calm. That was all."

"Pull over right here!" Margarete shouted. They were out of the town now. "Through that field."

Reed turned sharply into a hillside of corn, the stalks

falling beneath the wheels of the truck. They bumped over furrows, followed the field uphill and crested the hillock. They drove through a pasture now, waves of grass almost waist-high blowing like an ocean. In the distance they could see a building, probably a barn. It was old and run down. Daylight flowed through its walls here and there. Margarete directed Reed to slow down, and the difference in their speed seemed to calm everyone. They approached the building. It was a house, long neglected and overgrown, not much more than a stone chimney and rotted walls, still balanced and standing like magic. A few feet from the front door was a water pump, its rusting handle rising at an angle above the tall grass. The truck drove once in a circle around the building for a cursory inspection, then parked just beyond the pump.

No one said a thing. They remained in their seats, still in a state of shock. In just a few seconds, in the time it took to pull a trigger, all reason, all planning and purpose had been shaken.

"Warner, I shall remain here with the President and Reed. Go find us a car."

Edison felt the truck door slamming. He lifted his lid and saw Warner walking off through the field. He glanced to his other side. There was President Harding. Escorting him into the house on either side were Margarete and Reed. Edison conceded that they had found a good temporary hiding place surrounded as it was by such vast countryside. On the other hand, they were vulnerable to attack from the most unlikely source. And squatting now inside that very Trojan horse was Thomas Edison, beloved by the world as a kindly tinkerer and benefactor of mankind. Few knew that the kindly old gentleman who had bestowed upon the world such luxuries and pleasures as the incandescent light and the phonograph had another side to him. Indeed, Edison was also the man who had invented the electric chair.

In his younger days, Edison acquired a reputation for his practical jokes. He enjoyed playing with electricity, and because hardly anyone else comprehended its principles at the time, he had a clear advantage there. While working as a telegrapher, Edison once hooked up a horse trough to the electrical current of a dry cell battery. He would watch from his office as a rider approached, throw a switch, then sit back and watch the fun from a distance. Edison was amazed at the agility the animals showed once their lips touched the surface of the water. And the talent that the riders showed by hanging on as the horse bolted through the air was equally impressive.

But that electrical current was relatively small. In contrast, the storage battery in the rear of the truck was like a dynamo. It generated enough power to operate the campground's various gadgets — the movie projector, player piano, radios and camp lights. It was capable of four hundred volts. Edison imagined a variation of the storage battery that was attached to a high-pressure water hose. The device would be used in warfare to mow down an approaching infantry as if they were ants.

He had decided what to do. He raised the lid slowly and climbed down to the far side of the truck with the string of light bulbs wrapped around his shoulder. It was heavy wire, almost the thickness of cable. He untied the bundle, kneeling now at the rear wheel where he cut off the last socket a few strands at a time with a pocket knife. He split the raw end with the blade and stripped the insulation from a foot of each piece. He crawled beneath the truck and spied on the door of the old house. He could see nothing inside. There was a bucket hanging by a hook on the outside of the truck, the bucket Halverton had sat upon between rounds during his boxing match with Ford. Edison took it down gingerly, unaware really whether he was as quiet as a falling feather or crashing like a brass band. He was on his hands and knees, then on his belly in the grass. The grass was tall, and with the mild wind, his movement through it was well camouflaged. He carried the bucket with both hands, holding it in front of himself as he moved forward on his elbows.

He made it to the water pump undetected. A metal grill was at the foot of its base, probably to wipe the mud off the feet of the water-bearer. That was good. One end of the split wire he now attached securely to the bucket's handle. With the knife he scraped a little rust off the base of the pump, the other loose end of the wire he wrapped around it. Delicately, Edison placed the bucket beneath the faucet. To complete the circuit from the storage battery, all he needed was for someone to hang the bucket on the pump. Or a stream of water between the two would do the trick. He uprooted a few stalks of grass and weeds and covered the wire as best he could in the immediate area.

He retraced his steps, dropping off loops of the wire as he retreated. Light bulbs were strung along the ground from the pump to the truck. Edison climbed back into his nest. The very end of the wire had a plug exactly like an extension cord. He felt the prongs with his thumbnail as if to clean them. Then, without ceremony, he plugged it into his storage battery, the camp's portable power plant. He watched from the truck, and hoped that the well wasn't dry.

Almost two hours passed. To Edison, every minute, and even the seconds, were stretched beyond their normal span like taffy. It was an eternal vigil. Once, Margarete had stood outside. She had even walked up to the pump, then had become distracted, arching and twisting her back to stretch before meandering back inside.

Later, Reed appeared, and Edison felt that he had one of them now. Reed walked directly to the pump carrying the submachine gun. He stooped over. Edison craned his neck to see what he was doing. He couldn't believe his eyes. Reed was moving the bucket, not hanging it on the pump, but moving it on the ground in order for the water to fall into the center of it. He was standing on the metal grate. His hand was on the pump handle. Hadn't he seen the wire on the bucket? Or would he even guess what it might be doing there?

Reed set the gun down on the ground. With both hands he took the handle and began to work the squeaky instrument. Three times, four, five, six. It was either a deep well, or a dry one, if the pump still worked. Reed stopped, looking over his shoulder into the house. He started again. Five pumps, six, seven, the strokes more vigorous now. Edison hoped that Reed was very thirsty. Ten, eleven, twelve, pumping faster and harder.

The water gushed out into the bucket. The lights in the grass flickered only a moment as the electrical current was closed by the stream. Reed stood there, still holding the pump handle. He was utterly motionless, looking more like a statue than a man. Then, his arms fell limply to his sides and he collapsed, falling dead in the grass.

23

EDISON HAD WAITED IN THE TRUCK SIMPLY BECAUSE it was the best place to hide. But now that his trap had been sprung and Reed had fallen, innocent-looking as a child turning a somersault, he saw his opportunity to storm the house.

He threw open the compartment, quickly unplugging the wire from the storage battery at the same time. He climbed down and placed his feet on the ground. His approach to the water pump this time required no stealth. He walked upright

and in plain view of whoever was there. He leaned over
Reed's body and picked up the machine gun, balancing the
weapon in one hand. Edison paused a moment and felt the
dead man's throat for a trace of a pulse. It was emotional for
him, and nauseating, to clutch his hand around the neck of
the man he'd just killed. He dared not give in to the feeling.
There wasn't the time.

He stood and faced the house, aiming the submachine gun
ahead of him. The grips fit his hands nicely, but the
instrument was absurd and foreign in Edison's grasp. He
walked straight toward the door, stopping just shy of its
porch. "You come on out of there," he called out. "I have
the young man's gun, Miss Fabry. You turn Mr. Harding
loose now."

Margarete appeared in the doorway against the dark
interior of the house. She was holding her purse. She leaned
to one side, peering past Edison to see Reed lying on the
ground. She made a comprehending smile and nod. Edison
held the gun on her. He looked embarrassed.

Harding brushed past Margarete and hurried to Edison's
side. He had already been freed of the handcuffs.

"I *knew* it!" the President said. "I didn't know who, but
I was sure someone was in the truck." He looked at the
corpse himself now. "How did you manage that all by
yourself?"

"There's time for that later," Edison said. "Miss Fabry,
I'm going to ask that you come with us. The President can
drive us into a town if he will."

"I'll be glad to," Harding said, beaming a campaign smile.
"You can take that gun out of your bag while you're at it,
too. She has a pistol, Mr. Edison. There's another fellow
working with her. He gave it to her."

Edison shook the weapon at her. "Throw that bag on the
ground," he ordered.

Margarete held on to her purse. She placed one hand on

her hip. "Mr. Edison," she said. "My esteem for you could hardly be greater. You see, you have solved a rather uncomfortable problem in Reed over there. Don't misunderstand. If you had been any other man under the circumstances, I would shoot you myself for what you did. But I regard you too highly to consider such a thing."

"Throw down that gun," Harding commanded, both of the men hesitant to approach her.

"It is true that I have a gun," she went on. "I asked Warner for it before he left. I thought we needed the protection. It is also true that my gun is loaded. Yours is not. Please, both of you, step back inside."

Harding and Edison looked at each other in a doubletake. The President, who was frightened by loud noise, nonetheless grabbed the weapon out of Edison's hands and aimed its muzzle into the dirt. He pulled the trigger, a single click the only response. When he turned to Margarete again, she was pointing the pistol at them.

"Inside," she said.

"When did you do that?" Harding asked. He was bewildered, his momentary freedom an illusion. "Why?"

"You have to ask why?" Margarete said sharply. "After you saw him shoot that poor man who approached us, do you really think I would allow him to carry a loaded gun in my presence again?"

Edison interrupted. "I never have had a gun held on me before," he said. "Would you like me to raise my hands up over my head?"

"That isn't necessary," she said. She seemed suddenly self-conscious, lowering the gun away from them.

Harding was outraged. "Who are you?" he demanded. "I know you're more than you have let on. I'm sure of it."

"Yes, I am," Margarete admitted. "You are quite correct. And perhaps it is time now that I tell you so that you will know this is not a parlor game. Not a charade. My true identity will show you our determination. Now, get in the house."

The interior was bare. Harding and Edison sat side by side on the dusty stone hearth in front of the fireplace, Margarete remaining just inside the door, where she could watch them as well as the approach to the house. It was still bright outside, and her figure was silhouetted as she waited and watched for Warner.

"I was born in Holland," she said. "I never saw a reason to deny that. My given name is Gertrud Margarete Zelle. I married an English army officer, and we were sent to Burma. There I discovered that I had a talent for languages. In time, I became fluent in Burmese, German, English, French, Italian, Spanish. I returned to the Continent without my husband and brought what I had learned of the native customs. I became a dancer, using the name the Child of Dawn. Then came the World War, and I worked with the Germans. I also found service with the French and British. You persist in asking who I am, Mr. Harding. I am many people: Gertrud Margarete Zelle, the good English wife Madame MacLeod, the German agent H-21. I am also Child of Dawn, a translation of the Burmese *Mata Hari*."

"Ridiculous," Harding scoffed. "Mata Hari was executed by the French."

Edison considered the story and admitted to himself that every word of it just might be true.

"How did you escape the firing squad?" Edison asked.

"I was visited in my cell the night before the execution by a priest and two nuns," Margarete said. "There are written accounts of this. A man and two women entered my cell, and when it was time, a man and two women left. In the morning, dressed as a nun, I witnessed the shooting. After the execution, the *coup de grace* was administered by a bullet to the back of the victim's head. The face of the dead woman was torn away by the shot. Her identity was now completely gone. In place of burial, the body was taken to a medical school, where, I assume, it was cut into tiny pieces."

"I don't believe you," Harding said. "Who would do such an unprofitable thing as to take the place of a condemned prisoner?"

"Perhaps someone who had convinced herself that it was a way to fly straight to heaven," Margarete offered. "Or perhaps she herself was dying slowly, her fate already sealed by a dread disease, and was afraid. I asked myself of her motive. I concluded that what she did was important, not why. It was her decision instead of mine."

"I seem to remember reading some details about Mata Hari," Edison said. "She had a tattoo on her arm, I believe. My recollection was that it was a snake."

Margarete raised her arm and held it in the daylight coming through the door. "It is the wrist, sir," she said.

Harding leaped to his feet. "You monster," he said. "You monstrous whore. Responsible for the gassing deaths of fifty thousand soldiers. Fifty thousand young men, cut down like blades of grass. Countless others will be short of breath for the remainder of their lives. What you have done is unspeakable."

"That is French propaganda," Margarete said. "The numbers were not nearly so great as you suggest. The extent of my war service was the obtaining and passing along of information. Troop movements and positions, that sort of thing."

"Information gathered by your whoring your way through the ranks," the President said.

Edison seized him by the hand and pulled him down beside him on the hearth again.

"The French were pigs," she went on. "I was a very beautiful woman at the start of the war. After a year and a half in the dungeons of Vincennes, kept alive on a diet of potatoes, you can well imagine how that once beautiful woman appeared. Splotched, pale-skin, overweight. It was dehumanizing. The French had found their scapegoat whom they charged with responsibility for all their ills."

"You have no regret for your actions in the war?" Harding asked.

"My actions in the war," Margarete explained, "Were meant to shorten the war."

Harding dabbed the sweat from his forehead with the back of his sleeve. "So now you're a humanitarian," he said. "Excuse me if I seemed to question your noble impulses."

"Why did you get involved?" Edison asked. "Surely the war would have run its course without one spy's intervention."

"There is that word again," Margarete said. "Mata Hari the spy. I will tell you why. I was thirty-eight at the outbreak of the war. Already my appeal as a dancer was waning. I would not be in demand for very much longer, as a dancer or a courtesan. The Seven Veils was hardly new anymore. Much of my popularity was the novelty of dancing nude. I tried to be taken seriously. I wanted to dance with Diaghilev's company. The Russian pig demanded an audition. My reputation would not allow that."

"And what bigger stage," Edison said. "Than the theatre of war?"

"Yes," Margarete said. "Yes, exactly. On the day that war was declared, I had the chief of police in Berlin drive me through the city. I knew then that all my previous performances were just a prelude. The atmosphere in the city was truly electrifying."

President Harding raised himself again from in front of the fireplace. He was composed once more. He appeared dignified, persuasive, in spite of his ordeal. "I would like to remind you of an offer I made that still stands," he told Margarete. "In my capacity as President, the power of executive clemency can be invoked for any crime, past or present, admission of guilt or not. I extend a full pardon to you once more in the name of decency. You will not be responsible for my kidnapping. You will not be charged with the murder of that poor citizen, or even for any crime against humanity you were a part of in the World War. Please, Miss Fabry, your position is hopeless. It is obvious that your plans are altered by the hour. Do the right thing. Accept the offer."

Margarete was silent for a moment. "Do you think I told you of my past for nothing?" she said quietly. "As far as I'm concerned Mata Hari died six years ago. This is 1923. Every hour since 1917 has been a bonus to me. My usefulness did not die. And if by chance I fail to bring you to the destination, then it is you I pity, not me. You offer me a kind of freedom with the best of intentions. But I am giving you your life. Mr. Harding. It is possible you will see the White House again if I am successful. But if I am taken prisoner, if I am killed or thwarted, your life is finished."

Harding considered her answer. She spoke in grim threats and generalities. He imagined a widespread conspiracy in which Margarete played but a small role. Edison sat behind the President on the stone hearth, resting his elbows on his knees. He had listened to Harding's plea and Margarete's refusal. Harding turned to the inventor, shaking his head. "She's a woman without a conscience, Mr. Edison," he said. "She's turning down her only chance."

Outside, a Model T rolled over the horizon and into view in the field. Driving overland that way, it could only be Warner. Margarete left the house to meet him when he opened the car door.

Edison and Harding watched them speaking from inside, peering out from their seat. "What do the papers have to say?" Harding asked. "Is Mr. Coolidge safe?"

Warner looked perplexed. He walked slowly to Reed's body.

"The papers don't say a thing," Edison answered. "The world still doesn't know what has happened."

"That's best, I suppose," the President nodded. "I only hope that they increase the security around the vice president."

"They probably have."

Warner stepped onto the porch of the house. He leaned his head inside, "Mr Edison, is there a shovel in the truck?"

"I believe so," Edison answered.

"Will you be kind enough to get it for me?"

"Be glad to."

Edison accompanied Warner to the truck.

"Up there in that compartment on the right," he directed. "Want me to get it down for you?"

Warner looked over his shoulder at his nephew's body. "I guess I ought to get it myself," he said. "But let me ask you something. Have you been on our trail from the outset, or did we just interrupt your vacation?"

Edison had turned his back. Rather than lie, which he disliked under any circumstance, he walked back inside.

Side by side at the fireplace again, Harding and Edison watched Warner digging the grave. The ground was hard, and it was strenuous work cutting through the soil. He was digging in the yard of the old house, some forty or fifty feet from its front door. Warner and Margarete had argued briefly. She had wanted to go on in the new car immediately, but the order had been ignored. "We're going nowhere until he gets a proper burial," Harding could hear Warner say.

Harding considered himself a doomed man, and he began to talk to Edison, slowly at first, then with increasing urgency. He related every detail of his abduction that came to mind: the freedom of a crow in the cornfield where he witnessed the disposal of the first automobile, his escape attempt and subsequent fear that he had suffered a heart attack, the horror he felt at the slaughter of the cattle, which made him think of his Great Uncle Perry's cruelty to Harding's dog when he was only a boy. He then spoke of his past life, ranging discursively over the events, both good and bad, that had led him to his present view of existence. It was if he were attempting a self-reckoning of sorts — some estimation of his true worth — in the final hours before death. Edison was a good and patient listener. Observing the digging outside, he took in Harding's words as best he could. He found it hard to believe how haggard and drained the man appeared, compared to how he had appeared that first day in camp. He was concerned for his health. Suddenly, he touched the President's wrist and hushed him with a halting motion of the other hand.

"Just a moment," Edison said as he studied the figures outside. "Excuse me, but please be quiet a minute or two."

Harding rubbed his forehead. "Of course," he said, misunderstanding. "That was undignified of me."

Edison sat forward and concentrated. Warner was facing the house while he worked. Margarete was beside him in profile.

"If something should happen to me," Margarete said, "you ought to know where to go, what to do."

Warner nodded.

"You should contact Captain Nicholas at the Fairmont Hotel."

"This captain works for Remus?" Warner asked.

Margarete brushed the hair from her eyes and shook her head yes. "He is the one who hired me. I don't know Remus myself."

"All right. Captain Nicholas. Good enough."

He had finished shoveling. Edison said the names to himself a time or two. "Nicholas or Nichols," he whispered. "Working at the Fairmont Hotel. Niagara Falls, most likely." He smiled.

Margarete and Warner had made the mistake of underestimating Edison's keen ability at reading lips.

24

WARNER STOOD THE SHOVEL IN THE MOUND OF DIRT he had made. He brushed his soiled hands on the seat of his pants and looked about absently. He moved to the well, giving the handle a few pumps. It seemed to dawn on him exactly where he was and what he was doing, for his composure suddenly flew away. He reached violently at the wire, still connected to the pump's handle, and kicked the connection loose from the base. The pump might have been a punching bag for all the abuse he was giving it. Warner's arm worked around it for a good thirty seconds. Then the flurry passed. He pumped water into his hands and splashed his face.

Margarete was nearby. Every now and then she looked over at Reed's body like someone studying a sculpture. From inside the house, Edison and Harding couldn't tell whether she was affected one way or another by the scene. Warner straightened his shirt and walked quickly past her to the front-door stoop. "Mr. Harding?" he called inside. "I'd like to ask a favor if I may."

"Shoot," Harding said.

"I'd like a few words spoken over my nephew," he requested. "Nobody else here seems too right for the task, if you think about it. I truly would appreciate it."

Harding considered it, and consented. "Rather unusual," he said. "But, very well."

"I can't offer you much in return," Warner said. "I can guarantee that you won't be handcuffed anymore."

"You can do a great deal more than that and you know it." Harding said. He punctuated the statement by spitting tobacco juice between his shoes.

"No," Warner said. "There's no turning back at this point. There can be no compromise."

"Then promise that no harm will come to Mr. Edison."

"I never considered such a thing," Warner said. "He is safe."

Harding stood away from the fireplace now. He approached the doorway, and Edison followed him there. "Do you realize who you're working with?" he asked Warner. "Has she told you that she's Mata Hari?"

"No, she hasn't...but it comes as no surprise," Warner said. "It would take someone of her caliber to accomplish what we're doing."

"Did you fight in the World War?" Harding asked.

Warner shook his head, and after a moment, they all walked into the daylight.

Margarete was standing over Reed's body, waiting. Reed was laid out beside the hole. His hands were folded on his chest. His clothes were rumpled, and his hair was blowing in the dust. His face seemed to express astonishment. He was dirty. There was no mistaking him for someone asleep. He was dead.

The three men took their places in a semicircle around the grave. Warner nodded at Harding, and the President started the eulogy.

"Here lies the body of Reed...pardon me, what is the deceased's full name?"

"Reed Parker Smoot."

"Here lies Reed Parker Smoot, Lord. He killed a man earlier today. He was also a kidnapper and a thief. I am certain that you know him better than anyone assembled here. Some of Your servants You make to be good men, others not so good. Reed Parker Smoot once received a knock on the head, years back. That may be the reason he did some of the things he did. I am tempted to judge him harshly, but that is not my duty. Lord, we appeal to Your infinite mercy and goodness toward this recently departed soul." Harding looked about at the assembled, appearing a bit surprised that everyone's heads were lowered. "We deliver Reed Parker Smoot into Your hands, Lord, whether You want him or not. Amen."

There was a moment of silence and inactivity. Then Warner bent down and lifted Reed in his arms. He carried his nephew a few steps to the shallow grave and began to cover him with shovels of soil.

"I could have done better with a little rehearsal," Harding said.

"It was fine," Warner said.

Margarete was standing between Edison and the President. Edison was feeling fairly miserable over his part in the previous proceedings, and even more so for the fact that no one seemed to blame him for the death.

"What do you plan for Mr. Edison?" Harding asked Margarete.

"He will remain here," she said. "We're several miles from a town. I'll have my driver make the truck useless. It will give us a substantial lead."

Harding was plunged into gloom. He tried to smile for Edison. He patted the inventor on the shoulder and gave a baleful twist of his mouth that nearly brought on the tears. Edison wasn't one to chatter just to hear his own voice, but he broke his silence now to lift the President's mood.

"Is there anybody you know who always makes you laugh?" he asked.

The President shrugged his shoulders.

"Someone that you're always glad to see because they make you feel so good."

Harding was looking at the horizon. His face suddenly relaxed, and for a while, he didn't look so tired.

"Who is it?" Edison asked.

"Ring Lardner," Harding answered. "The sports writer. I play golf with him twice a week, and he never fails to crack me up. One of the few friends who has never asked a favor."

Harding laughed out loud now. "Except once. He wanted me to make him ambassador to the Court of Saint James. Brought it up on the golf course and kept after me about it for five holes. I finally asked him why he wanted the job. He said that his wife was tired of living in Great Neck."

Edison shared the laugh with him. "I have worked with men who have struck me the same way," he said. "It is a great comfort just to think of them when I feel down in the dumps."

Harding nodded his head. He could see that Warner had finished his task. "I appreciate your trying to help," he told Edison. "It is such a pitiful shame, the circumstances of this trip. My favorite play has always been Richard the Third, where the king travels the countryside disguised as a commoner to meet his subjects. I don't compare myself to royalty, but it has always been a fantasy of mine to make a trip in a similar vein. It appears that this doomed Voyage of Understanding will be as close as I come to fulfilling that pipe dream. You are a good friend, Mr. Edison. I only wish that we had met earlier. If you had entered politics, we would have had another Benjamin Franklin. As it is, I suspect that this country and the world has a great deal more in plain Thomas Edison."

Edison shook his head, both repelling and accepting the compliment. He grasped the President by the wrist. Warner was under the hood of the camping truck. He was cutting through every wire he could find.

Margarete touched Harding and parted the two men. She led the President silently toward the automobile. She returned to Edison with the pair of handcuffs. Let me see your feet," she said, and snapped the restraints around his ankles. He was a number of miles from the nearest road, and his feet were virtually welded together.

Having disabled the truck, Warner was now performing a final chore as he sat on the running board. From his view on the porch, Edison watched the man's fingers working away as he emptied box after box of cartridges and fed them one by one into the spare canisters for the Thompson submachine gun. Warner placed the weapon in its case and tucked it under his arm like a piece of luggage. In the Model T, he slid the gun beneath the driver's seat and took his place behind the wheel. Edison didn't fear the conspirators. He didn't have the time to devote to that emotion, for he was already calculating how he could walk to the distant road when his feet could move in only half-inch strides.

Margarete directed the President into the back seat and sat beside him before closing them inside. Harding leaned forward as the engine started. With both hands clasped together, he waved a good-bye gesture to Edison. Edison wanted to reassure him, to let him know that all was really relatively safe and that he was aware of their destination. But he wasn't certain. He had read Margarete's whisperings and added them to the assumptions the rescue party had set out with. What he had was just a mound of bones. The actual size and shape of the plot was anyone's guess.

Warner slipped the car into gear. He drove in the direction of the cornfield, where, Edison assumed, he would guide them back into the highway with the thousands and thousands of other black Ford Model T's. They disappeared from view over a ridge.

Edison stood in the yard, and as he did so, the change in his position tightened the cuffs on his ankles. It was painful. Slowly, he dropped to his knees, catching himself with his hands. Gradually, he scooted and crawled toward the rear of the truck. At the tailgate, he raised himself up, and his hands rummaged through the rear compartment for the tool box. He found it in a few moments beneath one of the pair of boxing gloves. Dumping the contents out into the open, he was frustrated at not finding a file, or even a pair of wire-cutters. Edison wasn't Houdini, but with electricity, he didn't have to be. He grabbed Ford's soldering iron, and plugged it directly into the storage battery. And in a matter of minutes, Edison was relaxing on the tailgate, the heating element of the soldering iron glowing steadily against the sturdy brass chain that bound his feet.

When he had at last coaxed the weakened metal apart and regained his freedom, Edison climbed into the cab of the truck, digging around until he found his jug of drinking water. From that vantage, he studied the near horizon. He took several swallows, tasting the mint flavoring each sip. He climbed down to the ground, located a box of Cracker Jacks in a storage compartment and slipped it into the pocket of his jacket. He walked away from Henry Ford's nickel-plated camping machine and passed Reed Parker Smoot's shallow grave. It was late afternoon. Clouds were massing together and threatening a rain. Margarete, Warner and the President were gone now, but Edison steadily closed the distance between himself and Niagara Falls one seventy-six year old step at a time. Like Halverton, he paced himself by loudly humming a tune. Only the melody was not a silly jingle blaring raucously from radios all over the country. It was the strains of Beethoven's Ninth Symphony that propelled Thomas Edison toward civilization.

25

HALVERTON WAS DISMAYED TO DISCOVER THAT there was little he could do to encourage the sheriff to work at a faster pace. The sheriff, who was a talkative man, seemed to slow the vehicle ever more as a story he was relating progressed, as if a crawling car emphasized certain remarks where a hand gesture wouldn't do.

The sheriff, whose last name was Boty, knew everyone in the county. He wasn't only the local bootlegger. Sheriff Boty's delivery rounds kept him in touch with the outlying rural votes. He couldn't just drive up and drop off a bottle. The sheriff had to hear about cows giving sour milk, boys with broken arms, babies overdue in the world.

Halverton was waiting for him with a cigarette at the side of the car. He found the sheriff's name a bit odd, but somehow fitting. Boty the bootlegger, he was thinking to himself. Boty the bottle bootlegger. He snuffed out the smoke. If only he had his own car, or at least the money that had ridden away in the pocket of his trousers when the truck was stolen. Then he could have taken a train, or a bus or had the security that the money might tease him with. At last, he saw the overweight county official waddling gingerly down a path toward him.

"You're tired of waiting on me. I can tell," Boty said. "You wish I'd shake a leg and move a little faster, don't you?"

"It's all right," Halverton said as they both entered the car.

"That gentleman I was speaking with is my brother-in-law. Married to my sister Mabel. My little sister. Nicest fellow in the world, except he drinks a quart of Scotch a day. Now, do you think Prohibition is the interest of folks like Tim? He was fixing to move to Canada when the law was voted in. Well, I convinced him that was nonsense, that I'd supply him with all he needed, said just don't buy it from someone he don't know. Wood alcohol is a killer. I deal only in the finest Canadian liquors. It's a pure product. As sheriff, I can run out any bootlegger that tries to move in on the business. This is my county. Nobody's going blind from bad whiskey as long as I'm in office. These people know that."

Their automobile had inched around a bend in the road. It was now making approximately ten miles an hour. "And there's hardly any crime here?" Halverton asked.

The sheriff bit down on a fat cigar he'd removed from his pocket, his stubby fingers holding a match to it while he took a couple of full-cheeked draws. "None to speak of," he said out the corner of his mouth.

The following customer lived less than two miles from the last one. Halverton was truly exasperated to leave the road again so soon. He decided to wait by the car for five minutes. If Sheriff Boty hadn't returned in that time, he would leave in search of another ride. No sooner had he made this decision than the sheriff was in sight again. He no longer had a bottle in his hands. His face was flushed and urgent. He was almost running. Halverton sat on the seat and closed his door. Boty flew past him and jumped in on his side of the car. As soon as he sat down, he turned on the ignition, hit the starter and threw the car into gear, closing the door as they took off.

"What is it?" Halverton asked.

"You know how I said that nothing ever happens around here? Well, there's been a shooting, right on Main Street. First murder in the county since 1906. Unprovoked, as near as I can tell. A motorist in some kind of fancy truck shot a man on the sidewalk. It happened just a little while ago. Lucky for me these people just had a telephone put in out here. I'd be gone all day otherwise."

Halverton felt he should hide his face, because he could feel it burning. He was absolutely certain that Ford's camping truck was the vehicle involved, and his sense of dread for Edison closed up in the rear of it was overwhelming.

"That's terrible," he managed to say.

Hands clenched tightly on the wheel, concentrating straight ahead and bouncing with the bumps in the road, Sheriff Boty was too caught up in his driving to notice any reaction by his rider.

"I'm letting you out when we get to the road," he said. "I've got to go back into town."

Boty slammed the brakes as they left the last customer's

winding access road. Halverton scooted out, surprised a bit that the car didn't immediately speed away. Boty was letting the engine idle. He leaned toward Halverton's side of the vehicle and addressed the open window.

"These are violent times we're living in," he said.

"Sad but true," Halverton responded. "I wish you luck in catching that killer. Be careful."

The sheriff nodded. He removed the cigar from his pocket once more, and the two men went their separate ways.

What could Halverton do? Alone on the side of the road again, he could scarcely imagine the circumstances that had deposited him there, much less believe them: Margarete's betrayal, the suspicion with which he was dealt by agent Starling, traveling across two states almost without sleep in the company of three American emperors, bickering with Henry Ford and losing the camping truck and now Boty the bootlegger. What could he hope to do but to find another ride and continue toward Niagara Falls?

He ended up walking the five miles to the next town, with no inclination by any driver to advance him in that direction. Halverton tried several variations of the hitchhiker's thumb. He jerked his arm like he was snagging a fish. He saluted with a smile. He knew that he must look more than foolish to travelers. He probably appeared downright crazy. Still, one particular car nearly broke his heart. He had raised his hand, flying it from one side to the other like a crashing kite, receiving in response a long and ducklike toot on the horn. He watched the automobile after it had passed him. A young couple had been inside. The rear of the car bore soap lettering on the windows, and the vehicle was dragging an array of pots, pans and shoes. They were newlyweds, and Halverton couldn't stand the fact that they were in all likelihood driving straight to his intended destination. He wanted to cry.

On the outskirts of the town was a cluster of tourist cabins. This was still a recent phenomenon in 1923. These forerunners of the roadside motel, made possible by the new-found mobility acquired in the development of the automobile on an affordable scale, were extremely popular. The cabin on the highway was convenient. Not only that, but it gave the traveler something in common with others. The fellow in the next cabin was just like you. One could compare routes with him, as well as road conditions. Halverton hoped to find a ride there, and he marched onto the porch of the office to see if that was possible.

It was the one real stroke of luck he had encountered in what seemed like ages. A handsome middle-aged man and woman were inside the office checking out. Halverton introduced himself to them and explained his need for transportation. He told them that his own car was "out of service." The twosome apparently had no objection to his looks or his story. The weren't going to Niagara Falls, but they would be able to take him part of the way.

"We have a date in Batavia," the man explained. "Two days at the Orpheum Theatre."

Halverton picked up a piece of their luggage and walked with them to their car.

"What kind of date do you mean?" he asked.

"Have you ever heard of Clarissa and Edwardo Hicks?"

The man looked a bit disappointed when Halverton shook his head.

"That's us," the woman said. "He's Edwardo, if you were wondering. I'm Clarissa. We sing a little, dance a little. Recite verse."

"You're vaudeville performers?" Halverton asked.

"That's right," answered Edwardo. "It's a shame you didn't catch us earlier in the year. We played Niagara Falls."

"It was a great audience," Clarissa added. "Newlyweds are so nervous that they'll laugh at anything. You can take your worst jokes to Niagara Falls and knock them dead."

"Whereabouts is Batavia?" Halverton asked them.

"Right about midway between Buffalo and Rochester. It's only forty miles or so from Niagara Falls."

Halverton helped put the luggage in the trunk. He held Clarissa's door for her, then found a seat for himself in the back. "I've always thought that would be an interesting way to make a living," he said. "I play the piano myself."

They were driving away now. Halverton felt good to be moving again. He had been tired even before the walk to the tourist court. The car seat supporting his weight was a luxury. He studied the driver and wondered how the man had become an Edwardo. He hadn't a trace of Latin features. He was, in fact, redheaded and blue-eyed. He didn't fit Halverton's concept of an Edwardo at all.

"Why didn't you pursue a career in music?" Clarissa asked.

"I don't know. I suppose I decided it wasn't dignified. Not for me, anyway. It would embarrass my family."

"What line of work are you in?" Edwardo said.

"I supervise the manufacture and construction of canvas. The company I work for makes anything that contains canvas."

"Tents?" Edwardo asked. "Tarpaulins? Boat sails?"

"Among other things," Halverton answered.

"I always thought that would be an interesting life," Edwardo Hicks stated. "Never thought it was dignified. For someone else, maybe, but not for me."

"Knock it off, Eddie" Clarissa said.

Halverton was amused in the back seat. "Sorry if you took offense," he said. "I'm from Houston, Texas. It's hardly a springboard to show business."

Edwardo eyed the rear view mirror. "Three years ago we played Houston's Majestic Theatre," he said.

By the time they reached Batavia, New York, Halverton had listened to the extent of Edwardo and Clarissa's act. He liked them, the way they could feed each other lines of memorized dialogue or unabashedly break into a two-part harmony. Their voices were like a weak radio signal. Hardly a note was on key. Halverton tended to blame the noise of the automobile on their sourness and was sure that their dancing made up for any deficiencies in other areas.

They drove downtown to the theatre. "We have to check our billing," Edwardo explained. "A matter of pride, you know."

The car pulled to the curb, and the three of them examined the marquee. Of the ten acts, they were listed eighth. "Look who we have to follow!" Edwardo shouted. "Baby Louise and Her Spaniels. Good Lord!"

Halverton read the program for himself, thinking he had misunderstood. "That's bad?" he said.

"It ain't good," Clarissa answered. "Never follow a kid or animals. We got both."

"I'm sorry."

"You got nothing to be sorry for," Edwardo laughed. "Hell, this is Batavia, not Broadway. Say, you want a pass to the theatre tonight?"

"No, I really have urgent business in Niagara Falls. Thank you just the same, and I apprecite the ride this far."

"It's all right," Clarissa told him on the sidewalk. "You're a good kid, and we don't mind doing favors for good people. We've needed a helping hand a time or two ourselves."

Halverton turned and waved when he was a block away. He decided that Edwardo and Clarissa Hicks were a very happy couple.

He walked along the streets of Batavia, a town he had never planned to see. He had never felt more like a stranger. It was as if he'd fallen there from the clouds. If there was anyone he felt he could confide in, someone to whom he could tell the whole truth, he would feel differently. As it was, no one would believe a word of it, not even Edwardo and Clarissa. He was certain that anyone in their right mind would conclude that he was completely out of his. Harding, Edison, Ford, Firestone. Indeed.

He walked along some railroad tracks in a direction he guessed was northerly. A freight train was switching tracks, backing slowly one minute, then pulling ahead a short distance, only to stop and repeat the procedure again and again. Far ahead of him, he saw in profile a flow of automobiles. The pavement itself was hidden from view, and it presented an odd picture for him. The cars, and the people in them, looked like a shooting gallery, small toys being pulled back and forth along hidden wires. The train had behaved the same way in town, expending a great deal of energy without any progress to show for it.

Great gusts of winds were beginning to stir the air, and Halverton could smell the rain in them. Overhead, enormous thunderheads were massing. The tracks were elevated from the ground surrounding them, and he ran downhill from them in the direction of the highway.

He stood on the edge of the road, his thumb a plea in sign language. Leaves and dust were flying everywhere. He thought that someone would surely stop and offer him a ride in such ominous-looking weather. But Halverton didn't consider what a picture he must present to the driver. Whether he believed it of himself at the time or not, he did look seedy. Though his clothes were relatively clean, they were badly wrinkled. He needed a shave. His exhaustion had carved dark circles around his eyes. All that he knew was that he was desperate to move on, and no one was stopping.

He heard the train whistle and made up his mind in an instant. He had never before dreamed of jumping a freight train. It was unsafe — something you drilled children never to attempt because the danger was so great for them. But he had seen hoboes riding the rails, and they hadn't looked particularly more skillful in anything than he. He found his legs pumping madly toward the tracks. He moved up the embankment and ran alongside the train. A closed boxcar passed him, then another. He knew that the third one would have to be it, for he was slowing down just as surely as the train was gaining speed. Kicking through the gravel, he raised his hands high, missing the handle on the front of the car. He saw the middle of it approaching. Its door was open wide. He leaped, the door handle slapping hard in the grip of his hand. His legs did dangle freely in the air for a moment, only long enough for him to gain his balance. He pulled himself up and into the boxcar, panting heavily.

He lay on his back on the dirty wooden floor. It was a great relief, and the rocking motion of the car with the wind rushing through the door and all around him felt good. He sat up and watched the scenery outside. It was just starting to rain, and in a few minutes, the sprinkles became a downpour. Streaks of lightning ricocheted across the sky. He leaned his back against the wall of the car and amid all the noise of the moving train and the crashes of thunder, fell asleep.

The train halted hard, sending Halverton sliding across the floor. He was awakened as violently as if someone had shaken him by the shoulders. The first thing he noticed was freight cars booming loudly against themselves like echoes of a slamming door. He stood at the opening of the boxcar. The light outside was fading into evening. The sight bewildered him, for stretched before him as far as he could see in the hammering rain and hard-driven wind were deep blue high-peaked waves of water, whipped into whitecaps reaching high into the air like a furiously boiling kettle.

"Lake Erie?" he said aloud. "Or is it Lake Ontario? Which one is it?"

He leaned out of the car, clutching his jacket tightly around his neck. Coming toward him on the ground was a brakeman in a slicker suit carrying a lantern. Halverton didn't know how long he might be delayed should the railroad find him there, and he didn't wait for an answer. He let himself down and trotted away from the tracks. He splashed through puddles and mud, the rain already running down his neck.

"Hey, you!" he could hear one time, but he never once looked over his shoulder or broke his stride. The raindrops stung his face. If it had been a clear day, the sun could give him directions. But on this day there was no sky at all, just a fading overcast with flashes of light in it. Whichever of the Great Lakes it was, Halverton ran directly away from it. Whether it was a matter of a few hundred yards, or several miles, he knew that a relatively straight line would eventually take him to a road. He moved through fields and woods. The storm was tremendous, the rain coming down in waves.

He was miserable, walking now, cold, tired and hungry. His walk was slow, but steady. He passed a barn and was tempted by its refuge. But if he fell asleep, be might not awaken for days.

The weather would not let up. It was only a summer thundershower, but a relentless one. Halverton now almost wished he wouldn't encounter anyone until it was over. He was painted with mud to his knees, and his trousers had ripped open on a snag. The sight of him in the night, lit up by a flash of lightning, might frighten someone to death. He looked like a ghost.

Finally, he could go no farther. He ached all over and allowed himself to fall at the base of a pine. He had abandoned the freight train some two hours earlier. How far had he managed to go? Eight miles? Ten perhaps?

He pulled the wet jacket around himself and leaned against the tree trunk. The soaked bark was somehow soft on his face. The rain was only dripping now, but in the distance the thunder continued its deep and steady rumbling. Closing his eyes, he made out the sound of a country dog barking far away to his left. A few seconds later, another howl far to his right sounded in the darkness. Halverton thought how dogs could relay a bark for miles and miles that way. If only he could travel as fast.

He began to sleep soundly.

At daybreak, the light in his face prodded him awake. The sky had cleared, but there must still have been lightning. He could hear the thunder. Half asleep, he felt his damp clothes, then slowly rose to his feet.

"That's not thunder at all," he said.

He wiped his face and ran his hands through his hair. He walked, slowly at first, then like someone obsessed, moved faster and faster around trees, over rocks and ground cover. He crossed over a paved road, not a hundred yards from where he had slept. Constantly, his eyes were searching as far ahead of him as the forest would allow. He saw the river now, wide and strong as God himself. Halverton became overjoyed at the sight of it. "The Niagara!" he cried out and leaped into the air. He ran along the plain above the riverbank. The noise was growing louder and louder until it was all that he could hear.

It was enough to take his breath away. There, not a half mile from where he stood, Halverton caught his first glimpse of Niagara Falls.

26

THE SHEER VOLUME OF THE NOISE WAS SO incredibly overwhelming that it was as if the Falls were the Earth's gaping mouth. And the planet heaved such moans and groaning tremors from there that it must have been in a great deal of pain. The sight itself was tremendous. The impression of a wall of water hundreds of feet high, supported by a cushion of mist that obscured the river, was like something from a fable. The beauty of the natural wonder was awesome. But it was the sound that moved Halverton. His entire being seemed affected by the scene as he sat on a bench at the observation point. He found little comfort in the warming effect of the morning sun. The area surrounding him — the pavement, railings and bench and probably the trees and ground as well — was induced by the Falls into a gently vibrating hum.

The other side of the river was Canada. A cable was suspended above the Falls, crossing the river and connecting the two countries. Halverton wasn't positive what it was until a car rode out of the daybreak on the wire. Women and men in hats and expensive clothes could be seen high over the water, peering their faces out of the windows. They were like children on a carnival ride, behaving far less dignified than their attire would lead one to expect. Halverton stood and placed his hands on the railing, holding it tightly to peer down at the base of the waterfall. A boat was making an excursion down there, looking as fragile as a toy. He edged back to his seat on the bench. The cable car let off some of its passengers on the shore. It took on a few more, and the new group embarked across the river once more. They were not far from him. He waved nonchalantly in their direction, and one or two returned the greeting.

More than anything, Halverton wanted to be with Firestone, Edison and Ford again. If only Firestone would stroll up and join him on the bench, then his misery would have a salve. He allowed himself the thought for only a moment, for it was utterly useless to dwell on it.

He saw a magnificent hotel a short distance away, which was three or four stories high. A high porch skirted its exterior, and awnings covered all the upper windows. It wasn't a large place, but there was an elegance to it. And who could have chosen a better location? Halverton straightened his clothes as best he could. Some of the mud from the night before had dried into cakes, and he slapped them away in a few strokes. He could do little more to improve his ratty appearance. His hair even felt matted. Still, he walked to the hotel and climbed the steps one at a time with his back as straight and his head as high as anyone he'd seen in the cablecar.

Paintings of sailing ships graced nearly all the interior walls. Halverton closed the door behind him quietly, as if entering a private museum. To one side of the lobby was a small restaurant, all white linen and silver, its windows looking out over a trim lawn where croquet hoops were set in the ground. Beyond the lawn, of course, was Niagara Falls, Mark Twain's Garden of Eden.

The desk clerk was not impressed by Halverton's entrance. He was, in fact, giving him a most baleful look, one he probably used on tramps before directing them to the kitchen entrance in the rear. The clerk had been doing some paperwork, but it was idle before him now. Envelopes and papers were spread over the counter. Halverton stood before him, running his hands over the Biblical-looking register.

"Yes?"

"I have a bit of a problem," Halverton said, looking mostly at his hands between glances at the clerk. "Please excuse the way I look. My car broke down last night, and I got caught out in the storm. I've walked quite a distance."

"I'm very sorry. How may we help?"

Halverton looked to either side, as if to take the clerk into his confidence when he lowered his voice. "It's my dad," he said. "You see, I have reason to believe that he's honeymooning somewhere here in Niagara Falls, and I'm trying to locate him."

"I wouldn't think that a newlywed would wish to be disturbed."

"Well, it's disturbed the family a great deal," Halverton said loudly. He paused and spoke softly again. "My father is no newlywed. He goes on these honeymoons anyway, usually with a girl from his office in Schenectady. We have reason to believe that he's hidden away in a love nest right here in Niagara Falls, and..."

"*Love* nest?" the clerk said. "Now see here. This hotel —"

"Believe me, I'm no more condoning this behavior than the hotel management would, I'm sure. He's still married to Mother, you see, and it's a great embarrassment to us all."

"I suppose you want a look at the register."

"No, I wouldn't expect Dad to use his name. I could describe the two of them to you, and you could tell me if you've possibly seen them."

"I'm really not good at that sort of thing."

"The lady is tall, trim, about my height. Statuesque would apply to her. She has a presence about her, like a resting ballerina. Very dark eyes, intense eyes. Her hair is long and black, accented with a little grey here and there. She might wear it swirled up high. She's the kind of woman who draws the attention of everyone in a room. You wouldn't forget her." Halverton paused. He felt sad and looked away from the clerk. "She's very beautiful," he said.

The clerk was nodding and nodding at Halverton's description, ceasing at the instant the words did. "What about your old man?"

"My father?"

"What does he look like?"

"Oh, yes. He is sixty. His hair is grey. He has dark eyebrows. As a matter of fact, he bears a strong resemblance to President Harding."

The clerk shook his head. "I haven't seen anyone like that pair," he said. "Is there somewhere I can reach you if I do?"

"No, not yet. I still have to repair my car."

"You say he looks like President Harding?"

It might have been Halverton's imagination, but as soon as he turned away from the desk, he felt that the clerk was more suspicious about him than when he had come in. The change in the clerk had been at the mentioning of Harding's name. Halverton turned at the front door. The clerk was watching him closely and reaching for the telephone.

A tall and ancient Negro who looked as old as a river was sweeping the steps in front of the hotel. Halverton closed the door behind himself and asked the man directions to the most convenient public transportation into town.

"Streetcar stops right over there," the Negro pointed to the corner. "It's the end of the line."

Halverton waited beside the tracks. He was aware that, as things were now, he was very close to the end of his own line. The few coins in his pocket were nothing. They weren't even enough to take him home to Trenton. In town, he could locate the Western Union office and wire his father in Texas for money.

The streetcar stopped in front of him, and he stepped aboard. The fare was expensive, at least it was for someone who was nearly broke. He knew that his father would come through, yet he had to wonder. On the surface, there was no urgency in anything, certainly no emergency. The streetcar stopped every two blocks. People on the sidewalks moved at their leisure. But time itself had to be crucial. Where on Earth were President Harding and Margarete? For that matter, was Edison safe? Where were Ford and Firestone? A passerby would never have suspected Halverton of entertaining such thoughts. He had a seat in the streetcar to himself. Indeed, a section of the car was his. He looked like a hobo, old before his time, one to be avoided.

He could see the Western Union sign ahead through the windshield, and he disembarked with a group of people at the downtown stop. He walked in that direction, looking for a cafe at the same time that might serve a modest breakfast. Across the street was the Shredded Wheat plant, where a sign indicated that free tours were given on the hour, a meal included. Next door was a movie theatre. He passed them by.

DAD — SEND $50. WILL EXPLAIN LATER — SID.

"You'll be sending that collect, I take it," the clerk said after taking the telegram form from Halverton.

"That's right," he answered. "Do you know when I can expect a reply?"

"Shouldn't be more than a couple of hours if the addressee can be reached. I'd say at about one o'clock."

Halverton was outside again. The day was extremely bright and clear, considering the boisterous weather of the night before. He was hungry, but more than anything he wished to sit someplace and rest until his telegram was answered. If he had been crazy about Shredded Wheat, it would have been a different matter. As it was, he found himself next door to the cereal factory in front of the box office. He bought a ticket without bothering to read the marquee.

The house lights were just dimming as Halverton took his seat. As the organ music filled the darkening theatre, he was pleased to read the title — *Girl Shy*, starring Harold Lloyd. He thought that a good laugh might be exactly what he needed. It was easy to lose himself inside the theatre, and his expectations for the movie were high. But scenes that brought howls of laughter from the audience, Halverton found rather sad. An insecure tailor's assistant was onscreen, eating dog biscuits to avoid the suspicion of hiding a dog on a streetcar. He was a man who stammered pitifully when talking with women, whose sincerest efforts were ridiculed. A particularly moving scene was the one in which Harold Lloyd was seated on the bank of a stream. He was pining for the woman he loved, imagining her face in the water. But it wasn't a fancy after all. She really was there on a bridge above him, and she in turn was looking for him. It was a touching image for Halverton, and he was glad that the woman cared for Lloyd for what he was. What was happening here? Chaplin was supposed to be the serious comic, not Harold Lloyd. Halverton had never felt such emotion for a movie. Was he the only one who did? When, at last, Lloyd was forced into acrobatic action, no one rooted more loudly than Halverton. The girl Lloyd loved was marrying another, and he took advantage of every means to interrupt the ceremony. The little stuttering man with the round glasses was suddenly a dynamo. He leaped onto a passing car, then a truck, taking every frustration in stride. He drove another car over a road so bumpy that the vehicle fell apart under his hands. He commandeered a streetcar, the only man aboard, racing through the city at sixty miles an hour, seventy. Lloyd found himself on the roof of the car, still careening out of control through the city. He hung by his fingertips, falling finally into a passing automobile. Stepping on the driver's foot, he sped onward until a motorcycle policeman halted the car. Lloyd raced away on the cycle, smashing through fruit stands and street vendors' carts. He stole a wagon with a team of horses, leaping daringly onto the back of one of them when the buckboard shattered from the intensity of the chase. Even when the horses fell on top of him, the hero was undaunted. He rode the steeds onto the grounds where the wedding was taking place, broke into the house and there, from the top of the stairway, lost his stammer and shouted his love for the bride, fighting his way down the stairs to sweep her away out the door on his shoulder.

It was a marvelous sequence, one of the most inspiring sights Halverton had ever witnessed, even if it was only a movie. He would have attempted the same feat if he'd known which direction to take to intercept President Harding. Halverton was preoccupied, noticing for the first time what was on the screen now. It was transfixing. Would the film he was now viewing be the world's last public glimpse of President Harding? There the man stood on the platform of the *Superb* only a few short days ago, speaking into microphones in West Virginia. The sense of dread became terrible. The frustration he felt made him leave his seat. What would next week's newsreel have to say?

He stood outside the theatre and happened to overhear someone telling a companion that he had some letters to mail.

"The Post Office," Halverton said aloud. "Mr. Edison said if we became separated, to leave word at the local Post Office."

He broke into a run and caught up with the man with the letters in his hand. He asked directions and found that the Post Office was only two blocks away. It was lunch time, and by the time Halverton was inside, he was part of a crowd. He waited in line, and it was several minutes before he could be helped.

"I'm picking up some mail in General Delivery," he told the clerk. "It may be under my name, or it could be in my employer's."

"What's your name?"

"Halverton. Sidney Halverton."

The clerk turned his back and rifled through a stack of loose envelopes. "Nothing here," he said. "What other name should I look under?"

Halverton didn't want to shout the names out, but he had little choice.

"Try H.S. Firestone," he said. "If there's nothing there, it could be for Ford or Edison."

Patrons in line turned to have a look at Halverton. Even

the other clerks stopped what they were doing.

"Please," he said. "There isn't a moment to lose."

Halverton's clerk returned to the window in front of him.

"You're holding up the line," he said. "I haven't the time to check for Henry Ford and Thomas Edison. Please let someone else at the window."

"No," Halverton said. "I just want you to take a look. It's very important."

"Am I going to have to call a cop?" the clerk threatened.

"If that's what it takes," Halverton said. "Yes, go ahead and call a cop."

The clerk stormed out from behind the counter, and Halverton accompanied him outside. Down the street a mounted policeman was approaching, riding the horse in the street just a step from the sidewalk. Halverton at last saw a chance for a little satisfaction. He might be thwarted in every other endeavor, but he was determined to get his way with the postal clerk. The two of them walked side by side toward the horse and rider.

At the side of the horse was someone shading his eyes from the sun. When he lowered his hand, Halverton immediately recognized him. It was the deskman from the hotel by the Falls. How unlikely that seemed. Something told him to stop. The hotel man spotted him too. He was at the policeman's side in a moment, tapping on the officer's leg and pointing in Halverton's direction. "There he is!" he cried out. "That's him!"

It happened extremely fast, but at the same time, the action was as if in slow motion. The horse broke into a slow trot and closed the gap to Halverton completely. The animal could easily trample him. Halverton shuddered and twisted himself out of the way. The policeman had drawn his club, and Halverton could see him leaning down from the saddle. The club landed just behind his ear. Halverton felt himself falling. It was the kind of fall one has in dreams — slow, painless. The ground rushing toward him was not the slightest bit hard when he hit it.

27

HALVERTON COULD LATER REMEMBER BEING MOVED along the pavement. He was upright, dragging his feet, supported on either side to maintain his balance.

He was left in a room by himself. His head was throbbing, and he found it easier to sit than stand. What sense could he make of it all? Was he the victim of a mistaken identity? Besides the old Negro sweeper, the only people he had spoken with were a hotel deskman, the postal clerk and the telegrapher. Was there a conspiracy of clerks who welcomed strangers to Niagara Falls by cracking them over the head? Were any of them involved with Margarete?

He looked at the barred window from the bed. It was set high in the wall, and when he stood, he still couldn't see anything but clouds from it. He pulled himself up for a view. A stream of air blew against his face as he surveyed a portion of the street below. He was on the second or third floor. He let himself down and approached the cell's door. "Who's in charge here?" he called out.

The only response he could hear were the occasional coughs of men hidden out of sight and the running water of the building's plumbing. He could hear voices in undertones. Other prisoners, he suspected. Halverton gave up on an answer, returning to the bed to listen. He watched the clouds behind the bars. At length, there were footsteps nearby. They seemed to stop near his door.

"How about some coffee?" a voice asked.

He rearranged himself, sitting up in the bed. "Yes, please," he said.

A policeman unlocked the door and extended a mug toward him. "Your name's Sidney Halverton?"

Halverton took a slow sip, nodding his answer as he swallowed.

"The man at the Post Office gave us that name for you. I had to make sure."

"What am I charged with?"

"Vagrancy," the officer said. "And resisting arrest."

"In what way did I resist?" he asked. "Didn't I fall fast enough when the gentleman on the polo pony swung his mallet?"

The policeman smiled. "The arresting officer's report simply stated that you resisted. That's all I know."

"How can I get out? Can I post bail?"

The policeman closed the door to the cell and sat next to Halverton on a folded blanket. "I have a better question," he said. "What are you doing going around asking about President Harding and using the names of Edison and Ford? Are they pals of yours?"

"Will you let me out if I tell you?"

"Probably not."

"Who wants to know?"

"We all do. The captain on duty does."

"Thanks for the coffee. I've got nothing more to say."

Halverton was left alone in the room again. He was by himself long enough to wonder whether he had made a mistake in being uncooperative. It was costing him time.

He could hear a set of keys once more. When the door opened, it revealed an older man of a higher rank. Halverton's father, always involved in Houston's politics, had a number of friends on that police force. Halverton could tell that he was being visited this time by a captain. He got to his feet and backed away from the visitor, because the cell was very small. They were like two fish in a bowl. The captain removed his hat and began fanning himself with it. He was in his fifties, Halverton guessed. He had a bald head.

"Start talking, or grow old as our guest," he said.

Halverton was tempted to ask why a police captain was interested in such a lowly criminal as a vagrant, a term whose every definition he met at the time, but decided to remain silent for the moment.

"All right," the officer said, rocking back on his heels and looking very amused. "All right, I'll talk first. We'll trade information if you need prompting. The President of the United States is due here in a matter of hours, and no one is supposed to be aware of it. I passed the word around that if anyone so much as mentioned his name, I wanted to know about it."

"I'm looking for my father," Halverton told him. "I told a man at a hotel that he resembled President Harding. That's all."

"That's not all," the captain corrected him. "But go on."

Halverton shrugged and shook his head.

"You asked at the hotel for your father," he said, edging closer as Halverton backed toward the corner. "Then you sent a cable to your father two thousand miles away. You want to explain that?"

"I haven't done anything," he protested.

"You lied to me!" the captain shot back. "And that's damned suspicious in my book. Now, what do you know about Mr. Harding?"

Halverton sat down. He had a huge knot on his head, and he ran his fingertips over it before he spoke. "All right," he said. "Maybe you can help, now that I think about it. I'm certainly doing no one any good sitting here.

"The President disappeared from a camping party where he was a guest of Mr. Firestone, Mr. Ford and Mr. Edison.

I was a member of the camping party myself. For days now, I've been trying to locate a clue to Mr. Harding's whereabouts, and I haven't met with a shred of success."

"President Harding just disappeared? You're saying that the Secret Service and no one else knows anything about it? None of the newspapers do either?"

"Of course the Secret Service knows," Halverton said. "They were there. How much they know, you'll have to ask them."

"Where did Mr. Ford go when he found out? Where's Edison?"

"We all went our separate ways when it happened. I came here."

"You just happened to stumble into my town. Looking for the President of the United States, you say. Is that what you maintain?"

Halverton just at that moment realized the contradiction. Had he not felt so miserable, he would never have overlooked it. He felt like a fool.

"How did you know that Mr. Harding was coming here?" he asked. "How could you possibly know, unless you're a part of it all?"

The captain smiled. "If I were you, I'd make myself comfortable. For a day or two, this will *be* your home."

"And then?"

"Then your presence here will be academic. Your conscience will be relieved that it will not have to harbor a dark secret. A secret, may I point out, that might lead one to doubt your sanity should you speak too freely."

In a moment, the door was again closed, and Halverton was locked inside.

What had Edison said? To observe everlastingly and hope for a streak of luck? It was possible that the police captain had painted a picture of Halverton as utterly insane to the rest of the force, delusional at least. What could Halverton say to any of them, any one of whom could be part of the captain's team? The element of time, and the very logistics of the situation, erased all hope of an Edison streak. Still, if the streak was out of reach, was a single stroke too much to hold out for? Something to build upon, anything to start the momentum. The likelihood of the captain's complicity in the crime led Halverton to believe that someone outside the cell could also track their way inside the building's walls.

About an hour passed. Halverton spent the time sitting on the bed and thinking. He was so lost in concentration that he had blotted out the sights and sounds of his environment. His thoughts were speckled with ifs. If he could get out of jail, he might follow the captain. If he had stayed with Firestone, he wouldn't be in jail at all. If Margarete had only trusted him totally, none of it would have occurred. If if if. Suddenly, a face passed by the cell's door window, and the latch was moved. When the door opened, Halverton didn't know whether to jump into the man's arms or flee from him down the corridor. It was Harding's Secret Service agent.

"Colonel Starling."

"Mr. Firestone was concerned about you. We've been trying to find you."

"Where is he now?" Halverton asked.

"At a hotel. The three of them are waiting for you. They're all safe. Mr. Edison has quite a story to tell."

"That's great news," Halverton said as they started down the hall. "But there's a police captain here you ought to know about."

"We already do," Starling told him. "A couple of the younger boys have him in custody and are trying to get some information out of him right now. There's a good chance he'll help us out. He knows he's up for the death penalty as it stands right now. Did he reveal anything to you?"

"Nothing helpful, no."

They descended a flight of stairs and got into a waiting automobile.

"He did say that there were only a few hours left. We're running out of time."

Halverton rode in the back seat with Starling. He recognized the driver as the radio operator from the camp. A nod of the head and a quick glance were the only acknowledgement from him. The car raced down the streets, and Halverton could feel his pulse pounding in his ears.

"How did they contact you?" Halverton shouted over the throttle of the engine.

"We received a cable from Mr. Edison late last night," Starling answered. "We hadn't a clue until then. We only just apprehended Captain Lyons. Couldn't trust anyone else for the job. I know that this whole affair makes the department look pretty inept, but I don't care. We're up against a master criminal. If we can break even and get the President back safe and sound, I'd do it in a clown suit if I thought it would help."

Halverton held onto the armrests in the turns. He wondered what kind of information Edison could have supplied. What could he have learned?

The automobile halted in front of a magnificent building. The agent parked directly at the main entrance, and the three men practically leaped out of it. They hurried through a cavernous lobby of wondrous crystal chandeliers and entered a gilded wrought iron elevator.

"Sixth floor," Starling told the elevator operator.

During the short ride, the operator was shooting glances at Halverton and the two agents. Anyone could see that he was a bundle of nerves. Apparently, the younger agent didn't enjoy the attention, and he barked out at the hotel employee, "Well, what is it?"

"I don't know what's going on up on Six," the operator

said apologetically as he stopped the car. He let them out and drew the iron gate shut behind them, adding, "And I don't *want* to know."

"What did that mean?" Halverton asked as the elevator descended from view, but he received no reply.

Colonel Starling led Halverton through a suite of rooms. "We have the whole floor," he said. Men were passing on either side, all of them agents, one would assume. Somewhere in the bustle of activity, they separated from the other agent who had accompanied them. It was a series of opening doors. Deeper into the maze of rooms, Halverton followed Starling step for step. They came to a sitting area. A table was set up, its surface covered with maps of the area and rolls of paperwork. At the side of a chair was a silver platter of sandwiches. There was corned beef, chicken, roast, ham, cheese, even peanut butter and jelly. "Help yourself if you're hungry," Halverton was told. A telephone was ringing somewhere, and continued ringing long after Starling left Halverton there.

He sank into an overstuffed chair and destroyed a ham sandwich in four bites. As he served himself a second one, he looked through a doorway. Men were moving this way and that, crisscrossing his line of vision. He must have seen twenty people by now.

On the other side of the sandwiches was a tub of Coca Colas buried in ice. He reached into the cold and happened to see a newspaper next to the drinks. The front page had a photograph of mounted policemen and other officers leading dogs and swinging clubs. They were charging into a crowd of men. Halverton opened the paper to read the caption.

MR. ZERO'S JOBLESS ARMY ROUTED FROM BOSTON COMMON Beneath the picture, he read: "Urbain Ledoux, self-designated leader of the poor and unemployed, was removed forcibly from the Boston Common yesterday after his refusal to cease from selling jobless men to the highest bidder. Ledoux, known to his followers as Mr. Zero, dismissed the notion that he was practicing slavery. 'Plenty of men need work,' he was quoted from the Boston city jail. 'I just line the man up with the job. The money from the auction block is his salary, not mine.'"

Halverton looked at the photo again. The men were nothing but bums dressed in rags. They looked terrified of the police squadron. His own brief stay in jail made him sympathetic. At least now he knew who Mr. Zero was. He was a charity worker.

"There he is," Halverton heard the familiar Firestone voice. "Glad to have you with us again, Sid."

Halverton set the paper down and shook Firestone's hand gratefully. Henry Ford was at his side.

"I've never been so glad to see anyone in all my life." Halverton told them.

"Hello, jailbird," Ford greeted him as he extended his hand.

"How did you two manage to get here after the truck was stolen?"

"We took the train," Firestone said. "It took us a little while to get us back into a town, and then there wasn't another train due for a half day. So Henry made a phone call or two. He ended up buying a locomotive that was on a side track. We had a caboose attached to it, and were on our way."

"I needed a train anyway," Ford explained.

"Don't you have trouble finding parking spaces?" Halverton asked.

"By what means did you come here, Sid?"

"I took the train too. Where is Mr. Edison? I understand he's here."

"He'll be along." Firestone said. "He was looking for a dish of ice cream to go with his slice of pie just a minute ago."

Halverton finished the last of his meal. The three of them took adjoining chairs, but Halverton noticed that Ford and Firestone weren't very comfortable. Their clothes were probably hand-tailored, and the seats were nothing less than elegant. But they kept straightening their suits, fidgeting in the chairs, and their eyes darted toward a wall clock almost constantly.

"Have you been able to find out anything more on the situation?" Halverton asked.

"Yes," Ford answered quickly. "It seems that your Miss Fabry —"

"Not now, Henry," Firestone stopped him. "Al was with the President for a time, Sid, and with Miss Fabry. It was one of her cohorts who made off with the truck. I don't know all of the details. I'm sure Mr. Edison will be glad to fill you in."

"I don't suppose Margarete was forced into anything, was she?" Halverton asked. "She did it all on her own, didn't she?"

"It looks that way at the moment," Firestone told him.

"Well, I was afraid of that."

Ford had been studying Halverton since they had taken their seats. He must have concluded from his appearance that the younger man had gone through the mill, for out of the blue he made him an offer.

"Would you like a change of clothes?" he asked.

"Yes, I'd appreciate that," Halverton said.

"I'll see what I can scrounge up," Ford said, and he left the room.

They watched him walk through the door and disappear. Then Firestone turned his attention back to Halverton. "Henry's a pretty good guy when you get to know him," he said.

"Yes, I know," Halverton said.

"He's pigheaded and opinionated, and at times his ideas

don't have any rational base, but he's a pretty good guy all in all."

"How did you two meet?"

"He made cars, I made tires. It was inevitable."

Halverton took the last of the soft drink, placing the empty bottle on the table.

"Is President Harding still alive?" he said.

Firestone wiped his mouth with his fist. "That I don't know," he answered.

28

HALVERTON DRESSED IN A CORNER OF THE ROOM. Ford had brought him a change of underwear, a pair of socks, denim trousers, a white shirt, suspenders and a white cap. He was tucking in the shirt when Edison entered, wiping his mouth on his sleeve.

"How was the pie, Al?" Firestone asked him.

"As a connoisseur of fine pastries, I would rank it in the upper 10 percent," Edison said. "It was a fine apple pie, graced with hand-cranked vanilla ice cream. I intend to have seconds shortly."

He was in a good mood, and when Halverton approached to shake his hand, Edison greeted him warmly, extending his left hand and squeezing Halverton's arm. By this time, Halverton knew which of the old man's ears had the better hearing, and he spoke into that one now.

"I'm very glad to see you're safe," he said.

Edison shook his head and pulled Halverton toward the chairs in the company of Ford and Firestone. "Take a seat," he gestured. "I think you have as much a right, if not more a right than anyone here, to know where we stand now."

Firestone reached for a sandwich on the table, settling back with it as Edison began.

"We know that the police captain was Miss Fabry's contact in Niagara Falls," Edison said. "Right now, Colonel Starling and the other agents are dealing with him to ascertain the exact method they have conceived of transfering Mr. Harding. At the moment, Captain Lyons is denying all involvement, but we do have the goods on him. We can only hope that he will cooperate before it's too late."

"What if Lyons doesn't show up for the rendezvous?" Ford asked. "What will they do with the President then? That's what I would like to know."

Firestone sat forward in his chair. "And the demands," he said. "To my knowledge, there hasn't been a single word on the subject of a ransom. Not a single word."

Edison looked at them from one to the other. Then he turned toward Halverton. "Good questions, both of them," he said. "I don't have the answers. Do you?"

"You were the last of us in the President's company," Halverton said. "What happened there? How did you get away?"

"Now that's something I can answer," Edison said. "And it may shed a little more light for the rest of us to hear it once more. It's for your benefit as well as ours."

"I understand," Halverton said.

Edison described how he had been awakened roughly from his nap in the rear of the truck, how he felt himself in no real danger until the truck stopped the first time. He could hardly believe his eyes from that moment on. Just as he was considering letting himself to the ground, he saw the President hustled aboard at gunpoint. In every community that followed, he attempted to get the attention of passersby. He considered dropping notes to the street, but his hands were jostled too much to write on the paper pad he carried in his vest. Edison had bolted at the sound of the gunshot. He knew immediately what it had been. He described again seeing the poor victim lying in the street with the back of his head gone. "My heart was in my mouth," Edison said. "It was becoming worse by the minute, like a nightmare that you can't awaken from." It was at that point that he formulated the plan of electrocution. He didn't know who would be the one to be trapped and dreaded that he might even have to climb over the cab of the truck as it moved in order to extend the live wire to one of them. Then the truck had raced across country, and soon Edison's choice was down to Margarete and her young accomplice. He described in detail how he managed the trap. "It was the worst thing I've ever done," he said.

"Nobody blames you for killing him," Ford said.

Edison paused a moment before relating the aftermath of the killing. As he told of Margarete's extraordinary admission that she was the master-spy Mata Hari, Halverton felt his face flush.

"I don't think that she said that just to make us behave," Edison told him. "I believe it to be true. And if that is the case, then she would have found a way to Mr. Harding regardless of the circumstances of the camping trip. What I mean to say is, don't feel guilt for your part in this. You had absolutely no control over it. You were a stepping stone. If you had not been there, another one would be."

"I don't find much relief in that," Halverton said.

"I know," Edison said, reassuring him with a tap on his knee. The story was depressing. It only reinforced the utter futility Halverton felt about the entire adventure. He listened now to the details of Harding's life that had been confided to Edison. It all sounded like the confession of a man who knew that he was about to die. At first, Halverton felt like an intruder to be privy to such things. After all, the man of whom Edison spoke, a go-getter who roller skated and played the cornet as a boy, was the President of the United States. Then he realized that knowing all the fears and pleasures that Harding had allowed himself to tell just made him all the more human. It built Halverton's determination to do something to help this likable man out of his crisis. And the actual details of the kidnapping plot intrigued him too. He had wondered how in the world someone as recognizable as the President could be moved in such secrecy, concluding that blind luck had as much to do with Margarete's success as planning and stealth. And that encouraged him.

"Their luck can't hold out," he said to Edison, Ford and Firestone. "Their streak has to end someplace."

"Their undoing may be the fact that they allowed me to leave," Edison said. "I read lips. I thought they had said that a Captain Nicholas was involved. I only guessed it was Niagara Falls. Turned out his name was Nick Lyons. Pretty close, as it happened."

"Al telephoned the Secret Service in Washington," Firestone said. "Happily, our fears about their involvement in the plot were unfounded. They transported Al to Niagara. By that time, Henry and I were already in the city. We took over the sixth floor here."

"And now we just wait," Ford said.

"What did you tell that man outside?" Edison asked Ford. "Was he a reporter?"

"Yes, he was a reporter, as a matter of fact. I said that I was here because I'm always on the lookout for a good piece of land. I said that you were studying the future electrical potential of the Falls. He didn't ask about Harvey."

"I don't like lying like that," Edison said with disgust.

"But it's more or less true," Ford said. "Can you deny that a day ever passes that you don't think of electricity? And I always have an eye peeled for a good piece of land."

Edison got to his feet. "It's the deception I object to," he said. "But I suppose the circumstances demand it. The truth is too horrible to contemplate."

Halverton moved near a window, and he looked through it to the street below. It appeared that a crowd was forming on the sidewalk across the street. Thirty people, perhaps more, were standing still and gazing at the hotel building. He pulled a chair in front of the window and rested his elbows on the sill to watch the people down on the ground. Occasionally, a pedestrian would encounter the group, walking at a normal pace until he was stopped by one or more members of the assembled. Then the pedestrian would stop, strain to look upward and become one of the crowd. Halverton saw this happen again and again, and the size of the crowd quickly swelled.

A man on the street spotted Halverton looking down at them, and he cupped his hands about his mouth and shouted something. Halverton placed a hand behind his ear, gesturing to the man that he could not understand him. The man repeated himself, and to Halverton's surprise, he could hear him over the traffic noise this time.

"Is Mr. Thomas Edison in there?"

He looked over his shoulder. Edison had taken a seat and was drinking from a bottle of Coca Cola, looking at a newspaper folded over his knee. Halverton shook his head at the crowd. "Don't be ridiculous!" he shouted out the window. But not a single person dispersed.

"Sid, what are you doing over there?" Firestone asked, joining him at the window.

"Look," Halverton pointed at the crowd on the sidewalk. "They want to see Mr. Edison, I think."

Firestone nodded his head. "Well, he *is* a wizard, you know," he said. "This happens everywhere he goes."

A door closed in the room, and Halverton's attention, as well as Firestone's, shifted from the scene outside. Colonel

Starling was with them now. The agent moved quickly to the table and helped himself to a sandwich. He took a bite, and with his mouth full, announced, "Well, we've done it. This Lyons character is talking his head off. I'd say the chances of rescuing Mr. Harding are finally in our favor."

"Who is behind it all?" Ford wanted to know. "Did you find that out?"

"A man named Remus," Starling told them. "George B. Remus. You might have heard of him, the so called King of the Bootleggers. He made over forty million dollars in the illegal liquor trade."

"Sure, I remember reading about him," Firestone said. "Isn't he in prison now?"

"Exactly. He paid over two hundred and fifty thousand dollars in bribe money to Mr. Jess Smith, an associate of Attorney General Daugherty, over a period of time. Supposedly, the money was to obtain B permits, which you need to withdraw bonded liquor from distilleries and warehouses for medicinal purposes. Smith must have strung him along. When an investigation began, Remus contacted Smith again and was assured he would never be indicted. Money changed hands, but Remus was indicated anyway. He got back in touch with Smith. A few hundred thousand more had Smith telling Remus that conviction was out of the question, that indictment was just to make the investigators look like they were doing their job. Remus was convicted. Still, he sent word and more money to Smith. Smith told him not to worry, that a suspended sentence was the worst that could happen, along with a fine. We think that Remus gave Smith a bonus for that one, but we'll never know for sure since Jess Smith killed himself and all. Remus was sent to the Federal Penitentiary in Atlanta."

"How does the President figure in with all of this?" Halverton asked.

"It's bizarre," Starling said. "But Remus and his money are still a strong influence. He somehow blamed Mr. Harding for all his woes, as if the President knew anything at all about Jess Smith's wheelings and dealings. In apparent revenge, I would guess, Remus has vowed to send Harding to prison. According to this Lyons fellow, there is a cell awaiting our President in Cuba."

"Cuba?" Edison cried out.

"Cuba," Starling repeated. "Our guess is that they were to cross over to Canada where there was less chance of discovery. Lyon's job was to transport Mr. Harding along the St. Lawrence Seaway, or through the wilderness parallel to it. Once they hit the Atlantic, there would be a boat to Cuba. It's all very plausible, gentlemen. Remus proposed that Harding would be let go on the same day as himself, by the way. Failing imprisonment, Remus would opt for assassination."

"That part sounds like what Miss Fabry said," Edison said.

"Yes, but can we rely on what a crooked police captain says?"

"Do we have any choice?" Starling said. "The transfer is scheduled for tonight at 9:30 at Whirlpool State Park, in the picnic area. That's only five hours from right now. Lyons will miss his appointment, of course."

"Where is the state park?" Halverton asked.

"Directly below the Falls a couple of miles. Except for one road through it, the terrain is very tough in there."

"What are your plans to thwart it?" Firestone asked.

"Well, Lyons was to take a sum of money to the kidnappers, and then accompany Mr. Harding into Canada. There is about a hundred acre area we're dealing with, and I have only a dozen men at this time. Fortunately, some of them served in the cavalry under Pershing. That expertise will be invaluable for this kind of terrain. More men are on the way, but there is some question as to whether they can get here in time. I can't trust the local police, even though Lyons may be the only corrupt one among them."

Halverton listened to Starling uncomfortably. Surely he

was mistaken that there were only twelve agents in the hotel. All of their bustling about must have exaggerated their size.

"Because of our limited number, I propose that our present plan of attack be to station a number of men throughout the area to act as sharpshooters, supported by the remainder of the force on horseback. I don't think we could get closer to act otherwise. You have to consider the amount of land we have to cover."

"Shooting will put the President at risk, Edmund," Ford told him. "I know you're using it as a last resort. But even having your agents tramping about the countryside could endanger Mr. Harding should they be spotted."

"But what else can we do?" Starling gestured with the half-eaten sandwich. "Answer me that."

His hands were frozen in mid-air, and he looked like an outfielder who's lost a fly ball in the sun. Halverton considered Starling's proposal and his suggestion for an alternative. All this talk about cavalry and firearms clarified the approach Starling was taking. Obviously, his plan was an ambush. Halverton knew for certain now that not only were they taking a calculated risk with the life of the President, but that Margarete was already as good as dead. He didn't see the operation any more as merely a crack at getting Harding back in one piece. He wanted to save her life as well. Suddenly it became clear to him what he had to do.

"Let me pose as Captain Lyons," Halverton said. "It will be dark out there, and there's a good chance I won't be recognized. If I am, I don't believe Margarete will harm me. I may even be able to talk some sense into her."

"That might be a safer approach," Edison said.

"Let me try," Halverton siad. "You can always back it up with a plan of your own, but I think that sending me in there will be safer for President Harding. Using a total stranger might provoke them into something."

"I'll have to agree with you about the President's safety," Starling admitted. "That machine gun Mr. Edison told us of has been a particular cause for worry. A weapon like that could pin us all down. It looks like you're our man. Do you have a pistol?"

"He can have mine," Ford offered.

"I don't really want one," Halverton said.

"Well, carry it anyway," Starling instructed him, "Just in case there's no reasoning with the woman."

Halverton started to say something but then nodded his head.

"We'll need to see those maps now," Edison spoke up. "It will be to our advantage to know the lay of the land."

Edison stood at the table and spread the rolls of paper over its surface. He located Whirlpool State Park. "Here's their point of rendezvous," he said as the others gathered around the table. "That's about three miles north of the Falls, just south of Niagara University. The river turns eastward above the Falls, so it defines a border on two sides, the west and the south. The college is to the north."

"And the airfield is to the east," Starling pointed out. "I already have two men there."

"What do you have in mind, Al?" Firestone asked.

"I'm not sure," Edison said. "An escape route, I reckon. I'm used to taking years to solve a problem. We have to turn up an answer in a matter of hours. The river itself blocks escape to the west and the south. If the agents are able to cover the area near the airfield, that leaves only the direction of the college unguarded. In India, tigers are hunted by having dozens of beaters walking through the brush to drive the animal in the direction of the hunter. The chances of one individual getting injured by the tiger are very slim. I suggest that after our daring young man here has already gone into the state park, we back him up with such a drive." Edison cupped his hands around Whirlpool State Park. "By the agents from the east, and by ourselves from the direction of the university. The river will do its part as well. They shouldn't have chosen this site. The river has hemmed them in."

"But there are only three of us," Ford pointed out. "You

could slip a herd of elephants through us, and we'd never know."

"Yes, but I am about to venture outside and announce to the populace that Mr. Thomas Edison is pleased to accept the invitation to give a public lecture on electricity tonight at Niagara University. It should recruit a considerable number of people — each one of whom the kidnappers would wish to avoid.

"Yes, I would think so," Ford said.

"But can we endanger people that way?" Halverton asked. "What if one of them gets killed?"

"Then we would deeply regret it," Ford told him. "It would be a regret nearly as great as if we had done nothing at all. Either alternative is a terrible choice."

"It's an excellent plan," Starling said. "I should have consulted you gentlemen from the very beginning, back in those tents in West Virginia."

Halverton walked away from them and looked out the window once more. How long ago the camping trip now seemed, but it had been less than three days.

"Are you coming, Sid?" Firestone asked, and Halverton turned to see Edison slipping on his jacket, his uncombed hair going in every which direction. A candy bar was in his hand. Ford was already out the door.

"Yes, of course," he answered.

29

COLONEL STARLING REMAINED BEHIND TO BRIEF the rest of the agents as to their duties for the night. Edison, Ford, Firestone and Halverton moved together down the hallway for the elevator. They boarded the conveyance, and as they descended to the lobby, the elevator operator said nothing. He watched Edison for a long time, shifting his attention to Henry Ford just before depositing his passengers on the first floor. Despite everything that the two men had to be preoccupied with, they were talking about rubber, synthetic rubber. Edison stated that his tests with goldenrod had shown the plant to be the most promising of those in question.

"We've reached a point where we can say our experiments are successful," Edison said. "We had hopes for milkweed, but there was very little yield. My estimate at present is a hundred pounds of rubber to the acre of goldenrod. I expect to raise this to a hundred an fifty pounds eventually."

"How many plants did you investigate?" Ford asked.

"Oh, fourteen thousand," Edison said as they stepped into the lobby.

Halverton watched the elevator operator's reaction. The thunderstruck man's mouth had dropped open in disbelief.

A swarm of hotel employees greeted the foursome before they reached the revolving doors to the street. Uniformed bellboys stood in a row at attention. The hotel manager dabbed his forehead with a handkerchief as he approached. Guests were frozen in their tracks at the sight of Edison.

"Please, can we be of any service?" the manager asked. "Is there anything unsatisfactory in your rooms?"

"You need anything?" Ford shouted the relayed message to Edison.

"A phonograph," Edison nodded his head. "I would appreciate the loan of a phonograph for a few minutes."

"Surely, Mr. Edison," the manager said. "Was the one in your room not to your liking?"

"It was all right," Edison said. "I just didn't want to tote it down six flights of stairs. I would like it out on the sidewalk."

A dozen people were surrounding them now, and the remark sent a ripple of laughter through the group. The manager ordered a pair of his underlings into a room off of the main lobby, and they returned shortly, shuffling their feet across the carpet on either end of a phonograph.

"Outside with it, boys," Edison directed.

Halverton and Firestone preceded the bellhops in order to hold open the doors to the side of the revolving ones.

"Do you have any idea what he's up to?" Halverton asked.

"None whatsoever," Firestone replied.

When Edison and Ford, the most recognizable faces of the group, emerged from the revolving doors and stopped on the sidewalk, the crowd across the street caught sight of them. Immediately, the onlookers surged forward. Car and truck horns sounded, and vehicles were forced to stop at the rush of people. Literally, within thirty seconds, the entire block was shut down. It was a joyous interruption.

Edison motioned for the bellhops to move the phonograph to the curb, and he himself stepped onto the running board of an automobile stalled in the street. People everywhere were whistling and applauding. Halverton saw groups of them clustered around windows in buildings up and down the block, edging each other out of the way for a better look. Edison first shook the hand of the driver of the car on which he was perched, then calmed the noise with a hushing motion of his hands. It became almost unbelievably silent for an afternoon in a city. His three cohorts standing close by his side, Edison ordered the phonograph placed before him.

"Ladies and gentlemen," he announced, gesturing to his invention. "You see before you a tongueless, toothless instrument, lacking in both larynx and pharynx. It is dumb, voiceless matter, which nevertheless mimics your tones, speaks with your voice, utters your words and centuries after you have crumbled into dust, will repeat again and again, to a generation that could never know you, every idle thought, every fond fancy, every vain word that you choose to whisper against its thin iron diaphragm."

There was a roar of applause and laughter while Edison paused. Halverton nudged Firestone. "I never knew he was such a speaker," he shouted over the din.

"I never knew he was such a ham," Firestone answered.

"For an explanation of the workings of such mechanisms as the phonograph," Edison went on. "And for an extemporaneous and spontaneous diatribe on the wonders of electricity, I hereby extend an invitation to all of you to a public lecture tonight at Niagara University. My accomplices in the proceedings will be Mr. Henry Ford and President of the Firestone Tire and Rubber Company, Mr. Harvey Samuel Firestone."

Edison pointed out Ford and Firestone to the crowd and led a rousing volley of applause for them.

"The event will commence at the hour of nine," Edison continued. "Please leave children and little ones in the home, as the subjects addressed will be very dry indeed and of little interest to such active minds."

He waved his arms once to the multitude before stepping to the ground. Halverton and Firestone flanked him on either side, as Ford shook hands with the onlookers while bringing up the rear. In 1923, the three well-known friends were heroes. They were the sort of men loved by the decade that roared.

Out of curiosity, Halverton raised the lid on the phonograph as it was carried past him. He guessed to himself that if it contained a record, chances were even that its title would be *Yes, We Have No Bananas*, the anthem of absent-mindedness written by Frank Silver and Irving Cohn. He was wrong. The record label he saw was two years old. It was Noble Sissle's and Eubie Blake's pleasant little masterpiece, *I'm Just Wild About Harry*. Halverton could play the piece on the piano, and play it well. As he entered the lobby of the hotel from outside, ceiling fans stirring a light breeze above his head, he considered his situation. He had survived the World War, the tedium of ship duty broken only once by the sighting of one torpedo in the entire Atlantic Ocean. Tonight, in Niagara Falls, he would need to wrestle the President of the United States from the hands of Mata Hari. He promised himself that he would not just survive. He would rise above his emotions and any other obstacle. He would have to. And when it was over, he would play Eubie Blake until his fingers ached.

Halverton was driven to Whirlpool State Park that night by Colonel Starling. At his request, Harvey Firestone accompanied him.

"I'd like to ask a favor of you."

"Just name it." Firestone told him.

"If something should happen, if I don't come out of this alive, I would appreciate it if you got in touch with my father. Tell him what happened."

"Don't think like that, Sid," Firestone said. "You've got a level head, the element of surprise and Henry's Colt .45."

"Colonel Starling gave me an automatic pistol. He says it fires much faster. Will you do what I asked?"

Firestone nodded his head, closing his eyes as he did so. The automobile turned onto the park's service road and began to wind through massive pine trees, the headlights creating the sensation that they were driving in a tunnel.

"Just remember what Edmund told you. Get Mr. Harding aside if you can. Step between him and them, and if you have to, don't hesitate to open fire. Don't allow anything to happen to you, and it won't."

"I really won't know what to do until the situation arises," Halverton said. "There's no preparation that could possibly be of help." He paused a moment. "I appreciate you coming with me. Mr. Firestone, you're a good and generous man. I'm glad we had the opportunity to become acquainted." He was silent again for a few seconds. "Do you know what time it is?"

Firestone checked his pocket watch. "It's 8:30," he said. "That means you have about an hour to wait at the picnic tables. Just sit tight, and don't get frightened."

"But I'm already scared to death."

"I know. The butterflies in my own stomach are about to lift me right off the seat. You're aware that the park rangers have been pulled out of the area, aren't you? That means you might have people driving through the park like they always do. We just didn't want anything to spook Miss Fabry. A uniformed officer like a ranger might ruin the whole scheme."

"Can you handle the job?" Starling asked from the driver's seat.

"That's a good question," Halverton answered him.

"Sit at the table, with your back to the road," said Firestone. "Have the briefcase in plain sight. Hopefully, that will occupy most of their interest."

"Just how much money is in it?"

"A hundred thousand."

"Oh, Lord."

"Don't think about that. It's just pocket money for Henry. One look at the money, and they may turn Mr. Harding over to you, no questions asked. That's what we're praying will happen."

"How many people do you think will turn up at the college?"

"Hundreds, at least. Al will propose a walking excursion into the woods in this direction at about the time Lyons was scheduled to meet with Miss Fabry."

"And we'll start to close in from the other direction," Starling said.

"How much time will I have before either of you arrive?"

"Probably fifteen to twenty minutes."

"In other words, if Margarete is more than twenty minutes late, the entire state park will be teeming with people."

"We can't help that," Starling said. "There's no viable alternative. Please calm down. There are crowds of people here the year round anyway. The Falls are just a short walk from where you'll be."

Starling braked the car and turned off the engine. "There are the picnic tables Lyons mentioned," he said as he turned out the headlights.

"You're going to be all right," Firestone reassured him.

Halverton felt nauseous and was afraid he would swoon if he stood up. He leaned over and put his head between his knees, his face almost pressed against the leather briefcase beneath his feet. He sat up again and slapped his face three or four times as if he was splashing on cologne. "All right," he said. "All right, let me out."

Firestone opened the car door, and Halverton followed him out. The ground felt soft like putty under his feet. Firestone reached in and grabbed the briefcase, turned and gave it to Halverton standing in the road.

"This is it, I guess," Halverton said.

Firestone stepped forward and embraced the younger man. Halverton couldn't tell which of them was trembling more. The car started up again, and Halverton stepped out of its way.

"Wait a minute," he called just as Firestone had boarded it.

The vehicle's two occupants nearly jumped out of their skins. "What's the matter?" Starling asked.

"Do you have a cigarette?" Halverton requested.

Starling reached into his pocket. "Here's a whole pack," he said. "And some matches. I expect you to give them back later."

"I would love to," Halverton said. "You two be careful too."

He watched the taillights go around a curve. Then he was completely alone. He walked the twenty yards to the picnic tables, his eyes adjusting gradually to the darkness. He raised the briefcase onto the surface of the closest table, striking a match on the stone and concrete bench. He lit a cigarette, knowing that his shaking hands could never have rolled one himself under the circumstances. He sat down at the table and rested his arms on it. The bulge under his shirt was new and uncomfortable. He felt it with his fingertips, taking long pulls on the smoke. He kept the cigarette dangling from his lips and squinted from its irritation while pulling out his shirttail to hide the gun more completely. But it was all he could think of at the moment, all he could feel, the piece of metal attached to his side like the grasp of a cold brass hand. He reached beneath his shirt and removed the gun. He then slipped the shirt off over his head and lay it on the table beside the weapon. He reached behind his back and wrestled off the shoulder holster, throwing it as far into the darkness as he could. He put on his shirt and sat there with the pistol in both hands.

He stood up and took five careful steps away from the table's corner, counting each pace out loud. There was no moon. What little starlight there was on the clear night filtered through a roof of tree limbs before frosting the ground amid the shadows. He covered the pistol in leaves, mulching them between his hands. He returned to the table and tried to pick the weapon out in the darkness, but it wasn't possible. If he hadn't put the gun there himself, there was no way of knowing that it existed.

"Five steps," he said as he lit another cigarette.

A car roared around the curve at a high rate of speed, shattering the silence and the darkness. Halverton clenched his hands automatically, and he knew that his heart skipped a beat or two from the jolt of adrenalin. He knew how a deer must feel when a set of headlights freezes its movement. He took deep breaths. In two or three very long minutes, he was calm again. Still extremely frightened, but in control of himself once more.

It seemed like such a long wait that he expected to see the Secret Service at any moment or Edison's multitude sweeping through the woods. Their premature arrival could be disastrous. But perhaps it only seemed as if the confrontation was overdue. With the exception of the one automobile, there wasn't a hint of activity anywhere. That in itself was suspicious to Halverton. He just didn't know what to think anymore.

He heard a faint motor in the distance. It could have been a mile away, but in the density of the forest, it might have been just beyond his field of vision. As he listened, the noise grew louder, closer. Then the light from its headlights began to outline the treetops before the car could even be seen. There were a great number of curves and hills to the road, and the light appeared to dance one way, then the other, like the glare of an airfield's beacon. At the same time, the noise of the engine was becoming less and less muffled.

He saw the headlights, and apparently, he was seen as well. The car came to a dead stop some fifty yards from the table where Halverton waited. He quickly put a hand to his face, not only shading his eyes from the light, but hiding his identity from the occupants of the car as well. The engine idled a moment. Halverton could see nothing behind the lights.

The vehicle slowly eased forward, moving steadily and directly off of the pavement, across the grass and gravel toward Halverton's table. He took his hand away from his face now, turning his head slightly away from the glare of the light. There was little point in concealing himself now.

He stood at the side of the table, pushing the briefcase away from him. He stepped up to the bench and sat on the table, the car edging ever closer to him. When there was scarcely room to step between it and the picnic bench, the engine was shut off. Halverton opened his eyes wide in the sudden backwash of darkness.

Both of the automobile doors opened simultaneously. From the driver's side emerged a man who moved behind his open door. He appeared to be using it as a shield. Halverton glanced at him only briefly. The other door remained open, and then she too stepped outside. Margarete was dressed as she was for the hike she had taken with him in the Monongahela Forest — men's pants and walking boots, a shirt tucked in at the waist. He could hear her breathing, the quiet exhalations he used to awaken to while she lay at his side.

"Is this Lyons?" the man said across the roof of the car.

"No, I'm not," Halverton said. "But I've got the money, and if it's all the same to you, I suggest we make the transaction as if I were him. Come count it if you like."

"Hell, you don't even have a car. What were you going to do, walk to Canada?"

"We must be surrounded," Margarete said calmly. There wasn't a trace of panic in her voice.

The man closed the door to the vehicle and took a couple of steps toward the table. Margarete was looking suspiciously around the area, ignoring Halverton. She reached inside the car and produced a flashlight, shining its beam here and there in the near distance. Halverton could make out the outline of another person still inside the car.

"Let's see that light," the man called to her.

She tossed it to him, and he threw open the briefcase on the table. There were rows and rows of bound stacks of hundred-dollar bills. He shined his light across the money.

"It looks all right to me," he announced, then turned his attention to Margarete. "It looks all right," he said. He threw her a bundle of money.

She reached inside the car and led President Harding out by the elbow. The President had been ordered about for days now. That, combined with the intense drive to this destination that dictated a disruption of his eating and sleeping habits, had transformed the handsome and dignified air Halverton had earlier observed into a ghastly countenance. The change in Harding was frightening. His clothes were filthy. An undershirt with suspenders attached to a torn pair of trousers seemed to fit the man's pale and exhausted features that showed even in the darkness of the night.

"I'm ready to get the hell out of here," Margarete's companion said. "Get in the car and let's go."

Margarete slammed her door. "Go ahead, Warner," she said. "I've decided to stay here."

"Then help me divide the money."

"You keep it," she told him, holding the one bundle in her fingertips. "I have more than enough here."

Harding looked from one of them to the other as they spoke. Halverton had yet to move from the table. He was hoping more than anything that Warner would leave them. Someone else, Starling's group, or Edison's or the New York State police, could deal with him later.

"Suit yourself," Warner said. "I'm not hanging around to argue. The Feds will be on top of us in a minute."

He seized the leather case and leaped behind the wheel of the car. His motions inside the vehicle were jerky and abrupt. Halverton could plainly see the fear in his eyes. In a few moments, he had driven completely out of sight. He had taken an easterly direction.

None of them took a step, or made a move of any kind. Each seemed to be assessing the other two, Margarete and the President uncertain where Halverton's loyalties lay and Halverton himself with only a part of the problem solved.

Margarete was the first to speak. "It was Mr. Edison," she said. "Wasn't it, Sid? It had to have been. But how could he know the details of the park here?"

"He's nearly deaf," Halverton said. "He reads lips. The police captain was captured a few hours ago."

She walked forward and joined Halverton at the table top, just beyond his reach. "The man who drove away just now is fairly decent, but unremarkable. If he can get through this trap in a car, I'm certain that I can on foot. We are two canaries, hovering in a room full of cats."

"What trap is that, Margarete?" Halverton asked her.

"Don't insult me. The one that the three of us are in the center of even as we speak."

"Do you have a gun on you?" Halverton said. She made no answer, and he repeated the question to President Harding.

"I don't know if she does," Harding answered." They passed it back and forth between themselves so much that I lost track. He had it for awhile, then she had it. I never knew."

The sound of Warner's car was still audible. It was plain that all three of them were listening. The sound of the first gunshot rolled through the timbered surroundings like a wave of thunder. Harding reacted visibly to the noise. He was startled. Three or more shots could be heard in quick succession, followed by a burst of machine gun fire. For a minute or two it sounded like a battlefield, with rapid exchanges between the different-sounding weapons. There was the thunder of rifles, the short cracks of pistol shots and the echoing blasts of Warner's return fire.

Then there was only the silence of the forest once again.

Halverton kicked his feet in the leaves near the table and grabbed up the pistol. He aimed it at her.

"Whatever happened out there will be blamed on me," Margarete said. "A scapegoat, just like in wartime. But it's more serious than war, Sid. Leaders survive almost every war. You have sealed Mr. Harding's fate, as well as my own. Mr. President, I tried my best to save you."

"By abducting me," Harding answered. "At a cost of many lives by now. Do me a favor. Don't try anymore."

"Stay where you are, Margarete," Halverton said.

"Where would I go, my love?" she told him. "Where would I go?"

"Mr. Harding, please come over here by me. I think you're safe now. Those were Colonel Starling's men out there."

Harding was still conditioned to obey. Move here. Stay there. Eat this. He promptly walked around the table and stood behind Halverton without comment or question.

Halverton kept the gun trained on Margarete. "I would have stayed with you forever," he told her.

"I know you would have," she said. "But that's not realistic, Sid. We had a short-lived, but beautiful affair. I cherish the time that was ours. You should live for the beautiful and glorious moments, dearest. It is better to live on Earth for a few short and intense instants and to pass away than to drag about through old age without beauty or joy."

"I don't believe that," Halverton said.

"Then we are not as compatible as you thought," she said.

They heard a commotion from the trees and underbrush in the direction of the gunshots. It was as if the ground itself was being drummed. People could be marching, perhaps. Then, from down the road, four saddled but riderless horses galloped toward them in the night, wildly throwing their heads about, their sides glistening. Their sudden appearance was frightening. They were ghost horses, running without direction. They might have been panicked by the shooting, but it seemed just as likely at the time that they were in search of their riders for their appointment with the Apocalypse. One of the animals halted on the road, while another slowed to a walk as it encountered the humans near the picnic tables. The remaining two cantered out of sight around the bend. Halverton waved his arms and shouted in an attempt to drive the beast away from them, but it continued still. Margarete held out her hand for it as she stood on the bench.

"There, there," she was saying.

"Leave it alone," Halverton said, cocking the pistol as he spoke.

She reached for the reins and seized them tightly in her hand. The horse, frothing at the mouth and breathing heavily from its run, stood alongside the table. Margarete talked soothingly to it.

All at once she sprang on top of the horse and Halverton found himself aiming at Margarete's heart with his pistol. In the split second he hesitated, the horse surged forward, knocked him flat on his back, and bolted away. The President helped him to his feet.

"The other horse," Halverton said.

They managed to get on either side of the skittish animal, both men moving slowly so as not to spook it. They moved in closer, and Halverton was able to grab the reins. The leather was wet and sticky, and he realized with revulsion that it was probably blood. He placed his foot in the stirrup and climbed up.

"The gun's on the ground over there," he said to Harding. "I just couldn't use it on her. I'm sure that help is on the way, sir. Can you wait for them here?"

"Get going!" Harding yelled as he slapped the horse's rear.

Halverton was not a good horseman, and he stayed in the saddle by gripping with his legs and hanging his arms around the horse's neck. Tree limbs were passing just inches from his head, and he buried his face in the hair of the mane. He prayed that he could get through, that he was being watched

over to triumph over all obstacles in the manner of Harold
Lloyd. A laugh or two at his expense would be little bother
indeed if he proved successful.

With kicks to its ribs, he drove the poor horse onward
down the same walking trail Margarete had taken. He could
scarcely see a thing in the night, but he had to find her.
There was nothing ahead but the river. Behind him was the
onward push of Starling's agents, or what was left of them,
and Edison's army from the university.

He broke into an open space. It was a meadow, and on the
far side of it he could make out the shape of another horse
and rider in open stride. What he could see of the territory
looked familiar. Halverton recognized the area as where he
had spent the previous rainy night. That could only mean
that the Falls were very close. He came upon another stretch
of woods and lowered his head again. When he galloped out
of the trees, he drew back tautly on the reins. The Falls were
illuminated brilliantly in orange and green floodlights. Halverton searched for Margarete somewhere in the scene. He
could see the observation platform, the hotel in the background, the cable car. Dozens of people were strolling here
and there. Lit like they were, the American Falls, and Horse-
shoe Falls on the Canadian side, resembled mountains of
green and orange cotton candy. Halverton was looking across
the careful landscaping of the luxury hotel when Margarete's
horse broke across his line of vision after passing the observation point. He slapped his horse and flew after her.

Halverton galloped across the hotel grounds, the hooves
tearing out huge patches of grass. Outraged pedestrians were
shouting to him, but he couldn't make out their words. He
ran down the length of a sidewalk, the horseshoes throwing
sparks along the pavement. In front of him, people who had
just missed being run over by Margarete were darting out of
his way now.

"Stop that woman!" he shouted. "Stop her!"

Margarete dismounted and pushed herself into a small

crowd. Halverton saw the cable car over the river. It looked as if it was hovering in the air, floating toward the ground where the cluster of people waited on the steep and rocky bank.

He climbed down from the horse and tried to run in her direction. Out of nowhere, a huge man grabbed Halverton by the lapels. "You almost trampled by wife!" he shouted in his face.

"Let go of me," Halverton said. "We have to stop that woman. The one who just rode up."

The man refused to lessen his hold on him and began shaking Halverton now as well. Halverton brought his knee up hard between the man's legs. It seemed to knock the wind out of him, and Halverton pushed him aside, running literally over him as he forced his way deeper into the group of people. The cable car had landed, and everyone was moving slowly in its direction. Halverton shoved and elbowed his way forward, and called out her name repeatedly. He could see her only a few feet in front of him. Margarete looked over her shoulder and saw him.

She drew out the pistol, and in the same motion, raised it above her head and fired. "Get back!" she shouted. "All of you! Get away from me!"

People screamed, and their surge away from Margarete prevented Halverton from getting any closer. In fact, he lost ground in the temporary panic. A man in a uniform stepped from the cable car onto a small embarking deck. Margarete aimed the gun into his face, and he walked sideways around her like a crab, saying, "I'm moving, sister. I'm moving. She's all yours if that's what you want."

Margarete motioned him farther away with the gun. She raised herself on her tiptoes for a look inside the vehicle, then backed aboard it while keeping the crowd at bay.

"Just close the door and throw that switch," the conductor instructed her.

The contraption was built like a motorized bicycle, only

upside down. The capsule took the place of the bicycle seat, and the cable was strung between it and the overhead wheels. She closed herself inside. The thing jolted at the start. Halverton pressed forward now. He could see Margarete's smiling, beautiful face, her hair falling all about her from the ride on horseback. The cable car maneuvered gracefully through the air over the turbulence of Niagara Falls, the large metal spokes of its wheels carrying her away. She never took her eyes away from him. She threw him a kiss.

A swarm of men on horseback came barreling out of the woods, along the paths and past the hotel. People scrambled for safety once more from in front of the cavalry charge. Halverton could recognize Colonel Starling in the lead. By the time the squadron had met up with him, he saw that Henry Ford and Harvey Firestone were among the riders.

"Where is she?" Firestone called out, and Halverton gestured to the cable car high above the Falls.

"The Mounted Police are waiting on the other side," Starling said. "I told them this afternoon what was up."

The glass-encased gondola was midway across the river when it abruptly halted. In the bright orange and green lights, the mechanism suspended on the wire scarcely looked real. It was the landscape of a dream, a deafening ocean boiling on the surface and an odd transport swaying high overhead.

The door to the car opened over the water. "Oh, Lord, no," someone called out.

Halverton realized with horror what was about to happen. He watched helplessly from the bank along with the rest of them. He saw Margarete's figure outlined in the gaudy haze, standing in the cable car's doorway. Then, she was flying in the air, falling, end over end over end. People around him were screaming and crying at what they saw, but Halverton closed his eyes tightly and kept them closed.

He had a room to himself on the sixth floor that night, and in the morning Henry Ford asked if he would drive himself, Firestone and Edison to the train station. Halverton replied that he would be happy to.

The depot was teeming with people, since word of their presence had preceded their arrival. Not only that, but everyone knew that President Harding was in the city on a surprise visit. Rumor had it that the President had so greatly enjoyed his short vacation on the campout that he had extended the visit with his friends by three days. This was the explanation in the newspaper. Who was to say otherwise?

On side by side tracks, the Presidential touring car, the *Superb*, and Ford's newly purchased locomotive awaited. Ford had had his personal train car shipped and attached to the engine during the hectic night.

As soon as they stepped out of the automobile, they were besieged by photographers and journalists. They were questioned on a wide range of subjects, both serious and light. A part of Halverton wanted to remain with them forever, these world-famous acquaintances that he still hesitated to call his friends because of their positions. At the same time, he realized that this was probably the last few minutes he would have to spend with them. And that was fine with him too. Before they walked to the train, they stopped to talk with the press.

"Mr. Ford, you've made a great deal more money than Mr. Edison."

"Money doesn't mean a thing, boys," Ford answered. "Al's done more good than anybody in his time."

"Do you think that John D. Rockefeller has done the proper thing with his philanthropies, his foundations and so on?"

"Why mention somebody else? That's for Rockefeller to decide. Let's keep to ourselves."

"Well, have you devised a plan for the disposal of your fortune?".

"No, I haven't," Ford said.

"Don't you know what you're going to do with it?"

"I have an idea. You're young men. You'll live to see it."

"Do you think that the accumulation of great private fortunes is a dangerous thing in this country?"

"Do you?" Ford replied.

"Well, it bequeaths to untried persons great reservoirs of power and wealth. For instance, your fortune may safely succeed for one or two generations. But suppose your grandson or great-grandson proves to be a wastrel?"

Ford smiled at the man jotting down notes on a tablet. "Well then, it goes, doesn't it?" was his answer.

"What's the finest thing in your life?" one of them asked.

"That I've got a job," Ford said.

"What do you think of Mussolini?"

"Mussolini," Ford pronounced. "So that's how you say his name. Lots of goods things come out of Italy. Take olive oil, for instance."

"But Mussolini," the reporter persisted. "He's a great one for discipline."

"Discipline's fine if you don't take it too far," Ford said. "But the best things are education and experience. The only trouble with experience is that the course is so long that the graduates are too old to go to work."

"Has your position on unions changed?"

"It's foolish to join one," Ford advised. "Skill is all the union a mechanic or a workman will ever need. Unions got the children out of the sweatshops and mines. They've done their jobs now."

At the same time, people hovered about Edison, all shouting questions over each other to be heard.

"When and what was your first experiment?"

"I developed the radio when I was eight years old."

"Wasn't that Marconi?" someone corrected him.

"So it was," Edison chuckled.

"Is the United States right in not keeping up with the development of aviation for defense?"

"No. Military aviation is the one thing that should be pushed."

"When do you plan to retire?"

"When the doctor carries in the oxygen cylinder."

"How does one break into the business of inventing?"

"To invent, all you need is a little imagination and a pile of junk."

"Do you have any words of advice for my readers, sir?"

"Yes. I would tell them that when down in the mouth, remember Jonah. He came out all right."

"Mr. Firestone, what is the key to success in business?"

"Own it yourself and keep plenty of cash on hand for investment."

The reporter laughed at the answer, caught up in the high spirit of the occasion. "I wasn't joking," Firestone said.

"Which of the three of you is the most successful?"

"You can't compare us," Firestone said. "We're in completely different fields, though those fields do overlap in places. But you shouldn't compare a salesman with a manufacturer, a clerk with a banker, an engineer with a merchant or an apple with a cabbage. I would say that each of us is an outstanding success in our individual fields. You may be planting a crop, or making a tire or keeping a set of books. Whatever it is, if you are doing it to the top notch of your skill and efficiency, and it's the thing you're best suited for, you are achieving success."

They walked away from the reporters now and stood between the two trains. Colonel Starling was standing on the platform outside the President's car, and he held the door open for them to climb aboard. Edison was first, followed by Ford, Firestone and Halverton.

The President was sitting in a chair with his shirt removed. Laddie Boy, Harding's Airedale, lay at the President's feet having his ears rubbed.

"Laddie's having himself immortalized." Harding said. "Children all across the country are donating pennies for a humane society program. Some of the pennies will be melted down for a copper statue of Laddie. Don't you think that's nice?"

Naturally, the four visitors concurred. Harding was still President of the United States. No one would disagree with him on such a point. As they stood there with him, a man entered the car. He was toting, of all things after Edison's remark to the reporter, a tank of oxygen.

"Gentlemen, this is Doctor Sawyer."

The doctor nodded his head and went about the routine of taking Harding's blood pressure. He also listened to the President's heartbeat.

"I wanted to thank each of you for what you have done, both for myself and for the nation," Harding said. He laughed. "You might say I am grateful for this return to normalcy. Seriously, though, I understand through the warden down in Atlanta that Remus denies any involvement in a scheme of revenge. We have no proof, so the matter is dropped. My trip to Alaska and back is underway again."

"You shouldn't go anywhere but back to a bed in the White House for at least four weeks," the doctor advised, returning his stethoscope to his bag.

"Impossible," the President said.

"Warren, what about the poor man who was shot?" Firestone wanted to know. "Is the government going to make adequate compensation for that? If it isn't, I'd like to help out his family."

"We can work something out," Harding replied. "It's no problem. It's a tragedy, surely. The man died. But we can take care of his survivors if he had any."

Firestone wished Harding luck, and the three others chimed in with their hopes for him as well.

"How are you feeling?" Ford asked.

"A little tired, but otherwise fine."

They stayed a few minutes more. None of them mentioned Margarete, probably because none of them felt at all well about what she had done or what had happened to her. They left the President, bade goodbye to Starling and crossed the cement to Ford's train. Ford, Firestone and Edison had said they were to spend a few days in Michigan for the remainder of their vacation.

"What are your plans, Sid?" Firestone asked. "You're more than welcome to come with us."

"I have to get back to my job," Halverton said. "I'm headed for Trenton just as soon as I can go. Mr. Ford, what do you wish to be done with the car I drove to the station?"

"The papers are in the glove compartment," Ford said. "I almost forgot to tell you. It's your car now. Good luck with it. The Model T is the finest automobile on the road today."

"The balloon tires aren't anything to overlook either," Firestone said. "By the way, Henry, what do you say about the balloons now? You promised an answer."

"I like the idea of riding on a cushion of air, Harvey," Ford said. "You sold me days ago."

Firestone smiled at the news. "Well, business is looking up," he said.

Edison had apparently heard little of the exchange. He reached out and pumped Halverton's hand. "Goodbye, my telegrapher friend," he said. "Goodbye."

Halverton stood outside and watched the trains leave the station. When they were out of sight, he drove his new car to the Western Union office, picked up the money that his father had wired to him and embarked for New Jersey.

Ford's train took an easterly route. In the Trenton papers, Halverton followed the progress of Harding's trip west for the next several weeks. The President went to Saint Louis for an overdue speaking engagement. From there, the Voyage of Understanding took him to Kansas City, then across the plains in the summer heat, where he spoke at every whistle stop along the way to whomever would listen. The World Court was the idea Harding stressed in every speech. The train moved on to Denver. Harding visited the Mormon Tabernacle in Salt Lake. His wife was having a marvelous time. The President addressed a gathering at Zion National Park. He spoke briefly at Pocatello, Idaho, in Helena and Butte, Montana. In Butte, he shook hands with some miners. The Presidential party spent a weekend exploring Yellowstone National Park.

Doctor Sawyer at this time advised the President not to climb any more stairs.

Jackson Hole, Wyoming saw the *Superb* through the Tetons. Then it was on to Spokane and Portland. In Tacoma, Commerce Secretary Herbert Hoover joined the party. Hoover later remarked that Harding ruined the game of bridge for him. Throughout Alaska, playing bridge was all the President wished to do between speeches. Hoover, patient but unenthusiastic, would never play the game again. For more than a week, Alaska and Harding entertained each other.

On their return to the States, Doctor Sawyer issued a bulletin to the press. The President, the doctor said, was suffering from food poisoning from bad seafood and would take two days to recover.

Harding seemed to make the recovery. His spirits were high. He even complained to Colonel Starling that they had not caught a single fish in Alaska, promising a return there just for that purpose. This was in San Francisco, where, on the second of August, 1923, President Warren Gamaliel Harding died at the Palace Hotel.

30

I AM RARELY SURPRISED BY ANYTHING ANYMORE. IT rained heavily last night, and this morning the sky is clear and cold. I fully expected this. It is that time of year. Autumn always puts me in mind of the events of 1923, even though those events took place in a sweltering summer. Perhaps 1923, like Autumn, signaled the end of something in me, and the natural change of the seasons reminds me of those times. Who is to say exactly what happened then? So much time has passed that there is bound to be a distortion. A distortion of memory already dependent on the powers of recollection of three people. In that broken country house long ago, Harding related his side of the events to Edison. In Niagara Falls, Edison relayed the message to me. Now there are all the years for the story to be filtered through. Who is to say?

Today did bestow a surprise on me. It arrived over the telephone. Instead of our usual agrarian conversation, Debbie suggested that we meet in a nearby park. I have talked with Debbie for more than a year, yet I haven't a clue as to her appearance. I told her that I would be pleased to meet her. She asked how she would recognize me. Look for an old man, I told her, being pulled like a water skier through the park by an Irish setter. Debbie laughed heartily at that image.

One might think that I would steer clear of parks. I met Margarete in a park. I lost her in one, too. I have to be realistic. Nineteen twenty-three was ages and ages ago. Since that time, I was blessed to find love once more. I married a fine woman. Together we had two offspring, in turn producing eight grand offspring. At present, I have a total of sixteen great-grand offspring. I am a widower. I spend a part of each day thinking of my wife, and almost as often, of Margarete. My love for one did not diminish that love for the other. It is like music. I enjoy listening to Beethoven just as much as I like to play Eubie Blake with these ancient fingers. Eubie Blake, by the way, was only five years older than I.

I tied a strong rope to Blue's collar, because she doesn't understand automobiles. In an enclosure, she is a dervish. Give her an acre, and she is an arrow. How inappropriate the word "setter" is when applied to Blue. An uncontained mass of energy like her is anything but a setter. An Irish torpedo is what I have at the end of the rope. We watch out for one another, Blue and I. Even on one of her wildest romps, she looks over her shoulder every now and then to see where I am. We have reached the park. I untied the rope, and Blue catapulted away.

It is a small park, just a city block. I could see Debbie parking her car on the other side of it and begin to walk toward me. I knew it was her before she said a single word. Debbie is a very good-looking woman. This doesn't surprise me.

"Good morning, Debbie," I told her, and she smiled because she knew me too. Blue was dancing in the background.

"Good morning, Mr. Halverton," she said. "Doesn't the cold weather feel nice for a change?"

"I brought you some broccoli," I said, handing her the paper sack. "I cut it this morning."

"Well, I wish you hadn't. I don't want you wasting your vegetables on me. It's your garden."

"To do with as I please. I want you to have it."

She thanked me, sat at my side on the bench, and we watched Blue burning up her calories. Neither of us spoke for the longest time. But we didn't have to. We do that on the telephone every day. So much talk is just chatter. Nine people out of ten will spot an old man like me sitting in a park and, before a minute has passed, will ask the same question that old men have been badgered with since time began. The question of course, is, "To what do you attribute your longevity?" And the other 10 percent? They don't say anything to you at all. They just want to take your photograph.

Debbie did speak up by and by.

"I ask just about everybody I meet the same thing," she said. "I don't think I ever mentioned it over the telephone. I always ask what the most significant event that person ever attended was."

"What have been some of your answers?"

"Some really interesting ones. One man was in Pearl Harbor when it was bombed. Somebody else saw Lindberg land in Paris. A friend of mine attended the last concert given by the Beatles in public. All sorts of things."

"Those are pretty good answers," I responded.

"What about you, Mr. Halverton? What was the most significant event you attended?"

"It was the summer of 1923," I told her. "I drove my brand new Ford Model T from Trenton, New Jersey to Marion, Ohio. I attended the funeral of President Warren G. Harding. Thousands and thousands of people were there. Pictures of the dead President were in all the store windows and in most of the houses. Black crepe paper hung everywhere. It was a sad time for most Americans."

"But wasn't he corrupt?" Debbie asked. "Was the country that sorry for him?"

"Oh, yes indeed," I answered. "None of the scandals of his administration had surfaced yet, and he was never directly tied to any of them. He was very popular. He was a good man who just had some bad friends. At the graveside services, there were more dignitaries than you can imagine. The new President was there, of course, Mr. Coolidge. Former President Taft was there. He was Chief Justice of the Supreme

Court then. And in a car nearby you could see former President Wilson. He was ill himself and too frail to walk about. Commerce Secretary Herbert Hoover attended. So you had Wilson, Taft, Coolidge and Hoover, not to mention poor Mr. Harding. There were others there too. Henry Ford came with his friends Thomas Edison and Harvey Firestone. Mr. Firestone was a good friend of the Hardings. He gave the President and his wife each a horse, I recall reading at one time."

"That's very impressive," Debbie said. "You know, this sounds awful. I should know my history better. But I can't remember what President Harding died of."

"You are not alone in that," I said. "I recall that he was examined by three doctors. His own physician said that it was a heart attack. Another said stroke. The third thought it was food poisoning."

"Do you know what the autopsy showed?"

"An autopsy was never performed. Can you imagine that happening in this day and age? Why, we would appoint a commission and spend millions of dollars to investigate. We still wouldn't find anything. That's the only difference between then and now."

Debbie shook her head. "Maybe it was foul play," she said.

We started talking about other things. The weather again, and the garden and television. I didn't tell Debbie any of the details about Mr. Harding or anything about Mr. Ford, Edison or Firestone. I neglected to say that when I talked with Mr. Firestone after the services, he informed me that the three of them were off for two weeks in the woods again, to his property in rural Maryland. He extended the invitation to me as well, but I declined. I had chosen that time to move back to Houston, where Dad's name graces the old library building to this day. I bid them all a farewell and never again saw them in the flesh.

Newsreels and magazines kept the country up to date on

their whereabouts and activities. The following year was their last campout, incidentally. Edison complained that the publicity had spoiled it for him. The three of them were filmed at Edison's eightieth-birthday celebration and again at his last birthday, his eighty-fourth. Not to mention the coverage they all received at the jubilee celebration of the golden anniversary of the light bulb in 1929. From a distance, I watched them age.

Mr. Firestone and I exchanged Christmas cards every year until his death in 1938. He was seventy when he died.

Henry Ford did not live to his predicted age of one hundred. Like Thomas Edison, he was eighty-four when he died. The year was 1947.

There was such public fascination with Mr. Edison that, when he died in 1930, tributes to his significance were voiced around the world. President Hoover wanted to extinguish all lights and electricity in his honor for a full minute. He was advised that such a thing would create a catastrophe. The world would no longer function without Edison's contributions for even sixty seconds.

Much was made of Edison's last words. The world loved him so much that it was sure his deathbed message was something more profound than an ordinary man's. Supposedly, Edison raised his head one final time and looked across the lawn of his estate. There are those who believe that he saw the afterlife through his window. Who is to say?

Blue is covering the ground in long, flowing strides. She is running past an oak tree whose limbs must span two hundred feet. The tree's leaves are falling like rain. The sun is shining through the the long red hair that hangs from Blue's forelegs and ears.

I nudge Debbie on the arm and point to the dog as she flies across the grass. I quote Thomas Edison just before he slipped away. "It's very beautiful over there."

"Yes, it is," agrees Debbie. "It's very beautiful."